LIOPLEURODON

The Master of the Deep

M. B. ZUCKER

HISTORIUM PRESS

Copyright © 2022 by M. B. Zucker

All rights reserved. No part of this book may be reproduced or transmitted in any form or by any means, electronic or mechanical, including photocopying, recording, or by any information storage and retrieval system, without written permission from the publisher.

First Edition published by Historium Press

Images by Shutterstock & Public Domain
Cover designed by White Rabbit Arts

Visit Mr. Zucker's website at
www.michaelbzucker.com

Library of Congress Cataloging-in-Publication Data on file

Hardcover ISBN: 9798218042318
Paperback ISBN: 9798986256450
E-Book ISBN: 9798986256467

Historium Press, a subsidiary of
The Historical Fiction Company, LLC
2022

Other Novels by M. B. Zucker

The Eisenhower Chronicles

A Great Soldier in the Last Great War

To Kalonji,

Michael Zucker

To my grandparents,
Skip and Carole

TABLE OF CONTENTS

Prologue	11
Chapter One – Venenum	15
Chapter Two – Restoration	54
Chapter Three – Go to it Laughing	66
Chapter Four – The Kaiser's Pet	115
Chapter Five – Falls the Shadow	146
Chapter Six – Alliances	199
Chapter Seven – Here Lies Wolfe Victorious	239
Epilogue	306
Acknowledgments	313
About the Author	

Consider the subtleness of the sea;
how its most dreaded creatures glide under water,
unapparent for the most part, and treacherously hidden
beneath the loveliest tints of azure.

—*Herman Melville*

Prologue

155,000,000 BCE

The rising sun revealed a thick layer of gray ash coating the ocean's surface, which threatened marine life for kilometers in every direction. Swallowing too much of the substance was lethal. Getting it stuck in a nose or gills meant strangulation. A five-meter reptilian head displaced the soot as it emerged from below. This was a Liopleurodon, the dominant predator in these waters. His triangular skull bore resemblance to a crocodile's, his three-meter jaws opened as he growled in frustration from the dirt and subsequent hunger. The nostrils on top of the Liopleurodon's head widened and snorted, blowing away ash that impeded the tracking device.

The Liopleurodon was amidst a journey north in search of new hunting grounds, leaving behind his territory in the location where the British Isles would eventually form. His ecosystem had undergone a radical change. The soot provided a clue. Pangea, the super-continent that comprised Earth's entire landmass, had broken apart. This shift of tectonic plates triggered a series of volcanic eruptions under the North Sea, preventing the Equator's warm water from reaching the North Pole.

Temperatures dropped and the resulting ice age forced local marine life to migrate to warmer waters. The Liopleurodon followed. He initially moved south in his search for food before detecting a prey-item to the north. He was desperate, having not eaten for months.

He spent several minutes treading the water, relaxed. Then his jaws opened and he inhaled air before submerging. A couple of thrusts with his four flippers, each four meters long, freed the beast from the dirt's clutches. The ocean's current removed residue soot, revealing the reptile's tri-colored skin. A black back allowed the Liopleurodon to stalk prey from below; his white underbelly blended with sunlight and camouflaged the predator when attacking from above. Vertical red stripes on the Liopleurodon's back and sides were meant to intimidate other large males and attract females. He had a history of vanquishing rivals, as the many scars around his jaws, neck, torso, and flippers attested. This process began with his own siblings, which he eliminated within his mother's womb. Mom was exhausted and needed calories after giving birth. She quickly transitioned from parent to hunter. The Liopleurodon escaped and exacted his revenge by preying on her after reaching maturity. He repeated the process with dozens of territorial rivals, only sparing females during mating season. He had not faced a challenger in years, having his pick of prey until the ice age's interruption.

The Liopleurodon did his best to track his victim for the next hour, his front and rear flippers moving in opposite, synchronized motions, propelling his 150-ton mass with speed and agility. The ash wasn't the only obstacle to his olfactory guidance. Rotting flesh from a Leedsichthys—a 27-meter fish—the Liopleurodon's previous kill, still clung between his meter long fangs. The Liopleurodon's nostrils picked up these fish pieces, compounding the challenge. Exhausted, he returned to the surface, rising above the soot-layer, and rested. He took a deep breath after a few minutes and swam to the seabed to wait.

His target registered 20 minutes later, incoming. The Liopleurodon's hunger tempted him to emerge prematurely, but experience told him to wait until making visual contact. He had transformed hunting into an art form; a master of his craft, he was the Shakespeare or Beethoven of preying on reptiles and fish within Jurassic waters. A five-meter long Ophthalmosaurus came into view. The Ophthalmosaurus looked like a dolphin with bluish-white coloring. Her long snout was ideal for catching squid. The Liopleurodon pushed himself off the seabed with his flippers. He gained acceleration as he attacked from below. The Ophthalmosaurus smelled the rotting flesh between the Liopleurodon's teeth and looked down, her large eyes identifying her attacker. She turned and dodged the Liopleurodon, who exploded from the ocean's surface and bit a mouthful of air. The master's hunger made him sloppy.

The enormous carnivore crashed back into the sea. He dove beneath the ash layer and saw the Ophthalmosaurus retreating. The Liopleurodon gave chase, desperate for food. He couldn't keep pace—the smaller reptile was too agile. Time, dirt, and cold temperatures drained prey and predator of energy. The Ophthalmosaurus slowed down, allowing the Liopleurodon to close the distance. She peered back, saw her attacker, and used what little strength she had left to swipe her tail to and fro. The Liopleurodon lacked the energy to catch up again. The Ophthalmosaurus escaped his grasp as the water surrounding both reptiles became colder and colder.

The soot hid an iceberg, a product of the glacial period. The cold-blooded marine reptiles, whose stamina was impacted by external temperatures, became motionless. The Liopleurodon, larger in size and with greater surface area, was particularly vulnerable and paralyzed from moving his flippers. The current pushed him toward the iceberg until he collided with the mass. A large chunk of ice broke off and landed on the beast. Water surrounding the Liopleurodon froze for the next several hours. He panicked but was too weak to do anything but watch, for once the powerless party. He was frozen by nightfall and entered suspended animation. Ash accumulated on the iceberg's flanks over the next year, causing it to sink below the ocean's surface. The ash coating and water pressure preserved the iceberg for millennia after the ice age ended.

History's greatest carnivore was preserved with it.

Chapter One

Venenum

February 14, 1911

Alice winced as the carriage rolled over a chunk of ice, disrupting her breathing and hurting her throat. She coughed and peered from behind the curtain to increase the air circulation. She blinked multiple times, frustrated and jittery from keeping still in a confined environment for so long, glancing at the brick and brimstone architecture that reflected older Queen Anne and Richardson Romanesque styles along with newer Georgian Revival ones. Massachusetts Avenue was grand by DC standards and less reflective of the patchwork look found elsewhere.

She opened her purse, eyeing her garden snake, coiled and passive, among her other items. Alice was careful not to touch the snake as she retrieved a cigarette and match. She lit the match on the carriage's interior wall. Her eyes closed as she inhaled the smoke and relaxed. The smoke stayed within the carriage when she exhaled.

"Must you smoke in here?" Theodore asked, sitting beside her.

"I'll do as I like, Father."

Theodore snorted and considered opening his curtain. "Still the same girl who smoked on the White House roof. My same bunny."

"Please don't call me that. I'm a married woman."

"And?" Theodore asked as he glanced at her. "That doesn't change the fact that I'll always be the big bear to my bunnies. Including you."

The carriage shook again.

"*Blasted* ice," Alice muttered. She squeezed her purse tighter so as to keep her snake still and calm.

"Be grateful we've come in the winter and the snow and ice are with us," Theodore said. "Summer brings horrid humidity to this city. Why President Washington opted to place the capital in a swamp makes me question the great man's judgment."

"I just wish we could have walked. I understand we'd be mobbed, but nonetheless. I would think you would feel similarly, Father, given your near-death experience when the Pittsfield streetcar—"

"On the contrary, I relish such brushes with—"

"Ah, yes. How could I forget?"

"Why are you in a mood? Surely, this can't just be about the weather?"

"Of course it isn't."

"Then what?"

"You know my feelings about Senator Lodge. He's a snob."

"No, he isn't. He's a warm boy."

"That opinion is unique to you."

"Then you needn't speak to him for more than a few moments."

"What does that mean?"

"You'll spend time with Constance when we get there."

"I will not! I'll sit in on the meeting!"

"You'll do no such thing."

"Then why am I here? I could have spent the day with Nicholas."

"You're excellent at social occasions. You know that."

"Then allow me to give you my opinion," Alice declared as she looked her father in the eye. "I know you've decided to challenge the President next year." Theodore did not respond. "I don't believe you'll achieve your desired outcome. You'll upset the party bosses and poison your chance to win the nomination in less controversial circumstances in '16."

"Nonsense," Theodore said. "I was the most popular President since Lincoln. And Lincoln had the war helping him. Think of the reception we received upon my return from the African safari last summer. The *acclaim*."

"And then you were held responsible for the Republican defeat in the midterms," Alice replied. Theodore's jaw clenched and he broke eye contact. "Your political fortunes are at a low ebb, Father."

"What will Nicholas do?" he asked softly.

"He'll play it safe—"

The carriage shook more violently than before. Alice gripped her purse and her seat as she briefly feared they might tip over.

"All right, back there?" James Amos, their African American valet, shouted from the driver's seat.

"We're fine, James!" Theodore replied. He looked to Alice, turning his head 90-degrees. His left eye was blind from a boxing match as President. "You were saying?"

"Nicholas will play it safe, like *usual*. Mr. Taft is his political mentor," Alice said. "He'll stand with him."

"And what will you do?"

"I'll do as I believe. Even if it costs me my marriage."

"It would come to that?"

"He already tells me to 'shut up' for defending you."

"You believe in me that much?"

"Of course I do, Father." Alice smiled. "Besides, how could I side with the family who banned me from the White House?"

"Did you ever receive an explanation for that action?"

Alice's grin grew wider. "They must have discovered the voodoo doll I buried of the First Lady."

"Alice…"

Alice smirked. Theodore sighed and thought of the estrangement between his family and the Tafts. Why hadn't Taft, or a member of the President's staff, greeted him upon his emergence from Khartoum in Africa? Theodore's friends and the press did. That was just one of a series of escalating events that built awkwardness and eventually—

The carriage stopped. The curtain on Alice's side opened after a moment.

"Ma'am?" Amos asked, offering his hand.

"Thank you, James," she replied as she took his hand and climbed out.

"I'll come get you in a moment, Colonel."

"That's quite all right!" Theodore announced. "I'm as fit as a bull moose!" He opened his curtain and climbed out. Despite his assertions, the former President was no longer as tan or fit as he'd been upon returning from Africa, having put on weight and appearing chubby. He glanced at the clouds, which were thicker than the ice clumps on DC's streets and sidewalks.

Lodge's home bore a Victorian style and was built of red brick with Greek columns holding up a balcony on the second floor. It was one of the nicer houses on the street. Theodore struck the door knocker. A glass knob turned, after a moment, and the black door opened. An African American servant was there to meet them.

"Greetings, Colonel!"

"Bully to see you, Mr. Marshall!"

Constance, Lodge's daughter, stood behind Marshall.

"Please come in, Colonel, Alice. Let us take your coats."

"You're most generous," Theodore replied before removing his winter gear. Roosevelt's characteristic energy returned to him as he moved like a big child to his favorite corridor of the mansion. A Spanish royal ensign was draped over the hallway and a display case contained a Spanish saber, a Puerto Rican machete, and a Spanish ship's porthole, among other things. Roosevelt analyzed them with glee.

"Admiring Bay's loot, I see."

Roosevelt turned to see Lodge standing behind him.

"Cabot!"

"Good to see you, Colonel!"

They embraced and then returned to looking at the trophies.

"Thank you again for writing that lovely introduction to his poetry collection," Lodge said.

"The honor was mine."

A tinge of melancholy set in.

"Do you still plan to vacation in Cape Cod this summer?" Roosevelt asked.

"I haven't decided," Lodge replied. "I'm not sure I can go without Bay."

"It would be good for you. You can sit outside and read."

"True. Shall we go to my study?"

"Let's." Roosevelt turned to Alice and Constance, who waited at the end of the corridor. "Ladies, please excuse us. We have important matters to discuss."

"Come, Alice," Constance said, "let me show you our latest renovations." Alice looked to her father to signal her unhappiness but he paid it no mind and followed Lodge to his study.

The study led to Lodge's library, one of the mansion's main features. Two cups of cocoa waited for them.

"You're so thoughtful," Roosevelt said. He glanced at the volumes placed in the library's forefront—*Don Quixote,* Homer, and Lodge's favorite, the complete works of Sir Walter Scott. Roosevelt took the seat closer to the door while Lodge sat across a glossy table, deeper in the room.

"I've been depressed by your absence," Lodge said.

"It's good to be back in Washington. The capital is a big, pleasant village. In New York, everything throbs with the chase for the almighty dollar." Lodge could tell that Roosevelt's anxiety was on the brink of boiling over.

"Shall we turn to the purpose of your visit?" Lodge asked. Roosevelt nodded. "So? What have you decided regarding next year's election?"

"I have a duty, Cabot."

"I see." Lodge glanced at notes he'd prepared on a yellow lined pad. "I assume this is primarily due to the Pinchot issue?"

"It is—in large part—though that's really just a symptom of a larger trend."

"Such as?"

"Cabot, you know as well as I that Taft betrayed our cause," Roosevelt said. "He's surrounded himself with corporate lawyers and was co-opted by the oligarchy."

"You're overreacting. He's had progressive accomplishments. Historic tariff reduction. Breaking up more trusts in two years than you did in seven."

"He and Ballinger returned one-and-a-half million acres in the Midwest to the public domain. How many millions have General Electric, Guggenheim, and Amalgamated Copper already made at the expense of our national treasures?"

"The executive order that you wrote with Mr. Pinchot stretched executive power to its limit," Lodge said.

"The Constitution doesn't prohibit it. The President is the only thing standing between the people and the capitalists." Roosevelt's hand swung before him like a karate chop to animate his action. "What we did was necessary."

"President Taft has a narrower interpretation of executive power. He's not alone in thinking your action required Congressional approval."

Roosevelt waved his hand dismissively. "I shouldn't dream of asking Congress' permission on the issue. It's in our national interest."

"The Interior Department hadn't even conducted a survey of the region."

"That's just an excuse to undo our action. Taft was meant to carry on my policies and he betrayed the progressive cause. Everyone in the movement knows this and says so." Roosevelt sighed after taking a sip of cocoa. "I didn't want this. He'd been my right hand when I was President. But he's been bought. Should have backed Mr. Hughes instead."

"Even if I were to grant you all of this, which I don't, but if I did, that still leaves the issue of actually *beating* him," Lodge said. "Taft controls the Republican leadership."

"Do you remember when George Cortelyou replaced Mark Hanna as party chairman in '04? That happened because *I* requested it. The party needs me more than I it."

"But then Parker accused Cortelyou of blackmailing corporations and you of corruption."

Roosevelt snorted. "Fine, but who remembers that detail?

My point stands."

"What people remember is that the party holds *you* responsible for the disaster in November. We lost the House for the first time since the '90s and almost lost the Senate. Plus dozens of state-level races. I won my runoff last month by a mere five votes."

"I only led our party's efforts in New York! It's poppycock to blame me for what happened across the country."

"Nonetheless, that was the public's perception and what you have to work with, Theodore." Lodge placed down his cocoa and leaned forward in his seat, resting his elbows on his knees. "You've never been so politically vulnerable and are in no position to challenge the President."

"I disagree, Cabot," Roosevelt asserted, taking a gulp. "My New Nationalism speech struck a chord with progressives across the country. The struggle for freedom for this generation demands a fight for popular rule against the special interests. That includes direct primaries and outlawing corporate contributions for candidates. Regulations for working women and children. Vocational training. And so on. Such a platform will generate far greater excitement than Taft's milquetoast conservatism."

"You should add Negro voting rights to the list," Lodge said.

"That will hurt me in the South."

"It's the right thing to do. You didn't mention your call for public referendums on judicial decisions. Did the midterm disaster change your mind?"

"Certainly not."

"It must, unless you wish to terrify most of the country and fade into irrelevance."

"Why should a five-to-four court decision shape whether progressive legislation is constitutional?" Roosevelt asked, his arms folded. "It is only right that public majorities should be able to recall such holdings."

"That would be a court of the crowd, Theodore." Lodge picked up his drink. "You would be destroying representative government for the whims of the populace."

"Wall Street has bought four dozen Senators as though they were yachts. Is that representative government?"

"You did not used to be *this* radical," Lodge said. "You used to call for *balance* between capital and labor."

"I still stand for the Square Deal, but it's now clear to me that fair play under the present rules of the game isn't enough. They must be *changed* if we are to achieve *true* equal opportunity for all Americans."

"You'll have to turn down your rhetoric if you want a *chance* of winning. You'll terrify the Eastern Establishment."

"I don't need them if they lack farsightedness."

"Casuistry," Lodge muttered. "Only six states allow for direct primaries."

"Then perhaps I'll run third party," Roosevelt spat back, "if the party leadership is going to rig the contest."

"And give the election to Bryan or whoever else leads the Robespierre wing of the Democratic Party?" Lodge asked in exacerbation.

"I suspect they'll back Woodrow Wilson. He just won the New Jersey gubernatorial race in a landslide. Conservative Democrats will back Champ Clark, since he'll likely replace Cannon as Speaker of the House in March."

Lodge broke eye contact and took a minute to think. "I suppose you couldn't simply *ask* Taft to step aside next year?"

"Not since he's been corrupted."

"And you wouldn't be interested in being Vice President in his second term? You would be set to run in '16 and shape his administration from within."

"I'll never hold that waste of an office again," Roosevelt said. "It ought to be abolished."

Lodge chuckled. "Do you remember when the Party leadership chose you to be McKinley's running mate in 1900? Henry and I had to lift your spirits." He referred to Henry Adams, grandson of John Quincy Adams. "He told stories of Washington in yesteryear. Of dinner parties where General Sherman would reenact his March to the Sea by pushing his silverware off the table with his spoon."

Roosevelt nodded despondently, losing focus as his insecurities set in.

"What's the matter, Theodore?" Lodge asked. "Not in the mood for trips down memory lane?"

Roosevelt resisted looking desperate as he restored eye contact with his friend. "How will history remember me?"

"As a great President."

"Will it?"

"Yes!" Lodge declared. "You confronted the excess of the industrial age. Established our nation as a great power in the world."

"But no one would rank me on par with George Washington or Abraham Lincoln."

"Well," Lodge said, framing his words delicately. "That's a very high bar."

"One I'm convinced I could meet if I was in office under the right circumstances."

"What do you mean?"

"Washington and Lincoln were great because they led the country during a once-in-a-century existential war. They successfully navigated those crises and *that's* why they're ranked at the top. It's not *my fault* that my administration lacked a major crisis. I'm proud of what I accomplished, particularly the canal in Panama, but that's not comparable to founding the republic or abolishing slavery."

"All of that is true, but it's beyond your control," Lodge said.

"Not if I win next year."

"And what does *that* mean?"

"Look at the situation in Europe," Roosevelt said. "The century of peace that Metternich built following Waterloo is ending. Bismarck destabilized the balance of power by replacing the German confederation of states with a Prussian-led giant, and *his* removal by the Kaiser has resulted in Europe devolving into rival blocks. Britain, France, and Russia are allied against

Germany and Austria-Hungary. The situation is unstable, particularly because of German aggression. A war more terrible than that of religion or of Napoleon is inevitable within the coming years. That's before mentioning the Japanese threat in the East and the decay of Russian society that will surely end in a bloodshed that makes the French Revolution look tame by comparison—"

"And you wish to be President during that war?"

"Can you picture *Taft* leading the country during a cataclysm of that scale?"

"No," Lodge said softly, conceding the point. "Is this duty or legacy?"

Roosevelt hesitated. "Duty," he said unconvincingly as he pushed his subconscious desires back in the box. "I seek to live a straight life and do good. I am not in the least concerned with my place in history."

Lodge sighed and took the last gulp of his cocoa, which was now cool. He consciously injected himself with more energy. "Enough talk of politics! Are you interested in a ride?"

"Is the path near the stable clear of ice?" Roosevelt asked.

"Yes."

"I would love to."

...

The plump man clutched his copy of *The Times* with his beady fingers, the paper covering all but his balding scalp. His black,

Edwardian wool hat sat atop the decorative cane that leaned against the table beside him. He briefly glanced at a story announcing that Neville Chamberlain, a manufacturer of metal ship births and former bachelor turned aspiring member of Parliament, was engaged to heiress Anne Cole before turning his focus to an article on a suffragette rally in Independence Square that provoked his scoffing. He was oblivious to the surrounding environment, which comprised a wall of half wooden panels and half flowery wallpaper, a large painting of formally dressed people enjoying their meal at a restaurant like this one, and secondary paintings. A dimly lit golden chandelier with several candelabras hung from the white ceiling, which had raised lines shaped like curved flower petals between the dim sky lights. The tables were set with white linen tablecloths, romantic lights, and comfortable upholstered seats.

The sound of approaching footsteps penetrated the man's bubble. He lowered *The Times*, revealing bespectacled eyes. A blonde couple stood on the other side of the table, the man in his late thirties and over a decade older than the lady, both pairs of eyes sharing a look of life's toll that sought to build energy for their social outing. The plump man rose to his feet and extended his right hand.

"Miss Painter," the man said in a Mid-Atlantic accent before taking the woman's hand and kissing it.

"'Kelsey' is fine."

The man nodded and hesitated before turning to shake hands with the blonde man.

"Dr. Ryan," he said.

"Dr. Ross."

"Please, sit," Ross invited, gesturing to the chairs closest to the couple. Ryan sat down before preparing Kelsey's seat. Ross monitored the action. Ryan sat in the middle and noted that Ross had already ordered five glasses of Merlot for the table, each next to a place setting.

"Appreciated," Ryan muttered. "I can't remember which is further back in time—my previous visit to Delmonico's or our last meeting."

"For which I apologize," Ross said. "It's a long walk to your office *down* the hall."

A brief flash of anger was the first, truest emotion to rise in Ryan's eyes, but he pushed it back down. "Careful, Benjamin. Let's be on our good behavior tonight." Ross gave a small nod, signaling his agreement without apologizing. "What do we know about Will's protégé?"

"All I know is that he wants to be a marine reptile specialist," Ross said. "A bit young for such a significant career decision, but that's kids these days, I suppose. Perhaps he's interested in my new article in *Science*. Other than that, I only know that Professor Harris claims that he'll be the star of his generation and is desperate to meet us."

"I suppose that's one word for it."

They exchanged an awkward laugh and broke eye contact. Kelsey flashed a brief smile.

Ryan glanced at *The Times*. "What's happening in the

world?"

Ross shrugged. "The lady agitators are in Independence Square again." He chuckled. "This doesn't seem complicated to me. The husband is the public representative of the family, but the wife still has input." He used hand gestures to make his point and looked to Kelsey. "Is that unreasonable?"

"I think the suffrage issue is in line with—"

"What if husband and wife disagree politically?" Ryan asked. "What if he's cruel? Should she not have her own say?"

"In that case, she should honor her husband's wishes. That's our heritage." Ross turned to Kelsey again. "How are your studies going at Cornell?"

"Lovely."

"Wonderful to hear," Ross said. "It's nice they have a program for women to enter the field. Have you started your thesis?"

"Yes, I have."

"What about?"

"Humanity's role in the mammoth's decline during the Pliocene," Kelsey said.

"I take it you think it had an impact?"

"I do."

"More so than other factors? Like the increase in global temperatures? Or what of other carnivores? Smilodon. The cave lion. Arctodus. Why humanity and not any of those options?"

"I have sections on all of those, and more, as contributing factors, but humanity was key because we had a radical impact on the mammoth's ecosystem. We were more organized, more intelligent. We used weapons and tactics."

"Surely, Smilodon had those."

"Yes, but they aren't comparable," Kelsey said. "It would be like pitting Alexander or Caesar against Sitting Bull." Ross smiled, impressed with Kelsey's defense. Kelsey relaxed and asked, "Who are we meeting again?"

"Will Harris is an old colleague of ours," Ryan explained, "but he had the wisdom to leave the museum system for the university. Less competitive. Less stressful."

"And less potential," Ross added.

"Will accomplished enough to satisfy the average man," Ryan said.

"Average. Yes."

"That's not very nice, Dr. Ross," Kelsey said.

"'Nice.' Excuse me, I forgot that people's *feelings* are in vogue these days. I suppose something is needed to pacify mediocrity."

Ryan glared at Ross. "I see why *you're* the only one to arrive on his own this evening."

Ross paused, an insecurity touched. "I'm more than enough company for myself."

Kelsey acted before an awkward silence set in. "You mentioned you published an article in *Science*?"

"Yes," Ross replied, seizing the lifeline. "Earlier this month."

"Congratulations."

"Thank you, dear."

"What's the topic?" Kelsey asked.

"I tried to make an evolutionary link between mosasaurs and snakes," Ross said. "You're familiar with mosasaurs, are you not?"

"I'm afraid to admit they're outside my specialty."

"Quite alright. They were the apex predator of the Cretaceous ocean. They peaked around 90 million years ago."

"What's your basis for their link to snakes?" Kelsey asked.

"Both had expandable jaws for swallowing their prey whole."

"How does that—lovely dinner conversation, by the way," Kelsey said. Ross laughed. "How does that prove a link?"

Ryan spoke before Ross could answer. "Perhaps mosasaurs developed that ability through a special need and passed it onto their descendants?"

"I will *not* debate this point with you again," Ross asserted. "Natural selection dictates—"

"Greetings!" an approaching man exclaimed. "Lady, gentleman, Dr. Ross." Ryan laughed. The man shook hands with the couple. "Kelsey, Sean, good to see you both." He sat beside Kelsey and noted the Merlot by his place setting. "I see the best part of the evening is already here. No offense, Kelsey. I hope we're not late. Fifth Avenue was packed." He took a sip.

"Good to see you, Will," Ryan said.

A younger man followed Harris to the table. He moved slower than the high-energy professor. He had let his hair grow out further than the professional men and had a stubble goatee.

He wore a sports jacket and a sloppy bowtie. He locked his eyes onto Ross, who arched his eyebrow in confusion. The student must have been intimidated, or perhaps excited. He sat between Ross and Harris.

Harris took another sip and raised his glass.

"A toast to the happy couple." Ryan and Kelsey took a moment to respond. Everyone raised their glasses. "Do I hear wedding bells in the offing?"

Ryan was flustered. Kelsey glanced at him and then looked at the others. "What about you gentlemen?" she asked. "Hmm? Dr. Ross? Professor Harris?"

Ross broke eye contact. He sank into his seat before restoring his posture. "I don't need distractions from my work."

"And you, Professor Harris?" Kelsey asked.

Harris smiled. "Too restricting."

"From your ladies of the night?" Ross asked. Harris gave a playful shrug and finished his Merlot. He grabbed his student's glass and pulled it closer. Ross' eyebrow arched again. This college student was over 18, wasn't he? Ross noticed the student was still staring at him.

"I'm afraid I didn't catch your name, young man," Ross said. He placed his right elbow on the table and put his weight onto it. "Can you give it to me again?"

"Luke."

"Thank you. I hear you're interested in marine reptiles."

"That's right."

"Did you read my article in *Science*?"

"Yes."

"What are your thoughts?"

"It was fine."

Harris, Ryan, and Kelsey all exchanged a glance.

Ross smiled. "A master of flattery, I see."

"Luke tends to be a bit shy," Harris explained.

"As are many bright young men at his age," Ross said. "Marine reptiles are an excellent specialty, though I advise you to keep an open mind. Paleontology is a booming field. A man—or woman—" Ross paused and glanced at Kelsey, "—could spend a career cleaning up the sloppy research that Marsh and Cope inflicted upon us with their juvenile race to identify as many species as possible. Misidentify is more like it. Or you can spend your career in the West, if you're unsure if you want a family."

"Is that a choice he would have to make at this point?" Ryan asked. "The railroad gives easier access to the West than in previous generations."

"Either way," Ross continued, "there have been major breakthroughs in that region in recent years. Majestic beasts like Allosaurus, Stegosaurus, and Triceratops will become household names before too long. It's so wonderful a man at your age has decided to enter the field. The opportunities are all around you. Reach out and seize them!"

Luke did not respond, as though he hadn't heard a word. He ran his fingers through the long pieces of hair near his neck.

Ross hesitated. "What does your father do?"

"You killed him."

Ryan and Kelsey exchanged a glance and then turned to Harris, who was mortified. All three turned to Ross. Ross took a breath and asserted control over his emotions before reestablishing eye contact with Luke.

"That's quite a claim, young man."

"I'm so sorry, Ben," Harris said. "I don't know what—mind expanding on that, Luke?"

"Gladly," Luke said, eyes locked on Ross. "Your career was launched by destroying my father's."

"I haven't a clue what—" Ross froze, blinking several times. "What was your name again?"

"Luke."

"Luke—what?"

"Luke Jones."

"Jones?" Ross asked, his voice louder than at any time since arriving at Delmonico's. He connected the dots. "*Andrew* Jones was your father?"

"Correct."

"You're the son of And—" Ross turned to Harris. "Why didn't you tell me that's who this is?"

"I thought you knew!" Harris exclaimed.

Ross waived his hand dismissively. "Of all the asinine—" He noticed Ryan smiling. "Did you know?" Ryan nodded and cracked up. "Why didn't you tell me he was Professor Harris' protégé?"

"And miss *this*?" Ryan asked between laughs. Kelsey looked

disgusted.

Ross turned back to Luke. "So what, this was an ambush?" he asked. "That's how you intend to enter the field? By ambushing its leader with absurd accusations?"

"Can someone provide context to what's happening?" Kelsey asked. "I'm lost."

"Happily," Ross spat. "Andrew Jones worked under the great Henri Émile Sauvage. He was on Monsieur Sauvage's expedition that discovered *Liopleurodon ferox*, a small pliosaur."

"A what?"

"A pliosaur is a short-necked plesiosaur," Ross said. "Head like a crocodile. Body like a turtle without the shell. They discovered Liopleurodon in the Boulogne region of France. Mr. Jones was a graduate student at the time. A few years later, he was on a dig that discovered an ichthyosaur, another marine reptile, that had been bitten in half. I don't remember the ichthyosaur's length. Let's say it was six to nine meters long."

"It was 11 meters," Luke said.

"*Eleven* meters. Excuse me!" Ross raised his hands to look like he was surrendering to the police before replacing his elbow on the table. "Anyway, the teeth marks on the ichthyosaur matched those of Liopleurodon and Mr. Jones extrapolated that pliosaurs, which have only been shown to be six or seven meters long, could grow to two or three times that size."

"Wow," Kelsey said.

"Don't be impressed," Ross replied. "It was *nonsense* then and it's *nonsense* now. He just made the claim to advance his career."

"It isn't—" Luke began.

"Save it!" Ross said.

"Well, wait," Kelsey said, "what else would explain how an 11-meter animal was bitten in half?"

Ross took a deep breath. "There are other explanations. It could have been a high-velocity impact, for instance. But Mr. Jones made an extraordinary claim without the extraordinary evidence to back it up. And yes, my first published article debunked his 'theory.'" Ross used air quotes.

"Debunked?" Ryan asked. "You eviscerated him."

"Which was *deserved*," Ross declared.

"What happened next?" Kelsey asked Luke. He took a moment to respond.

"My father's career was over," Luke said. "He fell into alcoholism and committed suicide when I was nine."

"I'm sorry."

"Thank you," Luke replied, "but you're not the one I want an apology from."

"Then *keep* waiting!" Ross said. "Don't expect it from me! Your father proposed an absurd theory and got what he deserved. It was even worse than Dr. Ryan's belief in Neo-Lamarckism."

"That's unnecessary," Ryan said.

Ross ignored him, his attention on Luke. "Your father humiliated his own university. They revoked his degree."

"Because of *you*," Luke said. "He only proposed a theory."

"It was *groundless*. I'm interested in science, not mythical creatures."

"It's not groundless. I can prove it."

Ross chuckled. "Well, I *am* a man of science. Go ahead. This ought to be good."

"The six-meter pliosaur specimens were adolescents," Luke said. "The growth rings prove it."

Ross formed a small smile. "Okay, that's fair. So, maybe they grew to eight or nine meters. Maybe ten, if they lived a long life. That still doesn't mean they were 15 meters or more."

"What about pliosaur teeth that are a third-of-a-meter long?" Luke asked. "Large theropods, like Tyrannosaurus, grew to 12 meters and had teeth *half* that size. That implies that, proportionally—"

"There's not a direct correlation between tooth length and body length," Ross said. "And there *are* tyrannosaur teeth just shy of a third-of-a-meter. Ask your professor or Dr. Ryan. They would know."

Luke turned to Harris, who said, "Ben's right, Luke." Luke turned back to Ross, who had a smug smile.

"Anything else?"

Luke thought for a moment. "My father and I are marine reptile specialists and—"

"Your credentialism doesn't impress me," Ross said. "Do you know what does? Science. You're—" Luke broke eye contact and looked at his lap. "*Look* at me. You'll learn something. You're making the same mistake your father made. You've found a conclusion that you like and you're forcing the evidence to support it. But your evidence isn't stable."

"You say the same thing about Neo-Lamarckism," Ryan joked.

"Don't get me started on that again," Ross said. He looked to Luke. "Anything else?"

Luke looked like he was ready to vomit as his face flashed green. "My father was a great man. He had a mind like Copernicus and he worshiped my mother."

"He was a crackpot, as you'll no doubt be, and he left your mother a widow."

"That's uncalled for," Harris said.

"He called me a *murderer*!" Ross said.

Luke grit his teeth and his right hand became a fist. Ross saw it and scoffed.

"You wouldn't dare," Ross said.

Harris grabbed Luke's left elbow. "That's it!" Harris declared. "Change of topic!"

Luke tried to calm himself. He'd been denied the victory he'd built up in his head, unable to force reality to bend to his will. He leaned back in his chair, stared at his lap, and his mind shut down.

"You'll have to forgive Luke," Harris said to Ross. "He has a vulnerable heart."

Ross did not respond for a moment. Then his face flashed red.

"I'm not done!" he declared, looking at Luke. "You should spare us all the trouble and not bother entering this field. Go be a joke elsewhere. Perhaps law."

"That's enough, Dr. Ross," Harris said.

"Fine," Ross said, crossing his arms. "I'm done." He finished what was left of his Merlot. "How *dare* he speak that way to the next Darwin?"

"With the self-image of the next Bonaparte," Ryan said.

"It isn't arrogance if it's accurate."

An awkward silence set in. A trio of waiters watched the table, unsure if they should approach to take orders.

Ross looked to the others. "Should we bother breaking bread?"

"I think we can get the evening back on track," Kelsey said.

"Lead the way," Ryan replied.

"Does anyone have any upcoming plans?"

The table became quiet as their thinking transitioned away from the argument.

"I have something," Ross said.

"Yes?" Kelsey asked.

"I'm going to Newport at the end of the week. The Navy wants to ask me some questions."

"That's exciting," Kelsey said. "What about?"

"They haven't said," Ross replied. "The government occasionally finds fossils they need identified. Or they'll try to get the museum to take them off their hands. It's not common but it does happen." He paused. "You're welcome to join me." Ryan looked confused. "That's extended to all of you." Ross glanced at Luke.

Luke appeared lifeless, devoid of the energy needed to think. He started raising his head, but Harris spoke first. "We'd be honored to attend." Luke looked to his professor in horror. Harris nodded, telling him to take the opportunity. Luke shrunk further into his seat.

"Will the Navy be okay with you inviting all of us along?" Ryan asked.

Ross shrugged. "They did a background check on me. I doubt they'll care. We're a bunch of professionals looking at fossils."

Ryan and Kelsey exchanged a glance. Ryan hesitated and said they also wanted to go.

"I'll just need to notify my academic advisor," Kelsey said. "It shouldn't be a problem."

"Wonderful," Ross replied. "Now, let's order an appetizer. It will reduce the effect of the Merlot."

...

February 17, 1911
Ba-dump, Ba-dump, Ba-dump.

Luke's body was compressed, the backs of his shoes placed at the edge of his seat, a notebook on his thighs. He'd kept calm during the train ride by drawing a picture of a pliosaur attacking a Cryptoclidus, a seven-meter long plesiosaur. The pliosaur's jaws were the piece's defining feature; they surrounded their victim and would bring death in an instant. The rest of the predator's body did not fit on the page. Marine reptiles, such as pliosaurs and mosasaurs, were his passion; their power over their enemies excited him. This one conformed to his image of the gargantuan carnivore, the mightiest beast to ever swim in the sea.

"Luke," Harris said, "we've stopped." Luke hadn't noticed, comfortable in his bubble. He filled with dread as he returned to reality, throwing his notebook in his bag and following Harris off the train. He stretched without thinking once he had the space; the ride from New York had taken six hours. "Careful not to slip." Luke nodded and stared at the icy concrete as he followed Harris out of the station.

They found Ross, Kelsey, and Ryan waiting for them outside. All wore coats and Ross balanced himself with his cane. Luke avoided eye contact. Kelsey amused herself by exhaling air made visible through condensation. She turned to Ryan.

"Sean, look, I can see my breath."

"Uh-huh."

Harris noticed Kelsey's disappointment. "Yeah, it's neat!" he exclaimed. She smiled, appreciating the attempt.

"Good to see you again, Professor Harris," Ross said.

"Likewise, Ben."

Ross turned and waved to a naval officer standing a short distance away. The officer had been hugging himself due to the cold and snapped back into a professional stance. He approached the paleontologists.

"Is this everyone?" he asked.

"Yes," Ross replied.

"Great. Welcome to Naval Station Newport. I'm Lieutenant Black. Can I get your names?" The paleontologists introduced themselves. "Terrific. I'll lead you to your destination."

"Do we have a ride?" Ross asked.

"It's within walking distance."

Ross grimaced but fell into line as Black guided them into the base. Evergreens sprinkled with snow that led to various gray and tan buildings with dark blue roofs flanked them. The paleontologists asked questions, as though on a tour.

"Can you give us any hints on what we'll be looking at?" Harris asked.

"I'd rather not disclose anything until we reach the mess hall," Black said.

"The mess hall?" Ryan asked.

"Yes. I ask that you reserve your judgment until we get there."

"What do you do in the Navy?" Kelsey asked.

"Mostly administrative work these days," Black said.

"Do you enjoy it?"

Black shrugged. "Can't complain."

"I didn't *stop* complaining during my tour," Harris said. The others looked at him in surprise.

"You were in the Navy?" Black asked.

"Years ago. Terrible fit."

"I'm sorry to hear that."

"Don't take it personally," Harris said. "You could have the best peach tree in the world and there will be people who hate peaches."

"A healthy attitude," Black said.

"What's that building?" Ryan asked.

Luke ignored the conversation, captured by his emotions. He'd failed. Failed to avenge his father's destruction. He'd built up what was going to happen in his mind for months—no, years. Dr. Ross had destroyed his father's career—and his life—to launch his own. Luke meant to return the favor. He'd wanted to humiliate Ross in front of his mentor and Ross' own colleagues at the Natural History Museum and reset the Jones family as a redeemed dynasty within the field. Now, it wasn't clear if Luke even had a future in the field. Ross had put him in time out—destroyed Luke's reputation—destroyed it. Before it had even been built in order to be destroyed. The last 12 years of his life—don't step on that ice—the last 12 years of his life had led to that dinner. No, more than that. Ross' article was 14 years old. Andrew Jones' psyche unraveled over the subsequent two years until his suicide, leaving Pamella, Luke's mother, alone to raise her son and abandon her career as a music tutor to make her way in the industrial world at an age past when most women entered the work force. Luke's meaning in life—destroying Ross and becoming a giant in paleontology—vindicating his father's memory—all gone because he'd suffered the same fate. For the same issue. By the same man. Now what? What was there for Luke to do? The last 12 years were about this. Only this. He'd hardly thought of anything else. And that mission was destroyed in an evening. The humiliation. It was just—God. Now what?

What would he do with his life? His career as a paleontologist was over. Should he change his college courses? Enter a different profession? Why? Why bother? Why bother having a career? To make money? What kind of life purpose was that? In what field? What field could possibly hold the same meaning to him that paleontology did? It was his whole life. His father captured his imagination with the incredible creatures of centuries past when he was four. It was all he wanted. All he ever wanted. What was he going to become? A lawyer, like his mother wanted? Why bother? A doctor? Eh. A writer? Hmm. Maybe he could write about—no, it wasn't the same. He wanted to be a paleontologist. What would he be if not a paleontologist who had secured his father's legacy? Would he just exist? Why? Why bother? What was special about that? Avenging his father gave him purpose. And he had failed. So why bother? Why bother going on? If he couldn't avenge his father—why exist? Frankly, slipping on ice and breaking his skull open would be an escape. Yeah. That's right. An escape from the horrible existence that Ross forced upon him. God. Ross. Ben Ross. And his arrogance. Just because he had status. Thinking he was better than everyone else. Because he could sell himself and sound smart. But he wasn't smart. A bag of hot air. He didn't know better than hundreds of others who wanted to be the lead researcher at the Natural History Museum. He didn't deserve it. So mad. Just wanted to hit him. And Harris. Harris was okay. Luke knew in the back of his mind that the professor meant well. But he kept telling Luke what to do. "Write your papers the way I want." "Do your citations like this." "Meet so-and-so." "Tuck in your shirt." God! Why was he so bossy? And that word he always used. Professional. Harris was always telling Luke to be more "professional." At least once a week. Was Harris even that professional? Really? He drank. A lot. And he made jokes. Why was Harris allowed to make jokes and Luke couldn't? Because Harris had power and Luke didn't? Was that fair? Because he could get away with it? Nonsense. Such nonsense. It just went to show that everyone was a snake. Even Harris. A snake. Like everyone else. Everyone only cared about themselves and fulfilling their core, animalistic desires. That was the point of existence—what everyone pursued. What society existed to provide. Society. Ha. What a joke. The powerful—like Ross and Harris—told everyone else what to do. Setting standards for everyone. So they could do as they pleased. Luke was different. He didn't care about those things. He was pure. An avenger of his father's death. Yes. That was it. He sought to redeem his family while—really should have worn a heavier coat—while everyone else only cared about self-gratification. And yet, they were in charge. Why? Age? That was part of it. They were also better at the things in life which bored Luke to tears—that bored him so much he didn't even know they bored him. They didn't register as boredom. That's how boring they were. A whirlpool that devoured his energy and ability to focus. Like schmoozing with professors or listening to other people's ideas and experiences. God. Who cared? Why did he have to listen to them? Just let him do his thing. Just let him read what he wanted to read. Write what he wanted to write. Otherwise, leave him alone. Unless it had to do with avenging his father. And now that was ruined. His entire life trajectory—in pieces. God. Why did that happen? What was his purpose now? Why exist? His family was doomed to be a footnote in paleontology's history. An embarrassment. Because Luke failed. He'd spent his life—no—if it was over, which it was, then that was it. Luke was done. Had it. He wanted a way out. He wasn't going to be a nobody. Wasn't going to leave his father unavenged. Wasn't going to be as powerless as others—

"We're here!" Black exclaimed. Luke blinked several times and returned to reality. He'd missed the entire trip through the base while the others saw housing units, a track field with a red band which highlighted the lanes against the snowy ground, and the road adjacent to the water. They approached Building 82, before which stood an officer with clumps of snow built up on his shoulders and on the rim of his hat and a large, snow-covered dolly which sat a few feet from the door.

"Thank you, Lieutenant," the officer said to Black. He turned to the paleontologists. "My name is Captain McIver. I'm the senior officer on base. I thank you for taking the day to come down here and help us out." The group entered Building 82, where McIver's aide handed the paleontologists nondisclosure agreements after everyone brushed snow off their clothes. "We could only conduct a brief background check on you all, given the time constraints, but we're not worried. You're all professionals."

The paleontologists scanned the agreements, signed them, and followed McIver to the meat locker. A skinny man in his late twenties sat in a chair by the locker's door. He had red hair and green eyes and stood as the party approached. Luke's face scrunched when he saw him. Then he lit up.

"Are you—" he muttered, "—who I think you are?"

The man blushed.

"I see you're already familiar with Mr. Noodie," McIver said.

"Call me 'Nathan,'" Noodie said as he shook Luke's hand. "Always nice to meet a fan."

"That's how old I am," Ross whispered to Harris. "I don't know who's famous anymore." Harris chuckled.

"Mr. Noodie is a 'professional adventurer,'" McIver explained. "He discovered what you're about to see." McIver's aide grabbed the locker's handle and turned it 90 degrees. "I have two questions when you see it—What is it? And is it alive?"

The paleontologists exchanged a glance. The aide opened the door and they entered the locker. Inside was the frozen Liopleurodon, trapped within its block of ice. The paleontologists were astonished. They ignored the drop of temperature and each circled the animal several times, carefully treading through the extra snow that the Navy had placed with the creature to keep it frozen. The Liopleurodon was mostly black with some hints of red. It had a crocodilian head and four flippers. Luke, in particular, couldn't take his eyes off of it. Wave after wave of energy surged through him. His head felt weird, as though he had ingested too much caffeine.

McIver decided the scientists had done enough oohing and aahing after a few minutes. "Is it a whale?" he asked.

"No," Ryan muttered, briefly glancing at the large door on the back side of the locker that the Navy had used to put the creature in the room. "It's a reptile. Look at its head."

"An alligator?"

"Closer, but still no."

"It's a *pliosaur*," Luke whispered.

"A what?" McIver asked.

Harris waited for Luke to answer, but his student was too absorbed in the monster. He turned to the captain. "A pliosaur is a short-necked plesiosaur. It was an ocean carnivore in the Jurassic Period."

"I see," McIver said.

"How did you find it?" Kelsey asked, her cheeks flushed.

Noodie stepped forward. "I, uh, I was in the Arctic…"

"On an adventure?" Harris asked, jokingly.

"Yeah," Noodie answered. "I was trying to touch a polar bear." The paleontologists gave him a funny look. "I thought it would sell a lot of article copies. A lot of photographs." He spoke with his hands.

"You're a braver man than I," Harris said.

"Thanks. I guess," Noodie said. "But I didn't realize the bear was a mamma with cubs. She didn't take kindly to my presence and I ran."

"That was ill-advised," Ryan said.

"You're tellin' me! Anyway, my team and I escaped okay, but then I saw something within an iceberg. Something green." The paleontologists looked at the Liopleurodon's green eyes. "I thought it was a jewel, at first. Wondered how it was so far north. I noticed the slit in the middle. That's when I saw the rest of the animal. Notified the gover'ment."

"How big is it?" Kelsey asked.

"25 meters," McIver answered. "80 feet."

"Wow."

"What was it called again?" McIver asked.

"A pliosaur," Harris said. He turned to Luke. "Do you know what kind?"

Luke's eyes widened. "I have no—maybe a Liopleurodon?"

Ross, whose face was cherry red, had had enough. "There's *no way* you could know that!"

"I mean," Luke said, "I'd have to look at its skull, but—"

"It could be a *different* pliosaur!" Ross claimed desperately.

"Come on, Ben. Don't be silly," Harris said. "That's not important right now."

"But how did it become frozen?" Ross asked. "The planet was *warm* during the Jurassic. Much warmer than today. There were no ice caps."

"Are you implying we faked this?" McIver asked.

"N-no," Ross muttered. "But the conditions didn't exist for this to happen."

"You're just trying to save yourself," Ryan said. He turned to

Kelsey. "You're the Pliocene expert! Tell him!"

Kelsey hesitated. "We don't know enough about the Jurassic to say anything conclusively. Tectonic plates and temperature changes zig and zag all over the place and—"

"Can you all relax and take a moment to appreciate the *biggest* discovery in our field's history?" Harris asked, trying to keep the peace.

"Yes, *Ben*," Ryan said with delight. "'Man of science' *Ben*. Isn't this *wonderful*?"

Ross turned from the others, constraining his anger.

Harris turned to Luke. "Is this a male or female?"

"At this size, it's definitely a male," Luke said.

"Good boy!" Harris said to the Liopleurodon, attracting funny looks from the others.

"Ready for question two?" McIver asked. The scientists nodded. "Is it alive?" The scientists looked at each other.

"It's possible," Luke muttered.

"Really?" Ryan asked.

"Yes. Reptiles can stop their heart beats if cold enough."

"I've never heard about anything like this," McIver said.

"Think about *Rip Van Winkle*," Luke said. "The Washington Irving story. A British subject during the Revolution, or maybe before the Revolution, drinks a potion that puts him to sleep for 20—"

"Think *Sleeping Beauty*," Harris said.

"Fascinating," McIver said.

Harris turned to Luke and pointed at the Liopleurodon. "I

expect this to be your senior thesis. Hell, I expect you have your work cut out for you for the next decade."

Luke beamed.

"Is he the expert?" McIver asked.

"He is," Harris said. "He knows more about marine reptiles than the rest of us combined."

"Are you his dad?"

"His professor."

"I see," McIver said. "I guess I'll ask you all a third question: Assuming it *is* alive—what should we do with it? I'd like to get it out of the base. Takin' up the whole meat locker."

"It's too dangerous to free," Harris said. "And I don't see it fitting in a tank."

"You can't kill it," Ryan said, looking at the Liopleurodon.

"Why not?" Harris asked.

"Life is life."

"But it could hurt people if it were freed," Harris said.

Ryan shrugged. "Trade offs."

"Lovely." Kelsey shook her head.

"If we kill it, would the museum want it?" McIver asked.

"NYU will be interested," Harris replied.

"I'm sure," McIver said. "The Navy will compensate you all for the trip back to New York. Remember the nondisclosure agreements. Don't say anything until we put it down. Then the museum and university can place bids."

"Will I get credit for discoverin' it?" Noodie asked.

"We'll make that clear in our press announcement in a few

days," McIver said. Noodie smiled.

Ryan turned to Ross. "This is *so* funny in light of what happened the other night. Tell me, how's the view from your office? Am I going to need a new desk—or, I guess I can just use yours."

Ross' eyes bulged. He cursed under his breath and stormed out of the locker, carrying his cane. Ryan smiled with delight while Kelsey shook her head again and McIver and Noodie exchanged a confused glance.

Harris turned to Luke and whispered, "Congratulations on 'winning.' I know how important this was to you, but try not to rub it in. It would behoove you to be the bigger man, and to blah, blah, blah."

Luke wasn't listening. His years-long mission complete, he felt purposeless for a moment before turning his attention to the next one. He stared at Kelsey.

Chapter Two
Restoration

February 21, 1911

The Liopleurodon rested on the ocean's surface, the midday sun increasing his internal body temperature. He'd spent the morning thawing from his icy prison. His breathing was slow but increased by the minute as he transitioned out of suspended animation. There was less oxygen in the air than during the Jurassic, making each breath worth less. His head jerked to and fro, his four flippers up and down, stimulating his blood circulation. He finally had enough stamina to take a breath and push himself underwater. Another thrust and the pliosaur's descent was underway.

    He barely made a ripple, despite his 25-meter length. This was due, in part, to his reinforced rib cage, an additional plate that was a ballast and a defense against enemies. The Liopleurodon's nostrils opened and inhaled. Water was brought to one chamber while scents the ocean carried went to another, allowing the reptile's olfactory nerve to map out his surroundings. It assembled an image of the North

Atlantic, his old territory to be conquered once again. The oceanic space between land masses was larger than the Liopleurodon remembered, while being narrower at the south end. The Atlantic lacked the funnel shape that he had known for decades.

Colder temperatures. Less oxygen. Different land masses. The Liopleurodon had to proceed with caution.

It took a few minutes for him to feel like himself and to be comfortable swimming. Once he did, he returned to his Jurassic-era priority. Food. He had failed to devour the Ophthalmosaurus and hadn't eaten for months prior. This was dangerous because he had to eat 1/50th of his own weight every day—a colossal three tons. The Liopleurodon felt insecure about this task because he sensed that he was no longer top of the food chain. This was a new environment filled with new carnivores and victims. He would need a steady supply of prey to survive and to rebuild his body weight and he risked being out-competed by his predatory successors.

The Liopleurodon smelled a potential prey item. He didn't recognize it but he moved in its direction. The reptile picked up others. A group. He still didn't recognize them. They weren't fish. Or sharks. Or reptiles. No matter. The Liopleurodon descended to the seafloor. He made visual contact with the animals within minutes, his black back disguising him. He restrained his desperation until his targets were in range. Then he flapped his flippers, rising from the depths.

His prey detected him. This was by far the largest attacker

they'd ever seen. They scattered, retreating toward the North American coast. The Liopleurodon was unusually fast for an animal its size, far faster than a whale, but the prey were faster. Well, the adults were faster. They could escape. The pups were a different story. The Liopleurodon made his first pick. The adults turned back, desperate to help but knowing it was suicide. They abandoned the younglings.

The pliosaur's flippers propelled him forward. His three-meter long jaws opened. The pups had no hope—until the Liopleurodon broke off his attack and retreated to the depths. The pups made it to shore, rejoining their parents as the barks of gray seals filled the air.

The Liopleurodon's instincts had overtaken him in panic, despite his hunger. He had never encountered mammals before. In the Mesozoic, they only lived on land as rodents among the dinosaurs, not conquering the ocean until after the asteroid strike ended marine reptiles' reign. This unfamiliar class increased the Liopleurodon's insecurity.

He swam out to deeper waters before taking a breath, returning to the seabed, and waiting for prey to come to him. Forty-five minutes passed when a two-meter blacktip shark swam overhead. A familiar sight. Sharks had been a favorite midday snack between larger meals during the Jurassic, something to munch on to satisfy cravings. He ascended and aimed for the shark's tail, a large target. The blacktip's ampullae of Lorenzini, a sixth sense that detected muscle movements, alerted the shark to its attacker. It dodged the reptile.

The shark panicked while the Liopleurodon tracked his victim through smell. He pivoted and lunged again. The blacktip banked right, narrowly avoiding the monster's fangs. The shark was more agile than its adversary and zigged and zagged while retreating. But it spent too much time darting around and not enough time building distance between the parties, allowing the Liopleurodon to aim his body and launch himself with a thrust of his flippers. The pliosaur bit down on the shark's tail with his tusk-like teeth, thrashed his short neck, and tore off the blacktip's caudal fin. The shark was too injured to escape. The Liopleurodon's jaws surrounded it and snapped shut. Thirty tons of force came down on the shark.

The Liopleurodon swallowed his kill, but he had wasted too much energy chasing such a small meal. He swam further out. He smelled a larger target—another shark, but this one was half the reptile's length. He had never encountered a shark this size before, misidentifying it as a small Leedsichthys. But the pliosaur had an easy way to learn the truth—taste it.

This attack's opening moves mirrored the last one. The Liopleurodon came from below, and the whale shark's ampullae of Lorenzini alerted it to the aggressor. The reptile's reinforced rib cage allowed it to out-maneuver his victim, and he grabbed hold of the shark's left pectoral fin. The fish's thrashing only sank the reptile's teeth deeper. The Liopleurodon shook his neck, tearing the fin off. The whale shark retreated, bleeding but not mortally wounded. The Liopleurodon swallowed the fin and gave chase. He had little trouble catching up with his victim and bit down on the shark's tail. The whale shark spasmed, its weight swinging upward, as the pliosaur increased his grip. The Liopleurodon thrashed his neck and tore the shark's tail loose. He then devoured the whale shark's remains.

History's greatest carnivore had returned.

...

February 23, 1911
Captain Owens watched as the trawl net deployed from the back of the *S.S. Animo*. Weights attached to the net pulled it under the surface. He smiled as it extended, knowing the school of tuna, the first the *Animo* found in almost two weeks, would soon be on deck and then for sale in markets. Such a catch justified the continued existence of his small operation. He glanced at Logan and Stephen Wade, a pair of Carolina brothers who'd worked for him for nearly three years. They positioned the mizzen sail on the *Animo's* mast to stabilize the ship's balance while the net deployed. Owens then monitored the crane-pulley system connecting the mast to the net, a vital piece if Owens hoped to bring the catch back aboard.

"Lower the woodbine!" he ordered. The *Animo* maintained its speed, risking the element of surprise and the tuna scattering. Owens looked to see Eddie Green, the scrawny young man and thorn in Owens' side for the past few months mindlessly watching the water. "Green! Get your head in the game!" Eddie blinked multiple times before rushing to reduce the *Animo's* steam. The steam cloud, channeled through a single high funnel, dissipated and the ocean's resistance slowed the *Animo's* momentum.

Eddie sighed. He turned to Owens, his fingers curling. Owens glanced at the net once more before turning to Eddie.

"I need you to focus, kid," Owens said. "All the time. But especially when we've found a catch."

"I *know*, Captain."

"It gets boring out here, sure, but that's not an excuse. What's going through your head that you can't pay attention?"

"On the contrary. I love the sea. It's why I wanted this job."

"Then what's the problem?"

"It's just—I wanted adventures of Scylla and Charybdis," Eddie said. "Tuna's a bit of a disappointment."

"Scy—what? What are those?"

"Surely you've read *The Odyssey*, Captain."

"I have little time for stories, boy."

"Even as a young man?"

"I couldn't afford such luxuries."

"Well—anyway—Scylla and Charybdis are a pair of sea monsters Odysseus encounters on his journey home from the Trojan War. Each dwells on opposite sides of the Strait of Messina. Scylla had—"

"This is not the time to discuss such things," Owens said. "Do your job. Back at it."

"Yes, sir," Eddie replied. He glanced at the Wade brothers, who glared at him before returning to their duty. Within minutes, the *Animo* was coasting, and the crew relaxed their shoulders. Stephen made his way to Eddie.

"So, sea monsters, huh?" Stephen asked. Eddie didn't respond. "Is that your thing?"

"My thing?"

"Everyone's got a thing. Somethin' that gives 'em meaning. Keeps 'em going."

"I don't know if it's my *thing*, but it's interesting."

"And you want to meet one?"

"I don't know what I want," Eddie said. "Adventure, I guess. Something more exciting than school or business."

"*This* is a business. And—you had a chance at school and you chose *this*?"

"Yup."

"That's—uh—that's somethin'."

"Why?"

"Because—why would someone *choose* this?" Stephen asked. "This is where men go when they have no other option. When they're tryin' to escape."

"I was trying to escape."

"That's not the same."

"It's valid."

"Not really."

"Whatever."

"Listen—we're getting off track," Stephen said. "It's swell you have interests—but realize the captain is stretched pretty thin. Larger operations take most of the loot. We're only a 20 footer. That's tiny. Plus, a fishin' operation is supposed to have a couple dozen trawlers. Do we look like a couple dozen?"

"I get it. I'm sorry, all right?"

"Don't be sorry. Just do what you're here for."

...

The Liopleurodon watched from below as weights opened the *Animo's* trawl net and the net grabbed over 40 tuna. He did not recognize this strange plesiosaur, with its long neck and expandable mouth that captured so many fish in a web-like substance. In the Jurassic, plesiosaurs were rivals for food, but were also lower on the food chain. This one was no different. The Liopleurodon had followed this tuna school 80 kilometers off the coast and would not allow the plesiosaur to steal his meal.

The plesiosaur had surprisingly little reaction as the Liopleurodon rose from the seabed. It must have been distracted with its catch. That was fine with the pliosaur, who opened his jaws and seized the tuna-filled net. The plesiosaur, seemingly oblivious to the Liopleurodon grabbing its web-substance, kept retracting its long neck. The Liopleurodon swung his body weight in the opposite direction, snapping the net loose without trouble and swallowing the tuna, pulverizing them.

The Liopleurodon monitored the plesiosaur as it shook on the surface. He remained confused. There was no way the plesiosaur still did not know of his presence. Yet it did not try to escape. Even stranger, it smelled oddly like the tree bark that

Jurassic storms sometimes threw into the sea. The Liopleurodon also picked up a new scent—metal—that he did not recognize. The plesiosaur also moved strangely—where were its flippers—and was uncharacteristically loud. Perhaps it was killed by the attack, but then, why didn't it sink?

No matter. Plesiosaurs were a favorite meal—a delicacy of medium size that provided the Liopleurodon a break from eating fish. He still needed to put on weight, and, as with the whale shark, he had a foolproof method of learning about new prey.

...

"What happened?" Captain Owens shouted, sweat running down the beard that covered the circumference of his chubby face.

"I don't know," Eddie said, rushing across the deck. He looked at where the trawl rope had disconnected from the *Animo's* mast. "The net must have come loose."

"That's not possible," Owens said. "The steel clamp is unbreakable."

Eddie saw a small metal object on the deck. He picked it up. "Are you sure?"

"Yes," Owens said. "And even if it was, the current is average strength today. Weather's normal."

"Maybe we grabbed too many fish?" Eddie asked. Owens and the Wade brothers laughed. "Or a shark?"

"What?" Owens asked after he stopped laughing. "You think a shark stole our trawl?"

"How else would you explain this?" Eddie shook the metal piece.

"I don't know," Owens said. "But there isn't a shark or fish in the ocean strong enough to rip the trawl loose."

"There must be some—"

Boom!

The *Animo* rose over the Atlantic's surface as though clutched by God. He carried it 40 meters to port before dropping the boat. Water came over both sides and coated the *Animo's* deck. Eddie felt disoriented, his teeth shaking, his head aching, as he opened his eyes to see the aftermath. There wasn't a man standing and Owens hugged his right leg, screaming. Eddie crawled to him.

"I landed on m' knee!" Owens screamed. "Broke the damn thing!"

"You'll be okay, Captain." Eddie didn't know what else to say.

"That's easy for you to—" Owens coughed uncontrollably. Eddie looked to the Wade brothers.

"Send an SOS!" he ordered Logan. Logan nodded and went to find the telegraph on the bridge. "Help me sit him up," Eddie said to Stephen.

Boom!

The *Animo* skidded across the water's surface.

"Hold fast," Owens said, pitifully. The three men rolled on top of each other, flopping around until they slammed into the boat's port railing. Owens took the brunt of the collision. He briefly lost consciousness.

The *Animo* capsized; the starboard side, now struck twice, dipped into the ocean. Eddie turned to Owens, trying to get the broken man to hold the railing. It took a moment for him to realize that Stephen was rolling back across the deck and to the water below. Eddie cursed as he lunged at Stephen and grabbed him with his right hand, digging his left into the deck and trying to establish a grip.

Stephen, bleeding from the nose, clutched Eddie's arm and dug his boots into the wooden boards, trying to slow his fall. He stabilized halfway down the deck. He and Eddie each took a deep breath.

"I got you," Eddie whispered. Stephen nodded.

An enormous, black crocodilian head emerged from the water. The Liopleurodon had binocular vision and watched the humans panic. His five-meter head was almost as long as the six-meter *Animo*.

"What the Hell is *that*?" Eddie shouted.

The Liopleurodon finally understood what was happening. These creatures were passengers on the plesiosaur, hitching a ride the way a bird might on an alligator. The plesiosaur had a strange outer-shell that smelled like tree bark, but these smaller creatures were vulnerable. The Liopleurodon flapped his flippers and lunged forward, coming part way onto the deck and clutching Stephen with the narrow front section of his jaws.

"No!" Logan shouted as he ran from the bridge to the deck, trying to keep his balance as best he could. Eddie gripped

Stephen's hand with all his strength but was powerless as the Liopleurodon pulled Stephen loose. Eddie heard bones crunching as the Liopleurodon withdrew and submerged.

Eddie's mouth hung open. He glanced at Owens, still clutching the port railing, solemn. Then he looked at Logan, halfway across the deck.

"I'm sorry," Eddie said.

Logan did not reply.

...

The Liopleurodon swallowed Stephen's body below the surface, tasting mammal flesh for the first time. The mammal's muscle had more protein than that of a fish or reptile, though this skinny one didn't have enough to be filling. Luckily, he saw three more mammals riding on that strange plesiosaur. The Liopleurodon circled back to the *Animo*.

Chapter Three
Go to it Laughing

February 25, 1911

President Taft held the tooth in his hands. Any blood or muscle tissue had been wiped away, revealing a weapon longer than his head and as sharp as a knife yet thick enough to puncture bone with ease. Taft shivered looking at it.

    He had gained weight since assuming America's highest office two years prior; now 320 pounds with a pasty complexion. The tooth represented the latest stress on the President. The Republican Party took a beating in the midterms, a tidal wave and holocaust rolled into one great cataclysm. This followed a rift with Roosevelt, his mentor. Taft had decided not to greet Roosevelt upon his return from Africa last summer, fearing it would diminish the presidency. In hindsight, Taft knew it could have healed their divide sooner. Taft tried to correct his mistake by inviting Roosevelt to the White House, but the cowboy declined, saying it was inappropriate for a former President to visit Washington. This new crisis evidently changed his mind. Taft was desperate to heal wounds; he spent too many days and nights worrying that Roosevelt would challenge him in 1912.

Part of him would like nothing more than to surrender the presidency. His temperament didn't suit the job, but Taft feared disappointing what supporters he *did* have. Nothing about the situation was fair—Nellie, Taft's wife, had helped Roosevelt push Taft into the presidency because she wanted to be First Lady, but Nellie suffered a debilitating stroke 10 weeks after they took office. This undermined Taft's presidency from its inception; Nellie had been his closest advisor and was set to be the most active First Lady in history. Now he had to tread Washington's dangerous waters on his own. Nothing he did satisfied anyone, particularly the progressive wing of the Republican Party to which he belonged, despite his efforts to restructure the government's means of collecting revenue by establishing income taxes on the wealthy and reducing tariffs paid by the common man.

Major Archie Butt, Taft's military aide, entered the Oval Office. "Colonel Roosevelt has arrived."

Taft sighed, feeling a jolt in his chest. He glanced at Secretary of War Henry Stimson and Secretary of the Navy George von Meyer, who sat on the other side of the Oval Office desk.

"He's early," Taft muttered. He looked at Butt. "Keep him busy if you can. Let him tour the White House and talk to the staff. Buy us some time."

"Yes, Mr. President." Butt left the room.

Taft had ordered the Oval Office's construction; it became operable in October 1909. He wanted it to be oval in honor of the

Philadelphia residence George Washington lived in as President. The Office had a simple Georgian Revival trim and the walls were covered in a seagrass green burlap.

"Where was this found?" Taft asked his advisors, gesturing to the tooth.

"It was pulled from an orca whale that washed up on a New Jersey beach," Meyer said. A notepad sat in his lap. "The whale had a seven-foot-wide bite in it."

"And this creature was under our control?"

"Yes, Mr. President," Meyer said with hesitation.

"Why wasn't I told?"

"The Navy Department was about to tell you when it disappeared."

Taft glanced at the tooth and then restored eye contact. "I assume the press picked up the whale story?"

"Yes," Meyer said. "It's received global attention."

"Who knows we had the creature?"

"The military and civilian personnel employed at Naval Station Newport have been instructed not to talk about it with anyone outside the base, since this is an ongoing situation. The adventurer who found the animal and the five paleontologists who identified it as a Liopleurodon all signed non-disclosure agreements."

Taft leaned back in his chair. He was concerned the scientists might talk. It would violate the agreements they signed, but it was difficult to anticipate the actions of so many people, especially if they could act anonymously and blame the others or were willing to bear punishment to achieve some other aim. The President focused on what he could control.

"The public knowing that we had it would undermine the government's credibility," Taft said. "Let's try to keep this information quiet, at least until it goes away. What was it called again?"

"Liopleurodon."

Taft sounded it out and twice repeated the word. "Do we have any idea how it escaped?"

"Our biggest clue is this." Meyer handed Taft a circular gold object that bore a crown's image.

"What am I looking at?" Taft asked.

"A German Army button."

Taft felt his throat and breathing constrict until he consciously overrode his emotions. He feared he was in over his head but didn't want to look weak before his advisors.

"Is that confirmation?" he asked.

"Can you rephrase your question, Mr. President?" Stimson asked, speaking for the first time. Taft took a moment to think.

"Does finding this button prove it was the Germans?" Taft asked. "Are we sure this wasn't left as a diversion—that this wasn't meant to throw us off a different trail?"

"The Germans are our prime suspect," Stimson said. "We're not ruling out other options, but we've long suspected that the Kaiser's spies have infiltrated our military and government as part of his strategy to promote his power at our expense. Including within the Western Hemisphere."

"But why free it?" Taft asked. "Why not take it back to Germany?"

"This might have been logistically easier. Or they thought they could deny involvement while still causing chaos."

"They may also be trying to sabotage your reelection," Meyer suggested.

"And get an isolationist like Bryan elected," Taft muttered, putting his finger to his lip. "Will they say they knew we had it to embarrass us?"

"They'd be shooting themselves in the foot," Meyer said. "They'd be accepting responsibility for freeing it and for any destruction it causes."

"Good point," Taft said. "It's probably useless to have Hill talk to the German government. They'd just deny everything." He referred to the American ambassador to Germany. "How dangerous is the animal?"

"We found the remains of a 20-foot long fishing boat," Meyer said. "There's no question the Liopleurodon destroyed it. The evidence was clear."

"The crew?"

"There were no survivors."

"My God." Taft again pushed down a surge of emotion. "I'll reach out to Secretary MacVeagh at Treasury. Have the Revenue Cutter Service work with local officials across the coast to shut down beaches and civilian marine traffic."

"That will be unpopular."

"What choice do I have?" Taft raised his hands and dropped

them to signal his lack of options. "I imagine other countries in this hemisphere will do the same. Maybe even Western Europe."

"We can also expect other governments to pledge to take action if it enters their waters," Stimson said.

"Even Germany?"

"Yes."

"We should do the same." Taft looked at the Navy Secretary. "Our territorial waters go for three miles off our coast. Have the Navy patrol that zone. Take action if they find the creature."

Stimson and Meyer exchanged a glance.

"This is a big animal, Mr. President," Meyer said. "It will likely spend its time further out to sea."

"We should consider an operation to track and kill it." Stimson completed the thought.

"That would be *offensive* in nature," Taft countered. "I would have to go to Congress to get authorization for such an action."

"That's a rather conservative view of executive power. Remember that Roosevelt sent the entire Great White Fleet around the world without asking Congress and made them pay to bring it back."

"I am *not* Roosevelt," Taft declared. "I'm going to do this by the book. I won't bend the rules."

"We're talking about an animal," Meyer said. "Not a state."

"It's still an offensive use of military force."

"Perhaps we should ask the Attorney General for his opinion."

"Leave Wickersham alone," Taft said. "I was a judge. I can

do my own legal analysis. The historical record is clear. Alexander Hamilton favored a strong executive as much as any Founder, and in Federalist 69 he wrote that the President could only direct wars that Congress declared, in contrast with the British king who could declare *and* direct wars. He said the President was nothing more than the 'first General and Admiral.' Or think of *Little v Barreme*, where the Supreme Court held that President Adams had exceeded his powers by ordering the Navy to seize French vessels *inbound* to America when Congress had only authorized the seizure of American vessels *going to* France during the Quasi War. Daniel Webster even questioned the Monroe Doctrine's legality because it acted as the President pledging to use force without Congressional approval."

"Then why not ask Congress for an authorization to use force against the Liopleurodon?" Meyer asked.

Taft's eyebrows ruffled in frustration.

"The animal's big teeth might be scary, but they're less important than my administration's agenda for this year." He looked at the tooth and paused, confirming his calculation within his mind. "I need what sway I have in the Senate to pass the two treaties that the State Department negotiated. Reducing the cost of living is one of the people's biggest concerns and lowering trade barriers with Canada on agricultural products and manufacturing will achieve just that. Canadian conservatives claim the treaty will lead to our annexation of their country and Prime Minister Laurier might dissolve Parliament to get a majority large enough to ratify. That would drag this out even more. That treaty and the arbitration treaty with Britain and France are my priorities. Not this sea creature."

"Would the people not rally around the President in this crisis?" Stimson asked. "It will capture their attention."

"The people seem determined *not* to rally around me no matter what I do. Ever since the Pinchot episode," Taft replied. "It's best to play it safe instead of opening Pandora's box."

"What if you sent naval vessels to escort a merchant ship across the Atlantic?" Meyer asked. "You could shoot the Liopleurodon as a defensive action."

"And what if it destroys the merchant ship?" Taft asked. Meyer nodded, regretting he raised the idea. "My decision in directing the Navy to patrol the coast is final."

"Yes, Mr. President." Meyer wrote down Taft's instruction.

The Oval Office door opened. Major Butt entered. "Colonel Roosevelt completed his tour. He's ready whenever you are, sir." Butt had held the same position for Roosevelt.

Taft took a deep breath and looked at the ceiling before nodding.

"We just finished," he said. "Send him in."

Butt widened the door and Roosevelt entered. The President and former President stood across the room from each other in a standoff, the three subordinates trapped between them. Eyes darted about. Taft was determined not to make the first move. He succeeded; Roosevelt slowly made his way to the Oval Office desk. Taft reciprocated by walking to the other side. Mentor and protégé approached each other. Taft gestured to the office.

"What do you think?"

"I like how you expanded on the West Wing."

"The Office was built on top of the tennis court."

"Aw, yes," Roosevelt said, melancholy in his voice. Memories of his time in office entered his mind. "The old tennis court." He pushed the emotion aside. "How's Nellie?"

"Good," Taft said with a small nod. "She's good. Her condition appears to be improving. She's begun planning the reception for our silver wedding anniversary this June. It's keeping her busy."

Roosevelt smiled. Taft opened his arms and they embraced, cutting the tension. Taft was a head taller. They released and Taft looked to Butt.

"Bring that chair over here for our guest."

"That's not necessary," Roosevelt replied. He grabbed it himself and brought it to the desk. He saw the tooth. "May I?"

"Of course," Taft replied. He, Stimson, and Meyer returned to their seats. Roosevelt remained standing while Butt exited the room.

"Extraordinary," Roosevelt said softly, swelling with energy. "A sea dragon."

"A Liopleurodon," Meyer said.

"The Jurassic," Roosevelt whispered. He glanced at Taft. "I tried to teach you about nature. About wildlife."

"I should have listened," Taft replied, smiling. Roosevelt placed the tooth on the desk and sat down.

"It's already destroyed a fishing boat," Meyer explained. "Do you know why it would do that? Eating a human would be like one of us eating a chip. It can't be worth the effort."

"This is about territory, not food," Roosevelt answered. "He's asserting his dominance of the sea."

"I'm sure you saw Hearst make a big deal about the whale attack in the *Morning Journal*," Stimson said. Roosevelt waved his hand, dismissively.

"Hearst is evil. His sensationalism got McKinley killed." He looked to the tooth and back to Taft. "Do you know where it came from?"

"An adventurer found it in the Arctic," Meyer answered. "He gave it to us." Taft grimaced. He was not sure he wanted Roosevelt to know the truth but had not told his advisors what to say in advance. A lapse in judgment from a fish out of water.

"I assume we didn't free him," Roosevelt said.

"Correct," Meyer said.

"Do you know who's responsible?" Roosevelt asked. Meyer gestured to the German Army button on the desk. Roosevelt recognized it. His eyes widened. "*Treachery!*" He looked at Taft. "What's your plan?"

"I'm going to instruct the Revenue Cutter Service to work with local governments in shutting down the beaches," Taft said. "The Navy will patrol our territorial waters for the animal."

Roosevelt's face scrunched. "You must act more aggressively!" He slammed his fist on the desk. "Chase him across the ocean!"

"I just explained to my advisors that such an operation would require going to Congress for an authorization to use force."

Roosevelt stopped his jaw from dropping. "Going to Congress will delay the mission. You'll be letting the Germans make the first move."

"What do you mean?" Taft asked.

Roosevelt pointed to the button. "Clearly the Kaiser wants it as a weapon."

Taft and his advisors looked at each other.

"If that were the case, why free it?" Taft asked. Roosevelt put his finger to his chin.

"The Army likely seized a narrow window of opportunity. But I know the Kaiser. He'll see it in action and want to use it against us and his other enemies."

"You're speculating," Taft said.

"No, I'm not," Roosevelt said. "It's entirely in line with the Kaiser's track record. Remember the Venezuelan Crisis of 1902. Venezuela defaulted on its debts to European countries and Germany initiated a blockade and bombarded Venezuelan coastal fortifications. They sought to establish a colony in this Hemisphere, rejecting the Monroe Doctrine. I deployed a fleet of 53 warships under Admiral Dewey to the region and threatened war. Germany retreated under the pressure." Taft weighed the sincerity of Roosevelt's argument. "The Kaiser is the most dangerous man in the world. He's anger-prone and thinks he's a descendant of Fredrick the Great. He even dresses like the Old Fritz."

"But going after the Liopleurodon would escalate tensions

with Germany," Taft said.

"On the contrary, a display of force would deter German aggression and enhance the peace. It would be our biggest display of power since the Great White Fleet."

Taft squirmed in his seat. "I'll instruct Hill to speak with the Kaiser and Chancellor. We have to keep stable relations with Germany until the animal's been dealt with."

Roosevelt sensed that Taft was cracking. He pushed into the opening. "You must show strength. Immediately. Don't wait for Congress."

"I won't violate the Constitution."

"Remember the Jackson-Lincoln theory of the presidency: national crises call for executive action, and it is the President's duty to assume he has the legal right to do what the needs of the people demand. Unless the Constitution or laws explicitly forbid the action."

Taft's jaw clenched. Roosevelt was venturing into his area of expertise. "When Washington sent troops to face the Indians or Jefferson sent the Navy and Marines to fight the Barbary Pirates, they ordered them to only act defensively until getting authorization from Congress." He paused. "I also don't want to waste political capital on this issue when I need it elsewhere."

"What's more important than this?" Roosevelt asked.

"The arbitration treaty, for one."

"I'm not familiar with it."

"That's because it hasn't been made public yet. It's Knox's big goal for this year." Taft referred to the Secretary of State.

"It's a treaty with Britain and France. It will establish an arbitration mechanism between our three countries. If it works, it will be a model for the whole world. A new global system that will end war. It's critical that it succeeds because tensions rise in Europe by the day. Surely, this is a more pressing concern than the animal."

Roosevelt devised his counter argument. "Is such a treaty in our national interest?"

"What do you mean?"

"We'd be surrendering our rights to a third party. It would be like watching a man slap your wife and letting someone arbitrate a solution."

"Theodo—"

"Death is not dishonorable. Men become mushy if they fear it. It's humiliating to adopt such a mindset."

"I thought you believed in peace," Taft said.

"Don't be outrageous!" Roosevelt exclaimed. "I won the Nobel Peace Prize. But there are some issues that *can't* be arbitrated."

"We ought to give this our best possible shot," Taft said. "We owe it to future generations."

Roosevelt shifted tactics. "These two goals work together, not in opposition. Killing the Liopleurodon will make you a hero. It will give you the political capital to ratify your treaty."

"Why are you so desperate I do this?"

"Because it's a threat! On its own and as a German weapon!" Roosevelt turned to Meyer and Stimson, both of whom had been quiet for most of the conversation. "Don't you gentlemen agree?"

Meyer and Stimson exchanged a look, silently confirming they held the same stance.

"The colonel is right, Mr. President," Stimson said. Roosevelt could tell the crack in Taft's armor had widened.

The door opened, and Major Butt burst in, carrying a paper.

"Mr. President!" he exclaimed. "Mr. President!"

"What is it, Archie?" Taft asked.

"Mr. President! The AP reported a new statement from the Ottoman Sultan. He said he wants to capture the sea monster and put it in a new aquarium in Istanbul."

Taft felt the urge to cry, imposing pressure on his eyes. He fought it, his eyes watering only lightly.

"The race has begun!" Roosevelt exclaimed.

Taft compressed in his chair. Roosevelt was right—the Liopleurodon represented global stakes and was attacking Americans. Doing nothing made him look weak—to America and to the world. Worse, it meant the end of his presidency. He had to act. Decisively. He looked at Roosevelt and nodded, accepting defeat. Roosevelt smiled. Meyer and Stimson exchanged another glance.

"We should ask the British to cooperate with us," Stimson said. "The Royal Navy is the strongest on Earth."

"No," Taft said. "Let's not make this more complicated. Our first step is to go to Congress."

Roosevelt restrained his frustration. He knew Taft would not be pushed from that point. He tried another.

"You should start putting our pieces in place so we can launch the operation as soon as the old goats in Congress can authorize what should be self-evident."

"I agree," Taft said. He turned to Meyer. "Who should lead the operation?"

Meyer had a name ready. "How about Captain Hawkins? He commands the *USS Delaware*."

"The *Delaware* is a dreadnought. Is a ship that size not excessive?" Taft asked.

"On the contrary," Roosevelt said before Meyer could speak, "it would flaunt our strength. Display the big stick." He turned to Meyer. "I remember Hawkins from when I was Assistant Secretary of the Navy. I would love to work with him again and serve on one of *my* ships."

"You want to go on the expedition?" Taft asked. Roosevelt turned to him, hoping he did not speak too soon. "Will Edith accept another period of separation? You only returned from your African safari in June."

"I would leave Edith on her hypothetical deathbed to go," Roosevelt answered. "I'll act as your *personal* representative. Make sure it goes smoothly. You can focus on passing your agenda and winning reelection. We'll keep the Democrats out of the White House for another four years. Forever, if possible. The party of slavery, secession, segregation, and socialism. They disgust me."

"I don't think it's wise to let the colonel go," Stimson said.

"It's not 1898 anymore and he isn't as young as he once was." He looked at Roosevelt. "Besides, we don't want you writing a sequel to *Alone in Cuba*."

"Oh, please," Roosevelt snorted. "The situations aren't comparable. My service in the Cuban war launched my political career. But my political career is over. You all saw how the midterms went. Now, I just want an adventure. Like big game hunting in Africa. But this will be the ultimate game. My magnum opus."

Taft nodded gently. Butt jotted down some words on the AP report and handed it to Taft.

"Please hold off, Archie," Taft said.

"This is an emergency, Mr. President." Taft sighed and looked at it. The message read:

TR wants to kill the monster as a launching point for a campaign against you.

Taft wrote the word "MAYBE" and handed the paper back to Butt. The President reached a decision. "I'd like you to go and represent the administration on the expedition. But *follow* Hawkins' command."

Taft's advisors couldn't believe it. Roosevelt contained his smile.

"*Thank you*, Mr. President. What reporters will attend? Who will be the Davis and Marshall of this journey?" He referred to the reporters embedded with the Rough Riders in Cuba.

"I would advise against a media presence," Meyer said.

"It's important for accurate documentation—"

"It's inappropriate for a military operation of—"

"What about the First Amendment?" Roosevelt asked.

"Please," Taft said. "The Lincoln administration established multiple precedents about restricting journalists from reporting on military operations."

"The corruption that Lincoln allowed in the Army and in government contracts led to the issues defining this generation!" Roosevelt said.

"Does your ring not contain a lock of his hair?"

Roosevelt grimaced, conceding the point. "You must learn how to use the press. Communicate your goals to the country *through* them."

Taft hesitated. "I suppose I've been derelict in my use of the bully pulpit. Nonetheless, I agree with Secretary Meyer. No reporters."

"What about bringing the other Rough Riders?" Roosevelt asked. "A reunion would—"

"Out of the question," Meyer said.

"At least let me bring General Wood!" Wood was the Rough Riders' commander.

"Wood is already Army Chief of Staff," Stimson said. "He's working on military preparedness and universal military training. These items are vital given the clouds gathering in Europe."

Roosevelt turned to Taft. "I ask that you place Wood on leave so the Old Icebox and I can work together on this mission." Taft kept his poker face. "Wood is great in a crisis. He kept calm when we were struck by a Spanish regiment in Cuba. He directed our counter attack."

"That would be more impressive if he hadn't led you into an ambush," Stimson said.

"It was the fault of a Cuban scout," Roosevelt countered.

"Wood can go," Taft said. Stimson and Meyer were even more stunned than before. What was the President thinking?

"Wonderful!" Roosevelt exclaimed. "Just wonderful!" He paused, thinking of a way to repay Taft. "I can give Hawkins advice on the Liopleurodon."

"I know. But we should consider adding an expert." Taft turned to Meyer. "Who was the paleontologist that identified the creature?"

Meyer looked at his notepad.

"It was a group of five. The only name I have available to me is Dr. Ben Ross. He's the lead researcher of paleontology at the Natural History Museum in Manhattan."

"Ben?" Roosevelt asked, excitement in his voice. "Ben Ross?"

"You know him?" Meyer asked.

"We went to Harvard together. What fun it would be to work with him!"

"We already did a background check on Ross," Meyer said, looking at his notes. "He's clean. We didn't have the time for full background checks of the others but Captain McIver says he wasn't concerned about any of them. One was a student. He was the real expert on the Liopleurodon."

"Inviting all five is smart," Stimson said. "We can get them to sign additional nondisclosure agreements and prevent any of them from talking to the media about the Navy having and losing the creature."

Taft chuckled. "Hawkins is going to have his hands full."

...

February 27, 1911

Luke stood on the *USS Delaware*'s deck, hoping to relax by watching the sunset over the harbor. The *Delaware* was a 158-meter long dreadnought. She was armed with ten 12-inch, 45-caliber guns in five twin turrets as well as secondary weapons and torpedo tubes. She, along with the five other ships that comprised the *Delaware* class, was the centerpiece of Roosevelt's naval buildup that established America as a great power. Most innovative was its oil-fired propulsion, which gave the *Delaware* a faster thrust, farther range, and more disguise than coal-powered ships.

His thoughts slushed around, breaking his focus on the sunset. He pictured a vivid daydream, imagining himself watching a 100-meter long trout slither down 79th Street. It carried half a dozen businessmen to the brothels. Its slime covered their pants. He saw this from the Natural History Museum's lobby, where Luke hoped to work but which had been converted into a courtroom. He sat in the defendant's seat.

Professor Harris was beside him, preparing files Luke could never hope to understand. Harris jotted down some notes, fine tuning his opening remarks. Luke glanced behind him and saw the faceless masses, awaiting his fate.

"All rise!" a clerk said. The Liopleurodon rose from the judge's bench, wearing a judicial robe. "People of Righteousness versus Luke Jones is now in session."

"***Be seated***," Judge Liopleurodon ordered with a hissing, snake-like voice. "***Are both sides ready?***"

"Ready for the people, Your Honor," Satan, the prosecutor, said in a deep, booming voice. It was the Satan of Dante, and not of Milton. Bat wings stuck out of his back and he had three heads, each of which chewed on a historical traitor—Judas Iscariot, Marcus Junius Brutus, and Gaius Cassius Longinus. All three traitors were alive while being punctured by Satan's serrated teeth.

"Ready for the defense, Your Honor," Harris said.

Judge Liopleurodon turned to Satan. "***You may begin your opening remarks.***"

"Thank you, Your Honor," Satan said before stepping over his desk. One head faced the jury while the other two watched the gallery. The middle head spoke. "The defendant's crime is coveting one 'Kelsey Painter,' who already loves someone else. The defendant seeks to sabotage the existing relationship, the relationship of others, for his own gain. Luke's job is to assert his logic over his heart. That is how righteous men operate. How civilization exists." Luke's arms vibrated. Sweat built up on his temples. "Luke has violated the Ninth Commandment and committed a crime against decency and against himself. He'll never be happy as long as he demands to be something that he cannot be!"

"I was made this way!" Luke blurted out. He heard Ross and Ryan laugh from the gallery.

"God didn't make you," Satan said. "*I* did. A being who will *never* be happy and who will take *everyone* down with him."

The gallery cheered. Luke was torn between feeling sick in his attempt to save himself and oddly content that he had no way out and could accept his fate.

"*Silence!*" Judge Liopleurodon declared. The room settled down. He turned to Harris. "***Begin your defense, sir.***"

Harris stood. "My client is powerless. I don't just mean against us, but against his own heart. He's a worm. He has no spine. He's a worm. His proper place is in the dirt under our boots. I acknowledge it was arrogant for him to attempt to take his place among the rest of us. To think he could ever belong. I ask that you allow him to return to his proper status in lieu of punishment. He's learned his lesson."

"*How do you know he has learned his lesson? Does he reject his infatuation for the girl?*"

"I'm sure he would acknowledge such if asked," Harris said.

Judge Liopleurodon looked at Luke and smiled. "***Let's test.***" Kelsey emerged from a smoke cloud. She had a bow in her hair and bracelets on her wrist; she wore a red dress with white polka dots. "***Well? What say you?***"

Luke fought his instinct and failed. "I'll never not love you, my queen!"

The crowd gasped.

Luke heard someone say, "I'm so disappointed in you." He wasn't sure if it was Harris or his father or a blend of the two.

"**Luke Jones is guilty of wanting what he cannot have**," Judge Liopleurodon said, bypassing the jury. "***You may see your love one more time.***" He picked up the gavel with his flipper and struck it. The table in front of Luke vanished. He jumped to Kelsey's feet, kissing them. The crowd laughed.

Satan plucked Luke from the ground and threw him to Judge Liopleurodon, who swallowed him whole. Luke fell into darkness, separated from Kelsey for eternity. He panicked, desperate for—

"Surprised to see you here. I thought your nose would be in a book."

Luke was jolted from his daydream back to reality. He turned to see Professor Harris behind him and then looked back at the harbor. The setting sun reflected off the water and into his eyes, forcing him to squint. Luke saw five other naval ships in the bay.

Their presence on the *Delaware* meant that Luke and Harris had already signed the contracts that Lieutenant Palmer, the *Delaware*'s lawyer, wrote for the paleontologists. The documents described their status as government contractors, pledged a small fee for their service, required a spot clarifying next of kin, and contained a nondisclosure clause. The contracts disclaimed any government liability resulting from negligence.

The scientists were told how the Liopleurodon escaped after signing the contracts.

"So," Luke said, "how do you think the German spy got it out of the base?"

Harris chuckled. "That's a very good question. I don't know if it was cunning on their part or carelessness on our part. Probably a blend of the two. These sorts of things have always happened. I bet historians can tell you similar stories of the Greeks and Persians."

"The government probably doesn't want us saying anything to avoid looking incompetent. Even though they are."

Harris *shushed* Luke and looked around, making sure no one heard his student. He briefly shook his head in exacerbation at Luke's lack of politeness before catching himself, knowing Luke didn't respond well to criticism.

"These are professionals," Harris said. "They make mistakes, but they're doing what they can. Some cloak and dagger stuff is going on. It's not our concern. Let's focus on why we're here. Giving scientific advice. Leave the politics to the politicians and the military."

"I don't understand why I had to come," Luke said. "What could I contribute—"

"You're the most important of any of us. You're the expert. They'll expect you to give a presentation."

"I hope it doesn't need to be formal."

"Do it as well as you can. We can talk it through in advance, if you want. The stars are aligning for you. Play your cards right and you'll rehabilitate your father's image and launch your career into superstardom overnight." Harris paused. "Don't repeat the scene from the restaurant. I don't know what you were thinking."

Luke sank into himself, losing focus from the pressure. Harris shifted topics.

"Are you excited to meet TR?" Harris asked. Luke nodded gently. His shoulders lowered. "*I* certainly am. A former President. And a good one. Do you remember when he was in office?"

"Of course I do. It was only two years ago. I'm not that young."

"Sure, but you don't remember when he became President, do you?"

"Not really," Luke said.

"Right. It was a big deal. McKinley was the latest in a string of corporate pawns and—it was tragic when he died—but there was excitement in the country when Roosevelt took power. He was younger. Progressive. Energetic. I remember being skeptical of him because of his war record, but just the fact that we had a President willing to take on the rich—even if he didn't do enough. It was the right direction." Luke was not impacted by Harris' nostalgia. "Is something bothering you?"

Luke took a moment to speak. "I'm nervous about being stuck on a ship with Dr. Ross. I'd rather get away from him."

"You're in the same field."

"But at least a break—"

"I'm sure he feels the same way," Harris said. "Probably more so. Discovering the Liopleurodon—its size—turned the tables on him. He's paranoid he's going to lose his reputation."

Luke grunted. "He deserves it."

"Building things is a nobler pursuit than destruction, Luke," Harris said. Luke turned away from his professor. "How have you felt since learning your dad was right?" Luke didn't know how to put it into words. "Better? Happier?" Luke shook his head. "It's because you're tangled up in negativity."

Luke wasn't sure that was true. He'd expected a celebratory atmosphere from validating his father that did not come, a silver bullet to solve his problems that did not fire.

"Do you remember my father?" Luke asked.

Harris sighed. "Luke, we talk about this every month." He noticed Luke shift from frustration to sadness. "Ben had already published his article by the time I entered the field. Your dad was on his downward trajectory, and I only met him a couple of times. He was clearly a man in pain. That's all I remember."

Luke nodded. "What do you think Captain Hawkins will be like?"

"I don't know," Harris said. "I'd heard of him when I was in the Navy, but I never met him."

"Watch him be a bureaucrat. A talentless Pontius Pilate who fell upward because he could sniff his way to—"

"Calm down." Harris shook his head again while Luke swallowed his anger at Harris interrupting him. Harris rubbed his eyes. "Feel like I go between not sleeping enough to sleeping so deeply that I'm still groggy. How are your other classes going?"

Luke's anger increased as he thought about school and the people he had to endure.

"Mind if I join you?" They turned and saw Kelsey. Luke gasped, causing Kelsey to smile and confusing Harris.

"I assume Sean's also on board?" Harris asked.

"He is," Kelsey replied. "He's arranging his room to be just as he wants it." She looked at Luke. "Sounds like you owe the Kaiser a 'thank you.'"

"Why?" Luke asked.

"An adventure centered around the animal you study," Kelsey said. "I'm so jealous."

Luke shrugged. "Who knows what else the Arctic is hiding?"

"True, true. It would be funny if there's a Noah's Ark of prehistoric life up there."

Harris nodded. "Probably a freak accident. And let's be mindful. Yes, this is exciting. But there are also lives at stake."

Kelsey couldn't control her laughter for a moment. "What terrible people we are!"

"No, no," Harris said. "Two things can be true at once. Though I doubt a raging mammoth would be as big a deal." He paused. "So, you're in the Cornell women's program, right?"

"That's right," Kelsey said.

"What do you hope to do with it?" Harris asked.

Kelsey shrugged. "Go as far as I can. Advance the field and our understanding of the Earth."

"And why the Pliocene?" Harris asked.

"The dawn of man, I guess," Kelsey said. "And the animals of the era are still recognizable today."

"Makes sense," Harris said. "I'm a theropod specialist because—well—they're big and scary looking." Kelsey laughed. "Who wouldn't like that topic? It's like asking why Shakespeare wrote about power. It's inherently interesting."

"Fair," Kelsey said. "Very fair. How'd you get interested in paleontology more generally?"

"Hmm. Well, I left the Navy, at least in part, to become a playwright," Harris said. "I thought prehistoric animals would be a good basis for fantasy tales, and, well, I never left."

"Did you ever write anything?" Kelsey asked.

"Yes."

"And?"

"I didn't have a lick of talent."

"You're being modest."

"No, I was bad," Harris said. Kelsey laughed. "Honestly. I would be embarrassed if either of you read it."

Kelsey laughed harder. She turned to Luke once she stopped. "Feel free to talk."

Luke froze. "I'm just listening." He hadn't found an entry point into the conversation.

"That's fine," Kelsey said. "Just know that you're welcome to—"

"Actually, I have a question."

"Yes?"

"How did you and Dr. Ryan get together?" Luke asked.

Kelsey looked to Harris, who shrugged.

"It was, uh, a contact at the museum through my program," Kelsey said. "I became his research assistant and—I don't know—it went on from there."

"What do you see in him?"

Harris glared at Luke but Kelsey chuckled. "He's brilliant," she said.

"Oh."

"We have common interests. Paleontology and all."

"Sure."

"And—you know—the Cornell program exists but it's still difficult for married women to be taken seriously and—never mind."

"No! What is it?"

"I—no—we don't know each other well enough to discuss personal issues like that."

"But what if—"

"Let's not pry, Luke," Harris suggested. Kelsey put her face in her hands and Luke glared at Harris, frustrated at his presence. "Why don't we change the subject?"

"Please do," Kelsey said.

"How about something uncontroversial?" Harris asked. "What does everyone think of the suffragettes?"

Luke looked to Kelsey to take the lead.

"They're a rowdy bunch," Kelsey said, "but I support their goal."

Luke nodded. "Me too."

"I would think young people would have more passion," Harris said.

"What makes you say that?" Kelsey asked.

"History will remember how slowly America worked toward its founding ideals."

"Well, a society needs time to adjust to these sorts of things," Kelsey said. "For—do you remember Julia Grant?"

"I'm not that old," Harris joked. "The Grants were before my time, but yes, I'm familiar with them."

"Right. Julia was considered an advocate for women's rights, but not even she was in favor of suffrage."

"Meaning—what?"

"That times change, and change is necessary, but these things are easier to absorb when they're not treated as wars on the status quo. Because people see it as a war on themselves and they get defensive."

"You should stand up for yourself more," Harris said.

"I do. I support the vote."

"But you're so nuanced about it."

"That's called maturity, Professor."

"Then you're more mature than I."

"You flatter me," Kelsey said.

"Happy to. But you referred to how married women can't get a job in paleontology. It must be frustrating having to plan for contingencies."

"It is. And I hope it changes one day."

"Or what about Mary Anning? How is what happened to her

okay?"

"Who?" Luke asked.

"Oh my—" Kelsey turned for a moment and shook her head. She came back. "She's who Dr. Ross wishes he was."

Harris turned to Luke. "You know her. 'Mary sells seashells by the seashore.' That jingle is about her."

"She did more for paleontology than anyone," Kelsey said. "She confirmed the existence of pterosaurs." Kelsey referred to flying reptiles of the dinosaur era. "She's the one who figured out that looking at fossilized dung would inform us what animals ate. She—she invented your whole subfield, Luke!" Luke's eyes widened, not sure what to say. "She discovered the first ichthyosaur and the first complete plesiosaur. She's why we know marine reptiles existed."

"What happened to her?" Luke asked.

"The men who comprised the British geological establishment took the credit," Harris said. "And now she's only remembered as a jingle."

"I don't appreciate being linked to the people who robbed my hero of her legacy," Kelsey said.

"I wasn't trying to. But you were qualifying your support for suffrage and I don't see the nuances," Harris said.

"Women have their challenges," Kelsey said. "But so do men."

"Like?"

"It wasn't women who died at Gettysburg."

"I guess," Harris replied. "I didn't mean to start such a

serious discussion. Tell me something embarrassing about Sean."

Kelsey chuckled. "Something specific?"

"I mean, not something he'd find mortifying. But something I can use against him if I need to or to get a kick. And I don't mean his theories."

"I don't know." Kelsey put her finger to her lip. "His sneezes look like whales discharging their blowholes?" Harris laughed. "Hmm. He takes himself so seriously. It sometimes feels like he thinks about Dr. Ross more than anything else."

"They're scorpions in a bottle," Harris said.

"Were they always like this?"

"More or less. I was there when Sean first arrived at the museum and he and Ben met. They circled each other like cats."

"How much of it is their scientific disagreements?"

"I think it's partially that, but there's a status element, too," Harris said. "Only one can stand atop the Mount Olympus of paleontology. It's kind of a small Mount Olympus to fight over —they're not exactly Caesar and Pompey—but it's what they have to work with, I guess."

"There are times I feel like I barely know Sean," Kelsey said. "What he wants. What he believes. And Dr. Ross—"

"Ben is… interesting. There are more sides to him than anyone I've ever met."

"Really?" Kelsey chuckled. "What's there besides arrogance?"

Harris smiled. "He's abrasive, sure. He's brilliant but not wise. I don't know, to me, he's clearly hiding within his intelligence. Don't misunderstand, he's the smartest man I know. But he knows he's bad with people. So he hides in his obsession of becoming a famous person in the history of science. Then he hits his limitations, causing a cycle."

"What's that based on?" Luke asked.

"Oh, just my observations."

"Does that explain what he did to my father?"

Harris was mad at himself for discussing the topic in Luke's presence. He should have known better.

"What Ben did wasn't okay. But I really hope you can release your grudge. Learn to move on. It would be best for—"

"Why should I?"

"Why shouldn't you?"

"Don't get cute with me, Professor. He destroyed my family."

"I know, Luke."

"You act like it doesn't matter."

"You know that isn't the case."

Luke broke eye contact but then restored it. "Do you think I'm more rational or emotional?" Harris didn't answer. "I try to be rational, but..." Luke's words petered off.

Kelsey filled the silence. "So, Professor—"

"Call me 'Will.'"

She nodded. "Will, do you have any theories about Sean? Can ya' help a girl out?"

"Sorry, but I don't know Sean as well as I do Ben. He's secretive. Our main experience together was in Wyoming two years ago. We were part of the Brown expedition."

Kelsey's eyes lit up. Luke felt a twinge of jealousy.

"You were there when Brown discovered Tyrannosaurus?" she asked. Harris nodded. "What was that like?"

"Oh, it was a career highlight. And a perfect moment to leave the museum behind to teach," Harris said. Kelsey laughed. "Who'd have guessed one of my first students would be this rascal?" He looked at Luke.

The sun disappeared from view. Darkness set in. Harris turned to the others.

"Let's call it a day."

...

February 28, 1911

A pod of five humpback whales migrated north, searching for plankton. They were led by two bulls, each around 15 meters long. The cows were both between 10 and 12 meters, while the calf, making the journey for the first time, was only four-and-a-half meters. He primarily drank his mother's milk. The males were tasked with defending the pod against potential threats. Their echolocation sensed something closing in on their position. Something big.

The aggressor was larger than any the whales had ever encountered, his speed greater than they could hope to match. The animal's black back provided camouflage; he was unaware the whales were tracking him, still unfamiliar with this new world.

The Liopleurodon hoped that preying on mammals would rebuild his body weight—still low from the Jurassic ice age—and that the mammalian blubber could compensate his energy level, which was stifled by the colder climate and reduction in oxygen. He opened his jaws, sliding his teeth together, sharpening them. The Liopleurodon's smell locked onto the five humpbacks—their sizes, their movements, their locations. He made his pick. He wanted the calf. He formed his plan of attack.

The whales initiated a defensive strategy. The females moved toward the calf while the bulls dove to challenge the Liopleurodon, their powerful flukes propelling them deeper. The pliosaur ascended, bringing all three males on a collision course. The Liopleurodon was as agile as a sea lion, using his flippers to effortlessly dodge the bulls without slowing down. He left them behind. The females placed themselves between the pliosaur and the calf. The Liopleurodon slammed into them, knocking them aside and shattering multiple bones in all three animals upon impact. He bit down upon the calf's fluke, breaking it. The baby struggled and the Liopleurodon thrashed his neck, trying to tear the calf in two.

The females came back, headbutting the Liopleurodon in his torso, but the reptile's reinforced rib cage absorbed the blows. The attacks were a distraction, however, and he dove deeper, his teeth gripping the calf's tail, trying to drown the baby and escape the females. This brought him back within the males' range, who each slammed into him. He lost his grip on the calf.

The calf's fluke was too hurt to function. The Liopleurodon was so large that his descent created its own current, dragging the calf from the surface. The bulls chased the pliosaur while the cows balanced the calf on their heads, trying to raise him to the surface to breathe.

The bulls pursued the Liopleurodon deeper, placing more distance between the reptile and the calf. The water darkened. The Liopleurodon tracked his pursuers with his smell; they tracked him with echolocation. He was satisfied that the males were too far away from the calf to interfere again. He turned back, dodging them once more, and closed in on the cows and calf. The cows were distracted by lifting the calf and did not detect the Liopleurodon's return.

The Liopleurodon grabbed the larger female's fluke in his jaws and dragged her away from the others. He released her once he felt she was no longer a threat. The mother whale could not balance her child on her own. He sank. The calf's lungs filled with water and he used his remaining strength to sing a death song to his pod.

The carnivore bit down on the calf's back, shattering its spine. Blood puffed from his mouth. The four adult humpbacks watched powerlessly as the ocean's returning apex predator swam away with the youngest member of their pod.

…

Dr. Branca arrived at Kurfürstendamm 1819 Berlin. He held a

cigarette in his gloved hand, smoke fogging his spectacles. A mink fur coat covered his dark suit, white waistcoat, and dotted necktie, while a Homburg hat sat atop his backcombed hair. However, his defining physical feature was his English mustache, jutting as needles on both ends. He glanced at the establishment, narrowed his eyelids to block out the sun, and dropped his cigarette, putting it out with his shoe.

Branca heard the *crack* of billiards from a side corridor as he entered the cafe. He scanned the crowded room. Writers, critics, painters, and composers conversed or worked at every table. Branca's patience wore thin when a hand rose above the mass.

He squeezed between tables and made his way to his destination, biting his tongue as he resisted imagining the germs touching his clothes. He took his seat at the soonest possible moment and breathed deeply.

"Sorry I'm late."

"You look traumatized." His companion was a woman in her mid-thirties.

"Don't be ridiculous," Branca said curtly. "I'm under a lot of stress today."

"Something at the museum?"

"No. Well, yes, but I took the day off from work. The Navy asked me to visit their headquarters at one and so I'll have to leave early. But these bi-weekly breakfasts are a *tradition* and I want the chance to check up on you."

"What does the Navy want? Does it regard that sea creature in the news?"

"Is that even a question? They'll want me to identify it, even though I'm not a marine reptile specialist. I can't say 'no' to the government, though, even if I wanted to."

"But you are the leading paleontologist in the country."

"Thank you. But I lack the time. On top of running the museum, I must plan the next fundraiser."

She looked confused. "Am I going crazy? You just had a fundraiser. It was wonderful."

"Don't be silly, Edith. I'm talking about the one for next year."

"Already? Give yourself a break!"

"These things take effort! I can't just display—is a waiter going to take my order?"

"You have to go up to the counter, Papa."

"Oh. I'll deal with that in a minute. What was I saying? Oh, yes. I can't just display the same specimens as I did this year. No matter how proud I may be of the Brachiosaurus." Branca smiled.

"Naturally."

Branca shook his head. "Why can't the government fund our efforts the way Vienna does for their program? This is why the Austrians are ahead of us." He shivered. "It's cold in here. I should have been a physicist. At the Kaiser Institute. I would get more respect. Like that Einstein-fellow. How about you? How's your painting?"

"It's going well, Papa."

"Have you sold anything?"

"No, but we're hopeful."

"You know I support you."

"I know."

"How about Hans? Has he made a decision?"

"Not yet."

"Uh. This isn't that complicated."

"He's weighing his options."

"He's not going to have options if the Army *drafts* him!" Branca stuck his index finger into the table to make his point. His shoulders hunched forward. "God, how many millions of our boys do they need? What is it now? 10 million?"

"They're concerned about the Triple Entente." She referred to Britain, France, and Russia.

"I know. But it's stupid. Nationalism is a disease."

"How do you *really* feel?"

"This is *serious*, Edith. Europe is hurtling toward war and your husband needs to either join the Lutheran ministry or come work at the museum. I'd prefer the latter but *either* is fine! I was in the Army before my studies in Strasbourg, and I don't want to see that happen to Hans. And to you. And to the children."

"I know, Papa."

Branca paused as he felt a wave of emotion. "I think about your mother every day. I sometimes catch my mind wandering to memories of the two of us when I'm not paying attention. And it hurts. Every time."

"I'm sorry."

Branca grit his teeth and pushed away the thoughts.

"I don't want that for you. I want you and Hans to live a long life together. For your children to have a father. It's so important that a decision be made."

"I understand," she said. Branca maintained eye contact. "Why don't you order breakfast? You don't want to be late for your meeting."

He nodded.

...

Branca fought to control his nerves. He sat at the far end of a conference table in German naval headquarters, which was in the Leipziger Platz in Berlin. The opposite wall held a blackboard and a world map. To his right were a wall of windows, showing a courtyard. To his left were portraits of Kaiser Wilhelm II and Admiral Alfred von Tirpitz, head of the German Navy since 1897. Besides these towering figures was an image so small by comparison its existence would not have registered if not for its excessive use of color. Branca stared at it for several minutes, passing the time by contemplating its significance. He restored his glasses, which had slid down the bridge of his nose, made slippery from sweat. He glanced at the clock over the blackboard. 12:58. He resumed staring at the tiny, colorful image.

"The Vice Admiral is never late," the man who had introduced himself as Rear Admiral Gunther said. Branca glanced at him and made a slight nod to acknowledge his comment. Gunther was only half of Branca's 67 years but his hair had already grayed—from military life crushing his soul, no doubt. Gunther sat at the midpoint on the right side of the table from Branca's perspective. Branca turned back to the small painting to pacify his thinking, desperate for his subconscious to remain calm and not embarrass him or offend his hosts. "Appreciating Tirpitz's dual beards?"

"I'm looking at the image beside him."

"Ah. The Vice Admiral has an eight-year-old who painted that for his birthday," Gunther said. Branca nodded again. "You're allowed to speak, you know. You have nothing to worry about."

"I understand."

A few more moments passed when the door beside the world map opened. A smiling man of 40 years entered. He carried a coffee mug in his right hand and a collection of files, pinned to his side, in his left. He wore a black cap, bearing the German naval insignia. An Iron Cross hung over his heart. Gold shone from his belt, from his wrists, and from the five rows of buttons framing his coat's torso. Under it all were a symmetrical, wrinkle-free white shirt and black tie. Branca looked at the clock. It was 1:00 precisely. The man walked to the front of the conference table, opposite Branca.

"Good afternoon, gentlemen," he said. Gunther jumped up and saluted. Branca, confused, followed suit. "That isn't necessary. Please, sit." Gunther and Branca returned to their seats.

The man placed his mug in the middle of the table, far from the edges, and proceeded to place his files in the exact order that he would likely need them. He spent two minutes doing this until he was satisfied. Then he made eye contact with Branca, a natural, disarming smile forming from his lips. Branca's shoulders relaxed.

"Dr. Wilhelm von Branca, I take it?" the man asked.

"That's correct."

"I'm very pleased to meet you. I'm Vice Admiral Michaelis. But you can call me 'William,' if you like."

"I would prefer to remain professional," Branca said.

"I respect that." He glanced at a form that lay before him. "You have an impressive background. Grew up in a family of merchants. Became a farmer. Oh." He grimaced. "A tour in the Army." He looked to Gunther. "Should we hold that against him?"

"Probably," Gunther said. Branca smiled.

"We'll see," Michaelis said. "That's very *suspicious*, Doctor." Branca snorted in amusement. "You didn't stay long, so I'll let it slide. Where was I? You left the Army and became a scientist. Postdoctoral work in Strasbourg, Berlin, Munich, and Rome. Knighted in '95. Very impressive." Michaelis briefly looked up and made eye contact. "And you've been the head of our Natural History Museum. Undoubtedly the perfect person to talk to about the current situation."

"Have you done much hands-on work?" Gunther asked.

"Yes," Branca replied. "I led the museum's expedition in the

East African colony."

"Eight years ago," Michaelis said, reading his document.

"That sounds about right."

"Some very impressive results," Michaelis said. "Though not particularly modest ones. Brancasaurus. Brachiosaurus. I'm noticing a trend."

Branca laughed. "I assure you, that's standard practice in paleontology."

"Uh-huh. I'm sure," Michaelis said. Branca laughed harder. "Brachiosaurus—that's the big one, yes? With the long neck?" Michaelis raised his hands and pointed them outward, his arms extended.

"Yes," Branca said. "It's the biggest dinosaur we know of. So far."

"My son and I saw it at the museum last summer. A very impressive beast."

"I agree."

"Do I understand correctly that you hosted a fundraiser at the museum earlier this month?"

"That's right."

"Seems a little demeaning. Having to play nice with the wealthy ladies of Berlin to advance our understanding of the Earth's history."

"It's a necessary evil, I'm afraid."

"The government doesn't fund you?"

"No," Branca said.

"A pity."

"It is. It would certainly make life easier."

"Well, it wouldn't be the Reichstag if their decisions made sense," Michaelis said. Branca and Gunther laughed. "Though I expect this is a global competition, like everything else."

"It is."

"And you're leading Germany's effort. Good for you."

"Thank you, sir."

"Of course," Michaelis said. "If you don't mind, Doctor, I'd like to turn our attention to the sea creature that's dominated headlines this week." Branca nodded. "Do you know what it is?"

Branca hesitated. "Let me start by warning you that I'm not a marine reptile expert. But I've followed this story. Everything I've read says it's a Liopleurodon."

"That's what I've read too. What's a Liopleurodon?"

"It was a marine reptile from the Jurassic. Think of it as a crocodile that only lives in the ocean. It's a predator. An air breather. I wasn't aware that members of this species could grow to this size, but again, this isn't my area of focus. It's likely very territorial and requires a large food supply. That explains why it targets human vessels."

"Is it a female? Is there a chance it could reproduce?"

"At that size I expect it's a male," Branca said.

"Will there be more?" Michaelis asked.

"I doubt it. It was probably a single occurrence. The chances that this could happen are less than one in a million."

"Fascinating. Truly."

Gunther cleared his throat. "Are we certain the Americans

had it?" His legs were folded, his hands clasped in his lap.

"Yes," Michaelis said. "Their government denies it, but our intelligence is confident."

"Such an arrogant republic," Gunther muttered. "How was it freed? Was it us?"

Branca's breathing tensed as he awaited Michaelis' answer.

"It wasn't the Navy," Michaelis said. "It could have been the Army, causing problems for us. That seems to be what the American government believes, to the best of our knowledge. I think it's just as likely that it was the American Democratic Party trying to sabotage President Taft in next year's election."

Gunther snickered. Michaelis turned to Branca.

"What would it take to capture the Liopleurodon *before* the Americans kill it?" he asked. Branca did not respond. "My sources inform me the wheels are already in motion. We're under time pressure if we want to make our move before they do."

"I—I don't follow."

"What would it take to capture it?"

Branca paused to think. "Didn't the Kaiser pledge to kill it? Along with the other North Atlantic countries?"

"He has, officially, but I suspect that he and Admiral Tirpitz will appreciate its application for the Navy."

"What does that mean?" Branca asked.

Michaelis chuckled. "Do you follow current events, Doctor, or is your time solely devoted to science?"

"I read the newspaper, though I'm sure I know less than both of you."

"Allow me to give you a primer." Michaelis moved his next document into focus. He spoke with a more serious tone. His smile tightened. "Admiral Tirpitz has dedicated his life to building the German Navy into a force that can challenge Britain's dominance of the sea. He believes that, by forming a fleet at least half as powerful as the Royal Navy, the British will be deterred from pursuing policies hostile to Germany and instead accommodate the Reich as a new great power. Unfortunately, the British are uninterested in sharing their place in the sun and have expanded their own Navy in response. They've also moved closer to the French, because apparently sharing power is more objectionable than allying with their historic enemy. Wellington and Blücher are surely rolling in their graves. Germany currently has 13 surface ships to Britain's 22. Five of those ships are dreadnoughts, including mine, the *SMS Thüringen*. The problem is that, as an island nation, Britain can focus its investments on the Navy, while we are forced to also fund a large army to deter the French and the Russians. This means, in the event of war, it is likely the British have the power to destroy or neutralize our fleet, and do it quickly, as Lord Nelson did to the Danes to keep the Danish fleet from Napoleon. Am I going too quickly?"

"No," Branca said, "but I'm missing where the Liopleurodon fits in. Surely, it couldn't destroy a battleship."

"No, of course not," Michaelis said. "But that's not my intention. Have you heard of Alfred Thayer Mahan?"

"I have not."

"Unsurprising," Michaelis said. "Every naval officer in the world reveres him. He's American, but his book, *The Influence of Sea Power Upon History,* is the Third Testament." Gunther chuckled. "The short version of his lesson is that it is *critical* to control strategic choke points, a concept he drew from Jomini. My vision is that we could unleash the Liopleurodon into a British port during a war. It could wreak chaos, disrupting British logistics by attacking supply ships and private vessels. Shutting down a British port would give us a decisive advantage in establishing superiority over the English Channel. That would sever British support for France and even open the possibility of an invasion of the British Isles."

Branca couldn't speak.

"I'm sorry, sir, but I thought the plan was to use the monster against the Americans," Gunther said. Branca turned to Gunther and then back to Michaelis.

"Yes, Rear Admiral, that is another possibility," Michaelis said. "You see, Doctor, the Kaiser is correct in believing that a single colony in the Western Hemisphere would be more valuable to Germany than the whole of Africa. For whereas Britain is a decaying empire, the United States is growing and is Germany's greatest rival for world hegemony this century." He pointed to the world map. "The Liopleurodon could help us conquer the Azores, followed by an invasion of Puerto Rico. That, in turn, would be a launch point for invading New York and elsewhere on the American East Coast. Unleashing the Liopleurodon in New York Harbor would enable us to march into Oyster Bay. We could greet Roosevelt at his front door."

Branca lost his battle with his nerves as pain swelled in his chest and throat. Gunther laughed.

"I can't wait to see the look on that Yankee's face. And to get revenge—" Gunther resisted water rising in his eyes. "I'm sorry, Doctor, but Washington's army killed my ancestor at Trenton. Bringing down that government is my dream."

Branca stared at Gunther and then turned back to Michaelis. Michaelis' smile widened again. It appeared disarming.

"Have I adequately explained the importance of capturing the Liopleurodon?" he asked.

Branca had trouble forming words. "H-how would you hold onto it? If you capture it?"

"A chemical concoction will keep the animal pacified. I've already instructed my engineers to draw up the blueprints for a holding tank. Perhaps you can work with our officers in training it—in shaping it into a weapon."

Branca resisted shivering. "Wouldn't—wouldn't turning the Liopleurodon into a weapon, as you describe it, increase global tensions and the likelihood of war?"

"We need every tool at our disposal to advance the Reich's interests."

"Is war in the Reich's interests?"

"It is if our alternative is submission to the Americans and British. Are you loyal to the Reich, Doctor?" Michaelis asked.

Branca's eyes widened. "Of course, sir. I am a proud, God-fearing German."

"Excellent. Then let's make a deal, shall we? Help me capture the Liopleurodon and I'll secure the Kaiser's backing for your purposes. You'll never have to hold a fundraiser again. It's a win-win."

"That isn't necessary."

"I *insist*," Michaelis said. "That is, unless you *don't* want to help our cause."

Branca vibrated with anxiety. "I'd be honored to accept."

"Wonderful. So, I repeat my question from earlier. What is the best way to capture the Liopleurodon?"

Branca raised his finger to his chin. Gunther spoke first. "What if we used the *Nautilus* to force it to the surface?"

"Like from Jules Verne?" Branca asked.

"Good catch, Doctor," Michaelis said. "The *Nautilus* is my crowning achievement, if you'll allow me a moment of immodesty. It is a small, one-person submarine that can be deployed from a dreadnought, such as the *Thüringen*. I believe it will revolutionize naval warfare."

"It could be the key," Gunther said. "We'd put blood in the water. The Liopleurodon would come. We would deploy the *Nautilus* and push the Liopleurodon to the surface, near the *Thüringen*. From there we could shoot it with a sleeper agent."

"Ketamine would work," Branca said. "It would knock the Liopleurodon unconscious."

Michaelis wrote down "ketamine." "I'll have it by tomorrow," he muttered. "I'd rather not put our submarine pilot in the ocean with the Liopleurodon, unless necessary. Do you have any other ideas for injecting the Liopleurodon with ketamine, Doctor?"

Branca looked down and then restored eye contact. "The simplest thing would be to put it in a canister, and then place the canister in a bag of chum. We'd get a bag that's too large for a shark to eat but easy for the Liopleurodon. The Liopleurodon will float to the surface. We could then attach it to the ship with harpoons and bring it back to Germany."

"Wouldn't the harpoons hurt the Liopleurodon's flippers? Could we not put it on the *Thüringen*'s deck?" Michaelis asked.

"I'm afraid not." Branca leaned forward. "It would suffocate under its own weight." Branca sensed Michaelis was testing him. He passed.

"Very well. I'll instruct the engineers to construct the canister for the ketamine."

Branca squinted. "Perhaps I can advise them."

Michaelis gave his widest smile yet. "I appreciate your enthusiasm."

"Of course," Branca said. "Anything for my Kaiser."

Chapter Four
The Kaiser's Pet

March 1, 1911

Taft's focus was locked on the ball. His left eye shut; his right narrowed, calculating the distance between the ball and the hole. His large hands gripped the club as he pulled back. He swung forward but struck the ball with restraint. Taft miscalculated. He had not applied enough force, and the ball, after an initial burst, stopped short.

"Damn," he whispered. He waddled toward the ball and paused. Distraction sabotaged his performance; a shame, because he did not attend the Chevy Chase Country Club as frequently as he liked. The President turned to his guests—Speaker of the House Joseph Cannon and Senate Majority Leader Nelson Aldrich. "Shall we get down to business?"

Aldrich nodded. "Why did you call on us?"

Taft put his weight on his club. He wore a cutaway suit and a straw hat. "I want Congress to pass an authorization to use military force against the sea monster." The legislators betrayed no reaction. "I want it to happen before the new Congressional session begins in three days. It can be the last act of the old Congress. Working with a Democratic House will be more complicated."

Aldrich took the lead. "I appreciate the respect you're showing the Constitution. It remains a breath of fresh air after seven years of Roosevelt. But—"

"I understand it's unusual to ask for an authorization of force against an animal," Taft said, "but I think it's important not to set precedents that degrade the separation of powers."

"That's not what I was going to say," Aldrich said.

"Oh?"

"This is an unusual procedure," Cannon said. "It will be tricky to pull off, given its significance and the time limit."

"It's not without precedent," Taft said. "Think of how Lincoln passed the anti-slavery amendment before the new Congress entered in '65."

"Even then the timeline wasn't *this* narrow."

Taft shrugged. "It's what I have to work with."

Aldrich looked to Cannon and back to Taft. "Why should we help you, Mr. President? I don't see how it benefits the Old Guard."

Taft had been in Washington long enough to know that appeals to patriotism or security wouldn't get him far. "We three haven't seen eye to eye on everything. But we've worked well together." He counted on his fingers. "The Payne-Aldrich Tariff. The Sixteenth Amendment. The railroad bill. Statehood for New Mexico and Arizona. Publicizing campaign contributions. The postal savings bank bill. The—"

"Why are you reminding us of your *progressive* agenda?" Cannon asked.

"It's what we accomplished as a *team*," Taft said. "The country is in a progressive mood, gentlemen, and I am as conservative a President as you can hope to get. It behooves your interests to keep me in power after next November."

"We might need more than that," Cannon said.

Taft turned to Aldrich. "We could make your Federal Reserve the main agenda item for 1913. Guarantee that nothing like the '07 Panic ever happens again." Aldrich sighed, considering the proposal. "Let me remind you of the alternative. Why do you think Roosevelt plans to challenge the two-term limit? Washington, Jefferson, and Jackson did not. Will he ever leave office? If Roosevelt is indispensable to the government *now*, will he ever *not* be? We'll have a King Roosevelt, a—"

"He's right," Aldrich said to Cannon. Cannon nodded. "But then, why let Roosevelt join the operation? What if he uses it as a launching point to challenge you next year?"

"That's what he intends," Taft said.

"So why risk having that cowboy in the White House again? He's more radical than ever."

"The treaties are where my reelection lie. They are items of substance, whereas the sea creature will be dropped from the headlines a week after it's dead. Getting Roosevelt out of the country will prevent him from influencing Senators during the negotiations for ratification and preparing enabling legislation.

That will guarantee my reelection is safe from Roosevelt, Follette, or the Democrats."

"The Old Guard isn't going to like either another tariff reduction or a surrender of our sovereignty to an international tribunal," Cannon said. "You can also expect the progressives to oppose *this* tariff because they're based in the Midwest and their constituents don't want competition from Canadian agriculture. The tribunal might have a better chance, but not if Lodge and his faction oppose it to hurt you and help Roosevelt. Frankly, Mr. President, you have an uphill battle no matter which way you turn."

Taft's jaw clenched. "The Old Guard *ought* to support me. Do you want Roosevelt to destroy the judiciary? He'll give its power to the momentary passions of the people."

That caused the legislators to pause. They took a moment to absorb how Taft was right in saying he was their best bet, their best protection from Roosevelt or someone even *more* progressive. Aldrich made eye contact with the President.

"This gamble is unusual for you," he said. "Risking him rebuilding his popularity by killing the monster. I didn't know you had it in you."

Taft smiled. "I don't know if it's wise to tell you this, but I have a contingency plan. An ace up my sleeve." He straightened his posture. "If Roosevelt challenges me next year, I'll instruct the Justice Department to sue US Steel for violating antitrust laws. Roosevelt signed off on Mr. Morgan buying the Tennessee Coal and Iron Company, in alignment with Rockefeller and

Carnegie, in exchange for Morgan bailing out the federal government in '07. All this would be made public. It will destroy Roosevelt's image among progressives."

Aldrich and Cannon exchanged a glance. Cannon snickered.

"You don't have to worry about King Roosevelt," Taft said. "Just get the authorization through as soon as possible."

...

March 2, 1911

Dozens of journalists and hundreds of supporters came to New York Harbor to see Roosevelt board the *USS Delaware*. Teddy flags bearing the former President's mustache and toothy grin waved in the air, as did moose flags and a long banner held by 10 women that read, "Get the Monster, Colonel!"

Roosevelt absorbed the adulation via osmosis. He doffed his sombrero, with its five inch brim, to acknowledge the crowd. It gave him the strength he needed to ignore the fact that Edith and his children had refused to see him off. William Shepherd of the *Milwaukee Journal*, one of his favorite reporters, approached him with a pen and pad.

"You seem in a gay mood, Colonel."

"I am *de-lighted* by the news that Congress passed the President's authorization to slay the beast that terrorizes our shores," Roosevelt exclaimed. He looked up, radiating in the light. "Let's also appreciate the sun that shines down upon us. It reminds me of my inauguration six years ago—another sunny day. I hope the weather remains wonderfully calm during this journey."

Taft and the Navy Department enacted a press ban during the operation, but their order said nothing about a media event *before* Roosevelt boarded the ship. Roosevelt knew he was stepping on Taft and Hawkins' toes, but he risked offending them to set the public perception that this was *his* mission.

"Is your hat new?" Shepherd asked. "I don't recognize it."

"Yes," Roosevelt said with a blend of excitement and sadness, "my old sombrero was kicked around enough during the New York election to warrant a new one for this hunt."

"Why do you want to be part of this operation, Colonel?"

"My purpose is two-fold: to act as the President's representative and to fight the monster. I will not stop until I have finished. Either he will die or I will!"

His answer triggered a *roar* of approval from the crowd.

"I heard you took the day off yesterday," Shepherd said. "How did you spend your time?"

Roosevelt puffed out his chest. "I rose with the sun and worked until breakfast. Then I took Mrs. Roosevelt for a long walk toward Cold Spring Harbor where I rowed for 12 miles. After luncheon, I went horseback riding and played six sets of tennis."

The crowd roared again. He continued.

"Please, take a look at this beautiful and majestic ship." He gestured to the *Delaware* behind him. "I cannot begin to describe to you the wonderful power and beauty of this giant warship, with its white hull and towering superstructure. I am all the more excited because the *Delaware* class began construction under *my* administration."

"Colonel, do you subscribe to the theory that the Germans want to capture the creature and use it as a weapon against us?"

Roosevelt smiled; his answer was ready—his allies had informed the press of his prediction. "We *know* the Kaiser and his lackeys regard the Monroe Doctrine as a hollow threat. Admiral Tirpitz has said publicly that he wants to build naval bases in the Caribbean and Brazil. Our naval superiority, built during my administration, has held back this aggression. The Germans hope that acquiring this monster as a weapon will alter the equation. We must deny them this acquisition and defend our hemisphere, not least the Isthmian canal."

"And what do you say to those who claim you're desperate for Mr. Taft's approval to stay relevant?"

"That's nonsense. The President and I have been friends for decades. I don't *owe* him anything. It was my friends and I who got *him* his current office." Roosevelt knew he had overstepped. "I am motivated by nothing more than a passion to destroy this adversary."

Shepherd had a final question. "Your critics accuse you of using this sea creature to rebuild your reputation after the Republican defeat in the midterms. How do you answer them?"

"My *critics*," Roosevelt jeered. He took a moment to think. His signature speech emerged from his memory. "It is not the critic who counts; not the man who points out how the strong man stumbles, or where the doer of deeds could have done them better. The credit belongs to the man who is actually *in the arena*, whose face is marred by dust and sweat and blood; who strives valiantly; who errs, who comes short again and again, because there is no effort without error and shortcoming; but who does *actually strive* to do the deeds; who knows great enthusiasms, the great devotions; who spends himself in a worthy cause; who at the best knows in the end the triumph of high achievement, and who at the worst, if he fails, at least fails while *daring greatly*, so that his place shall never be with those cold and timid souls who neither know victory nor defeat."

Shepherd nodded, conceding to Roosevelt's presentation. The crowd roared one last time before he boarded the *Delaware*. Once on deck, he shook the hand of everyone he could find, giving an explosive word of welcome to each. The *Delaware*'s band played "America." Then the sailors cheered Roosevelt's arrival for an hour as he stood and devoured every minute of it.

…

"How are you, Colonel Roosevelt?"

"I am disgracefully well!"

"Wonderful to hear. You look good."

"As do you."

"You're too kind." Captain Hawkins had silver hair that was in the process of turning white and a large skin cancer splotch over his right cheek that touched his eyelid, a consequence of a life in the Navy. He sat at the head of the table in the captain's dining room, which contained a spherical chandelier hanging from the rugged-looking ceiling and a black piano beside a curtain-covered exit. A white cloth covered the oval table and each guest sat in a leather-bound chair. Roosevelt was at the table's other end, General Wood sitting to his right. Dr. Ross, Professor Harris, and Luke sat between General Wood and Captain Hawkins, with Dr. Ryan and Kelsey on the opposite side.

Hawkins sized up his guests. He respected Roosevelt's deeds and energy, but also considered him a blowhard. Why did he insist on going on this mission? Duty? A glorified hunt? Please. Roosevelt undoubtedly had an ulterior motive. Wood was a capable man who lacked greatness; he was dragged from his duties to hold Roosevelt's hand.

Then there were the paleontologists. Why did Hawkins need five of them to kill a lizard whale? The student squirming to Hawkins' left was the expert and his professor was his mentor. That made sense. Ross was Roosevelt's friend and so nepotism explained his presence. Museum politics was why Ryan got a spot, and the girl, whose appearance in the dining room made Hawkins uncomfortable, was Ryan's date. Look at them. Barely restraining themselves from crawling on top of each other, even while in a professional setting and seated in distinguished company that included a former President.

Two African American sailors entered and distributed glasses of Domaine du Salvard Cheverny Blanc to the party, placing them next to their water cups. Hawkins took a sip.

"A time for drink and chatter is needed before any formal dinner," Hawkins said. "What say you, Colonel?"

"The drink portion of an evening shouldn't last long," Roosevelt said. "People get hungry."

Luke shifted in his seat as the narrow-bowled glass was placed before him, his forearms rising to his torso and forming a shield. Harris snatched it and placed the glass next to his own before taking a gulp and returning it to its place.

"Happy to take it off your hands," he said with a smile. Hawkins and Roosevelt both eyed Harris.

"Perhaps we should serve cocoa at the next juncture," Roosevelt said. He pushed his own glass back with his right index and middle fingers.

"What can I say?" Harris replied. "I learned my love of drink while in the Navy." He looked at Hawkins and Jenkins. "Some mentors taught me that it's a better servant than a master."

"When did you serve?" Hawkins asked.

"1903-ish. During the build-up." Harris turned to Roosevelt.

"What about you, Dr. Ross?" Jenkins asked. Light from the chandelier reflected off his bald scalp. "Were you ever in the service?"

"Oh, heavens, no!" Ross exclaimed. His face scrunched. "I would have been a terrible fit." He paused. "I might feel differently if I'd been an adult during the Civil War or a comparable existential crisis."

Roosevelt moaned. "To have served in that time."

Kelsey identified an entry point into the conversation. "Mr. Presid—"

"Call me 'Colonel,' dear."

"I'm sorry. Colonel, would you rather have served in the Revolution or the Civil War?"

"Oh, easily the Civil War."

"Why's that?" she asked.

"We've overestimated the actual fighting quality of the Revolutionary troops," Roosevelt said, "and have not laid enough stress on the folly and jealousy with which the states behaved during the contest. A very slight comparison of the losses suffered in the battles of the Revolution with those suffered in the battles of the Civil War is sufficient to show the superiority of the soldiers who fought in the latter. No Revolutionary regiment or brigade suffered such a loss as befell the First Minnesota at Gettysburg, where it lost 215 out of 263 men—82 percent. None of the European contests since the close of the Napoleonic struggles can be compared to it. The Light Brigade at Balaclava lost only 34 percent, or 247 men out of 673. Had the Americans of 1776 been united, and had they possessed the stubborn, unyielding tenacity and high devotion to an ideal shown by the North, or the heroic constancy and matchless valor shown by the South, in the Civil War, the British would have been driven off the continent before three years were over."

Kelsey glanced at the others, her hands in her lap. Everyone was stunned by the strength of Roosevelt's memory and how quickly and elegantly he formed such a detailed answer. She turned to Hawkins. "What of you, Captain?"

"Hmm. You're making me choose whether I would rather fight alongside Captain John Paul Jones or Admiral Farragut."

"Oh, Captain, Farragut is the easy choice," Roosevelt said.

"Is he now?" Hawkins asked.

"Yes! One Farragut is worth a thousand shrewd manufacturers or speculators."

"I'd have thought you'd take the opposite perspective, Colonel," Hawkins said. "Farragut had an institutional structure supporting him. Jones' accomplishments were won through nothing but self-initiative."

"Hmm." Roosevelt put his finger to his lips.

"Additionally," Hawkins said, "Admiral Dewey gave me first-hand accounts of Farragut. I feel as though I knew him, whereas Captain Jones has been a myth my entire lifetime."

"Admiral Dewey is a great man," Wood said.

"That he is. I hope we can utilize his services in the Navy's General Board for as long as possible."

"Were you with him in Manila?" Harris asked.

"It was the highlight of my life," Hawkins said. "I witnessed him destroy the entire Spanish Pacific Fleet in just six hours." Roosevelt smiled; his efforts as Assistant Secretary of the Navy had enabled Dewey's actions in 1898.

Harris completed his second glass of wine. "Were you in the Philippines during the insurrection?"

"I was," Hawkins said.

"How did you feel about it?" Harris asked.

"In regards to what?"

"Did you approve of our becoming an empire?" A brief awkwardness set in.

"Had we not established control of the Philippines," Hawkins said, "they would have been captured by the Germans." Roosevelt felt a surge of excitement go through him at Germany's mention.

"Sure," Harris said, "let's pretend the route to China had *nothing* to do with it. Sure. But wasn't our founding about being *against* empires? That we were *different* from the Europeans?"

"Professor Harris," Roosevelt said, "in what way were our actions in the Philippines different from our taming the North American continent from the Indian? Your position places you against our entire history!"

"*Your* words," Harris replied. "Though I'd assert one can be against our island policies without opposing the whole history of America." He looked at Hawkins. "Were you witness to Filipinos receiving the water cure for information?" He referred to waterboarding.

"I was," Hawkins said.

"Did you consider it torture?" Harris asked. "Did anyone?"

"Oh, please!" Roosevelt said before Hawkins could speak. "The water cure is an old Filipino method of *minor* torture, at most. It doesn't seriously damage anyone."

"President Taft condemned the use of water torture when he was governor of the islands," Harris said. "He instructed those responsible to be court-martialed."

"He also said the military mostly used compassion and restraint," Roosevelt said.

"He was being diplomatic."

"You're awfully critical for someone who *wasn't* there," Wood said.

"I didn't need to be at Moro Crater to know that what *you* did there was *atrocious*," Harris said.

"That is quite enough, Professor!" Roosevelt said.

"I'm sorry. I know I'm overstepping." Harris glanced at his empty glasses. He eyed Ross' to see if he could take it but saw that his colleague had already drunk from it. "I just get passionate about women and children being *massacred*."

Ross grabbed a loaf of bread from the middle of the table that no one had yet touched. He tore off a piece and handed it to Harris.

"It would be best if you sobered up," he said. Harris nodded. Ryan hid his smile. He loved every minute of this. Awkwardness set in again, until Roosevelt offered Harris an olive branch.

"I actually *do* think it's time we grant the Philippines its independence," Roosevelt said. "We've done what we can and it's a tempting target for Japan."

"Do you think Japan's a problem?" Ryan asked.

"Absolutely. Their aggressive designs were clear to me when I worked to end their war with Russia."

"How do you propose we deal with them?"

"Maintaining a large navy is the key," Roosevelt said.

Harris chewed on the bread but couldn't help himself from

pushing back. "What was the point of protecting the Philippines from the Germans if we're going to let the Japanese take it?"

"We've established a functioning society," Roosevelt answered. "Otherwise they'd have collapsed, as Haiti did a century ago."

Harris snorted. "I rue humanity's blindness toward those not like them. Imposing our ideals on a foreign culture that hasn't organically developed them reeks of Robespierre, not of Burke."

Roosevelt's eyes widened, the debate giving way to anger. He turned to Ross. "Did you know he was a member of the Anti-Imperialist League?"

Ross shrugged, unsure why he was being held responsible.

"I'm not a formal member," Harris said. "And I'm not some socialist or radical either, to be clear. I voted for you in '04. Along with everyone else."

Roosevelt bowed his head in appreciation.

"You two have beautiful voices," Hawkins said, "but I'd like to hear from others." He turned to Luke, who up to this point had been doing his best to not stare at Kelsey. "Young man, I've been told that you're the expert on the animal. How did that happen?"

Luke sighed. "It's been a lifelong—"

"To be clear, everyone," Hawkins interrupted, "this is the only talk of the operation that's allowed tonight. There'll be plenty of opportunities to discuss it in two days' time." He looked at Luke and nodded.

Luke mumbled, "My father helped—"

"Speak up, young man!" Roosevelt said. "I'm not sitting far

from you and I can barely hear you. A man must make his voice *heard* if he hopes to get anywhere in this world."

"My father helped discover the Liopleurodon in the '70s. He was a grad student at the time," Luke said louder.

"He must be very proud of you," Hawkins said.

"He died a lot of years ago."

"I'm sorry," Hawkins replied. Jenkins and Roosevelt nodded. "It's honorable that you followed in his footsteps. Advanced his legacy."

"Thank you," Luke said.

Ross looked at his hands for a moment, restraining feelings of defensiveness that converted to sadness and guilt.

"What classes are you taking at NYU?" Roosevelt asked.

"He's in my 300-level," Harris answered.

"That and finishing off some remaining courses outside the field," Luke said.

"Is that all you have to say about them?" Roosevelt asked.

"Cut him a break, Theodore," Ross said. He froze, embarrassed their shared history led to his using Roosevelt's first name.

"All I am saying is—"

"Do you even *remember* your courses, Colonel?" Ross asked. "You were the professor in all of them." Ross led the laughter around the table.

"What was it like to go to college with the colonel?" Jenkins asked Ross.

"It was as much fun as you'd think," Ross said. "He had a

great mind. He still does, but he had the extra benefit of youth. More energy than 10 men." Ross turned to Roosevelt. "Remember when you tried to have me join the boxing team?"

Roosevelt smirked. "It would have been delightful."

"I am a man of the mind, not of the body," Ross said.

"Without the body, the mind can only go so far," Roosevelt said. Ross' face flashed red at the sudden insult.

Hawkins cleared his throat, grabbing everyone's attention. "I would like to take advantage of having five paleontologists here. Can you explain where these large creatures, the ones in museums, where they came from? Where they went?"

Ross looked to the others and took the lead.

"Dr. Ryan and I disagree on the specifics, but I endorse the theory put forward by Darwin that different species are in competition with one another and the species that best adapt to their environment out-compete the others and produce offspring that carry their genes through the ages."

"What does that have to do with dinosaurs?" Hawkins asked. Roosevelt watched Ross with fascination as he answered.

"I'm saying that different species have existed over the course of the Earth's history," Ross said. "Dinosaurs out-competed their rivals for millions of years. Until they didn't."

"Millions?" Jenkins asked.

"Yes."

"I didn't know the Earth has been around that long."

"John Joly's calculations of the rate at which the oceans have accumulated salt from erosion determined they were between 80 and 100 million years old," Ross said.

Hawkins turned to Ryan. "What do you believe?"

Ryan glanced at Ross, who had never respected his theory, and made eye contact with Hawkins. "My argument is that species can shape their own evolution by acquiring new habits that alter their physiology."

"And those theories are in conflict?" Hawkins asked.

"They're incompatible," Ross said.

"I'm still having a hard time with this notion," Jenkins said. "There were animals that *used* to exist but *no longer* do?"

"Correct," Ross said. "The Liopleurodon is one example."

"But where did they go? Where were they in the Good Book?" Jenkins asked.

"That was my next question," Hawkins said. "How does this sort with God the Creator?"

"That question has been asked in one form or another since Aquinas," Ross said. "We're not going to resolve it before the appetizers are served."

"I personally see God as a guiding force," Ryan said. "He shapes the big picture, not the details. So these species existed but He didn't intend for them to last forever."

"Do you think He knows how things will play out?" Hawkins asked.

"Yes."

"As in predestination?"

"Not exactly," Ryan said. "There's some wiggle room. Like where I choose to go to lunch."

"Very convenient," Wood said. "Allow for God's omniscience and free will to exist together."

"I'm not claiming to have the answers," Ryan said. "This is just what makes sense to me."

"I *do* believe in predestination," Hawkins said. "Otherwise the universe lacks structure."

"You don't believe in free will?" Ryan asked.

"I think it exists but I think God knows where we're going in the afterlife before we're born," Hawkins said.

"I have a question," Luke said.

"Yes," Hawkins said. "Please."

"Why does God allow bad things to happen, if He does exist?"

Ross looked at Roosevelt, Hawkins, and Jenkins, to make sure no one was offended. None of them appeared to be. He looked at Harris, who was either too disinterested or too inebriated to intervene.

"That's where free will comes in," Ross said. "Individuals can make choices."

"Why?" Luke asked. "Why not have utopia on Earth?"

"Everything would be mindless. Like a machine."

"So He has the power to fix things but chooses not to? Like my father's suicide?" Luke asked. Hawkins and Roosevelt shared a surprised look. "Or the Civil War?"

"The Civil War was God's punishment for slavery," Wood said, reflecting Lincoln's Second Inaugural.

"But why allow it to happen?" Luke asked. "Or slavery, for

that matter?"

"Our decisions wouldn't be righteous if they weren't ours to make," Ross said.

"But He'll cast us into Hell if we make the wrong ones?" Luke asked.

"Don't forget that Adam and Eve ate the apple and separated us from God," Roosevelt said.

"But why was *that* allowed to happen?" Luke asked.

"Perhaps this is a discussion best saved for later," Ross said. "I can give you some literature on the topic, Mr. Jones."

"*Paradise Lost* is probably the best piece on this subject," Ryan said.

"Remember Job," Jenkins said, keeping the discussion alive. "We're tested to see if we'll follow Him no matter what."

"But why bother with that step?" Luke asked.

"If there wasn't suffering on Earth, what would be the point of Heaven?" Wood said.

"Does anyone have any thoughts on the *Jefferson Bible*?" Harris asked.

"What?" Ross laughed. "Jesus without God?"

"That's enough," Hawkins declared. "I shouldn't have allowed for a religious discussion. It's inappropriate."

The African American sailors entered with the first course—a piping hot tomato soup.

"Finally!" Jenkins exclaimed, smiling. They watched as the bowls were distributed. Roosevelt dinged his water glass and stood.

"I would like to make a toast. This is the cry the Rough Riders gave during the Spanish War, and I'd like to think that this group will hold a similar place in my life's story when all is said and done." He paused. "Rough, tough, we're the stuff/We want to fight and we can't get enough/Whoopee!"

The others applauded. Hawkins reached for his spoon. "Dig i—"

"Actually, Captain," Ryan said. "Can I say something before we start?" Hawkins pushed a rising anger and hunger aside as he sought to accommodate his guest. Ryan stood. "I have an announcement. This morning, Kelsey Painter, the love of my life, opted to make this mission even more special for us by making me the happiest man in the world."

Kelsey raised her hands, which had been hidden on her lap, onto the table, revealing a ring made of a low-quality gold band and a quarter-carat diamond. The others exchanged a series of shocked glances. They were that serious? Why on the mission? It was hardly romantic. Nonetheless, they applauded.

"Marvelous!" Roosevelt said. "Simply wonderful news!"

Luke looked at Kelsey with devastation. She avoided making eye contact. Ryan saw Luke's face and smiled.

...

March 3, 1911

The Liopleurodon glided over the seabed as the emerging sunlight penetrated the ocean's surface. He had digested the whale calf from three days ago and it was time to hunt again. He decided to kill two birds with one stone—having spent the night stalking the orca pod. The reptile studied his new environment in the 12 days since emerging from suspended animation, learning about it, and knew that the orcas were the apex predators of the North Atlantic, other than the metal plesiosaurs. He had clashed with the orcas once before, learning of their strength, speed, and coordination. Now, he deliberately targeted them, wanting to eliminate this rival group for food and territory.

His sense of smell allowed him to track the orcas' movements without seeing them. He'd learned from his mistake when attacking the humpbacks, now knowing that mammals could detect him from a distance. He swam directly under the pod and struck from below, targeting a female and her calf. The pliosaur slammed into the calf, pulverizing him. The adults delivered a series of clicks to each other, acknowledging the child's loss, and counterattacked.

The Liopleurodon shook the calf in his mouth like a rattle, releasing it once he was sure it was dead. He attempted to dodge an adolescent bull but underestimated the mammal's agility; it grabbed his tail in its jaws while an older female bit onto his front left flipper. The Liopleurodon was determined that he not be bitten by too many orcas at once. He aimed downward and flapped his flippers, dragging the two mammals deeper. The others hesitated. The orcas clung to him at first but panicked as the water darkened and they lost contact with their pod. They released their enemy. The reptile spun 180 degrees, snatching the male's fluke in his jaws, shaking it until the orca's tailbone snapped. He released the young bull, still alive. The female tried to retreat, but the pliosaur propelled himself into her ribcage, shattering it and flattening her lungs.

The pod's dominant male tracked the pliosaur from above. He sent clicks to the other adults, instructing them to attack the Liopleurodon's flanks as it rose to fight them again. The others hesitated but followed his command. They launched themselves at the Liopleurodon's sides; he dodged some while absorbing the blows of others. The alpha male attacked head-on, trying to grab the Liopleurodon's throat.

The reptile outmaneuvered him, grabbing the orca's dorsal fin between his fangs. The others bit at the Liopleurodon's flippers and torso. He was unconcerned, having suffered much worse during the Jurassic. The Liopleurodon flapped his flippers, rising past the juveniles and piercing the surface. He lifted the male orca over the water, still holding the mammal's dorsal fin in the narrow, front part of his jaws. Seawater dripped from the orca like rain. The orca considered fighting back by thrashing his head or tail. It would make him harder to hold but risked ripping off his dorsal fin, a fatal injury. The Liopleurodon turned and flung the mammal. The orca landed back in the ocean a short distance away.

The male sank; he was not mortally injured but was hurt and knew he was doomed. He ordered his pod to escape while the Liopleurodon focused on him. The others did not need to be told twice. The adults surrounded the calves and they fled. The male, sacrificing himself, awaited his fate.

The Liopleurodon did to the male what the orca had tried to do to him. He grabbed the mammal's neck in his jaws and crushed his throat, and then returned to the surface to breathe and rest, stretching his flippers. His injuries bled, but they weren't severe. The pliosaur descended after a few minutes to feed. He smelled a lot of commotion several kilometers to the northeast, including blood and metal. It didn't matter how many orcas or sharks he killed as long as those metal beasts and the mammals that rode them challenged his dominance.

The Liopleurodon, tired from battle, bit into the male orca's torso and ripped away its liver—the most nutritious part of an animal. He left to investigate.

...

A seagull landed on the *Thüringen*'s port side railing, startling Dr. Branca and disrupting his inhalation. He coughed, amusing nearby sailors. His anger spiked. Mindless buffoons. How dare they mock him? He was probably smarter and more accomplished than all of them combined. God, he hated the military. Why couldn't humans evolve to a more civilized means of resolving conflict? Or accept that everyone had needs to be met and grow beyond conflict altogether? Just live in peace. Then such institutions could be abolished.

Over three dozen German sailors stood on the *Thüringen*'s deck, all eager to see the monster. Most were giddy. It was far more exciting than their average day's duties. Vice Admiral Michaelis stood in the middle of the group, wearing an extra black coat to protect himself from the sea breeze, his left hand holding his right behind his back. His cap sat atop his head. He was stoic. At ease. In control.

Rear Admiral Gunther stood near the *Thüringen*'s bow. He peered through binoculars at an orange flag that flapped over the ocean's surface a kilometer away. The flag was clipped to a metal structure connected to the chum bag under the water. Its disappearance would signal the Liopleurodon's arrival. The sailors were ready to spring into action once the Liopleurodon digested the ketamine and rose to the surface. They would attach harpoons to its rear flippers and drag him back to Germany, as Branca had suggested. The Germans knew the Liopleurodon couldn't hope to threaten the *Thüringen*, which was 167 meters long and 24,000 tons.

Gunther's eyes and arms grew tired as the hours passed. The Germans had placed the chum bag in the water before dawn. Evening fast approached now, and their enthusiasm wavered. Branca glanced at Michaelis for the thirtieth time that day. Would he be held responsible if the Liopleurodon didn't arrive? The North Atlantic was huge, and a chum bag surrounded by blood was as good an idea as any for attracting the Liopleurodon. Perhaps its failure to appear was ideal, because that would keep it out of Michaelis' hands.

Gunther winced in pain from holding his position all day. Michaelis wouldn't keep him there all night, would he?

...

Almost two dozen sharks circled the chum bag. Great whites, hammerheads, sand tigers, and others all took turns biting it, only to lose teeth to its rough leather hide. They smacked it to and fro as the larger sharks sought to pierce the mass or break it apart. But the bag held firm.

The sharks scattered as the Liopleurodon rose from the depths, looking like a demon escaping Hell's darkness. He moved effortlessly, with no restraint, the master of his domain, arrogantly tracking the smaller predators. Sharks. No matter the era, they were the same cowardly nuisances.

The Liopleurodon slowed his ascent as he approached the chum bag, circling the object with his still-bleeding flippers. His olfactory nerve acted as a hand for the Liopleurodon to feel the bag's contents. A leather exterior. A bloody, meat-filled interior. A metallic core. The metal signaled danger but was not inherently a deterrent. After all, the strange plesiosaur from 10 days ago was delicious. He continued circling the bag. Something else restrained him from grabbing it in his jaws and swimming away—a highly objectionable smell—so disgusting that, if the Liopleurodon were human, he would vomit from revulsion.

The putrid scent clashed with his never-ending hunger. Finally, he rose to the surface, popping his head out of the water, and saw the *Thüringen* in the distance. More metal.

...

Gunther gasped as the crocodilian head came into view. "It's here!"

Excitement spread across the deck. Branca braced with anticipation, the wind playing with his mustache. He was obsessed with a desirable outcome but powerless to shape it.

"What did you say?" Michaelis said, loud enough for all to hear.

"The Liopleurodon!" Gunther exclaimed, his voice revealing weakness. "I see it! It's looking at us!"

"This is it, men! Steady does it!" Michaelis ordered. "The beast will be at our mercy within minutes." The Liopleurodon submerged. Half an hour passed. The Germans' excitement faded. "What's happening, Gunther?"

"I don't know," Gunther said. "The flag still stands."

Michaelis would have suppressed his anger, but he'd done it for so many years he didn't feel it anymore. He turned to the aide next to him.

"Tell Joachim to deploy the *Nautilus*."

"Are you sure, sir?"

"Don't question me, Lieutenant. I want to know what's happening."

...

Lieutenant Commander Joachim could barely see out of his

periscope as the *Nautilus* cut through the water. The lights shining from the submarine's nose didn't help. Sweat built on his temples and on the palms of his hands as they clutched a joystick. The *Nautilus* had six missiles, but Joachim wondered how useful they would be when battling the Liopleurodon, which was far more agile than this prototype vehicle. The universe of blue was penetrated by a dark mass in the distance that became clearer as the *Nautilus* got closer.

The Liopleurodon was still circling the chum bag, repelled by the stench inside of it but reluctant to leave until he detected a different food source in the distance. He smelled the *Nautilus* coming toward him and broke his circular formation to investigate.

Joachim couldn't breathe as the Liopleurodon came closer. He put his thumb near the red button that was the torpedoes' trigger, ready to fire if the monster attacked. But he did not attack. He stopped once he was a quarter of a kilometer away from the *Nautilus*. The Liopleurodon's four flippers moved in small, synchronized circles to keep himself in place. Joachim's heart was in his mouth, unsure what the Liopleurodon was doing.

The reptile looked gentle and inquisitive. His olfactory nerve mapped out the *Nautilus*. This was a large, metallic object that was under the water and had approached the Liopleurodon and his potential food. He had never known anything like this 12-meter long creature before.

A small flap of the Liopleurodon's flippers brought it closer. Joachim was motionless, watching the Liopleurodon and resisting the fear that clawed into his psyche. He couldn't afford to panic. He had to remember the torpedo trigger but didn't want to press it.

The Liopleurodon paused again. He had invaded the *Nautilus'* personal space and the *Nautilus* hadn't backed down. This was a worthy rival, the first the Liopleurodon had met since entering the twentieth century. The Liopleurodon wasn't interested in a fight; he was still tired from battling the orca pod. Besides, it wasn't clear which would survive.

Joachim saw the side of the Liopleurodon's head as it turned to leave. The Liopleurodon's jaws curved upward near the back, under his eye, forming a sinister grin. Joachim could no longer resist his terror. Tears fell down his cheeks, beyond his control. One more flap of his flippers and the Liopleurodon was gone, out of Joachim's view and conceding the territory to the *Nautilus*.

...

Joachim was on the *Thüringen*'s deck an hour later as evening turned to night. His body shook and his teeth clattered. He approached Michaelis.

"What happened?" Michaelis asked. Branca, who had moved closer to the Vice Admiral, had not heard him speak with as rough a tone before.

"That was incredible, sir," Joachim said. "I've never witnessed anything like it. It's the most powerful thing I've ever seen. Nothing can control or stop it. And that mouth—it looked like a demon. Are you sure it's an animal? It might be possessed by the Devil!"

"What happened?" Michaelis asked.

"Please don't put me in the water with it again, sir. I beg you," Joachim said. "I won't come back alive."

"Don't make me ask a third time."

"I'm sorry, sir. All I saw was the monster circling the bait. It kept circling it, over and over. Like it was debating what to do. Then it saw me and left."

"I understand." Michaelis smiled and put his hand on Joachim's shoulder. "Thank you for doing your duty. Take the night off. And tomorrow."

"Yes, sir." Joachim left.

Michaelis turned to the sailors. "Let's return to port. Today was disappointing, but tomorrow belongs to us. I'm very proud of all of you." The group dispersed. Branca allowed himself to breathe. His day from Hell was over. "A word, Doctor." What now? Branca walked over to Michaelis. Gunther joined them. "You are not needed here, Gunther. Direct our return to port."

"Yes, sir."

Soon, Michaelis and Branca were alone on the deck. Michaelis' smile disappeared. He had a dead stare, like a shark's eye.

"What went wrong?" he asked. "*Explain* yourself."

"I don't know, sir. It was a good plan," Branca said. "Perhaps the ship's presence spooked it."

Michaelis was not amused. "The engineers informed me that you instructed them to coat the ketamine canister with citrus. Why?"

Branca felt his breathing restrict again.

"It was good for the canister, sir. It protec—protects it from the chum. From the blood." Michaelis maintained his stare. "I'm s-sorry it didn't work. But I don't care about the money you promised for the museum. Let me just return home and we'll forget we ever knew each other."

Michaelis said nothing as he studied Branca's eyes.

"No." Branca froze. "I'm not done with you," Michaelis said. He retired to his cabin, leaving Branca alone on the *Thüringen*'s deck.

Chapter Five
Falls the Shadow

March 4, 1911

Luke waited anxiously on the opposite end of the corridor from the meeting room. He didn't want to be late—especially if it led to another Harris lecture—but he knew this was his best chance to talk to Kelsey before the *Delaware*'s operation was launched. His excitement led to another daydream:

Kelsey sat atop a Roman column in her living room. She wore a sleeveless white dress, her right leg folded over her left, a glass of wine in her hand. Her hair was pulled back in a ponytail. She took a sip as Luke entered the room. His head was at the same height as her feet.

"Have you completed your daily tasks?" she asked.

"Yes, dear," Luke said. "The children are in bed. The house is clean. Your bath is ready."

"Very good. What about the research for my next paper?"

"I've completed it. It's sitting next to the bust of Mary Shelley. You just need to write it up."

"Wonderful," she said. "You did well today, Luke."

"Thank you." He blushed.

"Why are you so good to me?"

"Serving you is my raison d'etre."

Kelsey smiled. "I knew you were the one from the moment we met. My relationship with Sean was set on its path to extinction."

"Let us not speak his name in our home."

"I will do as I like."

"O-of course, my love."

Kelsey smiled and he smiled back. His left hand held his right wrist in front of him. Dr. Frankenstein and his monster entered from another chamber, speaking inaudibly as they walked by and exited.

"Tell me again why you love me," Kelsey said.

"You're the most beautiful woman I've ever met! It was my honor to die for you!"

"Is that all?"

"What more can I say?" he asked.

She snorted. "A poet you're not."

Luke paused. "I feel like who I'm supposed to be when we're together. I feel safe. Like the forces that used to hurt me can't reach me anymore."

"That will do. Now help me down from here so I can take my bath."

She released her wine glass and pushed herself from the column. Luke caught her and they embraced.

Luke regained focus when he saw Kelsey, the real Kelsey,

turn into the corridor, panting. She glanced at the room number written on her notepad for the tenth time that morning. It started with a "3." The third floor. She cursed herself for forgetting that the floor numbers were the reverse of a normal building, meaning the top deck was floor one and each succeeding floor below increased numerically. She had even left with time to spare and was *still* late from getting lost. Ryan had checked up on her that morning and she had assured him that she could find the room without a problem. She looked up and saw the correct room number. Finally, some success! She huffed and closed in on her destination.

"Kelsey, I'm glad I caught you!"

She took a moment to process Luke's voice penetrating her reality. She looked at the meeting hall and then back to Luke. The young man was poorly dressed—his tie loose, his hair only partially brushed because he gave up after encountering difficulty.

"Uh, hi, Luke. What is it?"

"Can we talk?"

Kelsey gripped her notepad tighter. "Does it have to be now? We're already late."

Luke's face flashed with anger, but he suppressed his emotions. He implemented Plan B, raising a set of papers clipped together. "I wrote you a letter," he said. "I'd like you to read it, when you have the time."

Kelsey smiled. "That's sweet, Luke. Thank you. I'll read it this evening." He smiled like a puppy. She took the letter and waited for him to say something, but he didn't. "Why don't we take our seats?" He nodded and followed her to the door.

"Luke." He turned to see Harris. Luke was surprised, assuming the professor was already seated, but Harris moved at his usual, leisurely pace.

"Morning, Professor."

"Let's talk for a minute."

"Shouldn't we go in?"

"That can wait."

"Um—okay." Harris guided Luke away from the door, his left arm around his student's back. Harris looked Luke in the eye but struggled with his wording. "What is it, Professor?"

Harris whispered. "I don't know what's going on between you and Miss Painter, but it has to stop." Luke's brow furrowed. "Dr. Ryan is going to be your colleague and is a leading figure in this field. I understand that you're a young man with a crush, but trying to woo Dr. Ryan's fiancé is extremely unethical and unprofessional."

"You need to stop lecturing me as if—"

"Listen to me, Luke. I'm trying to save you from destroying your career before it's even started. Think about how far you've come. You proved that your father was right. He was *right*! That's all that you've cared about for as long as I've known you. And now you have the most extraordinary opportunity I've ever seen. Honestly—of *any*one in *any* field I've ever heard of—you'll spend 50 years as the world's most famous paleontologist —and I don't want you to blow it."

Luke glared at him. Harris shifted tactics.

"Let's say that two pterosaurs are flying over Laurasia." Harris referred to one of the two continents that existed during the Jurassic. "They look down and they see dozens of different dinosaurs wandering the land. One laughs. He says, 'poor things. If they thought a bit harder, maybe they could rise to the sky like us.' The other one says, 'that's not enough. They'd have to be light to stay in the air.' The first looks at her and asks, 'what's air?'"

Luke's eyebrow narrowed, softening.

"Remember a few nights ago when you said you try to be rational?" Harris asked. "It took me a long time to learn that I'm not the center of the universe. It's our default perspective and you're still young. You have the time to learn how to see things objectively and logically and with nuance. *That's* the key to maturity. *That* will get you far in life. In your career. In love. In whatever else."

Luke's shoulders relaxed. Harris smiled.

"It would help if you learn to dress like a man." He fixed Luke's tie. He looked at Luke's hair but didn't have the time to straighten that mess. "Come on. We're late."

They opened the door.

"This is a strategy session for a military operation. It's no place for a lady."

"But Captain—"

"I am sure you are *more* than capable to contribute, Miss Painter, but decorum matters on my ship."

"I *really* must insist that she be allowed to stay, Captain Hawkins."

"You are free to join her, Dr. Ryan, but I'm putting my foot down."

Ryan turned to Kelsey and shrugged. Her mouth dropped. She grunted and grabbed her notepad, pen, and letter and barged out the door. Luke turned to Harris for guidance on whether he should join her. Harris shook his head.

They moved to the other side of the table so their backs faced the small windows near the ceiling. The seating arrangement was similar to the inaugural dinner two nights prior. Hawkins stood at the end of the table that was opposite the door. A blackboard hung behind him. Commander Jenkins sat to his left and Lieutenant Palmer, who recently graduated law school on the Navy's dime, sat to his right. Colonel Roosevelt, who sipped from a large coffee mug and wore a cowboy hat, sat at the other end of the table. General Wood sat to Roosevelt's left. Dr. Ryan sat next to Palmer while the chair that Kelsey pushed out was between Ryan and Wood. Luke and Harris were flanked by Roosevelt and Jenkins, along with Dr. Ross, who sat beside Jenkins.

Hawkins resisted yawning as he looked at the men around the table. He briefly glanced at Roosevelt, who stared back at him. Roosevelt spent the morning twilight hours running around the *Delaware*, offering pointers on whatever he liked. He then prepared a document providing Hawkins with feedback. Roosevelt had wind in his sails; news of the German attempt to capture the Liopleurodon validated his argument and disproved Hawkins' suspicion that the former President was just playing games. Hawkins also noted that Wood wore his general's uniform and had the Medal of Honor, earned during a campaign against the Apache, hanging around his neck.

Hawkins saw Luke and Harris, his patience thinning as Luke organized his papers. He would be ready if he'd arrived on time. Secretary Meyer put renewed pressure on Hawkins to act quickly after the previous day's news of the German operation. The captain was determined to remain in control of events. Luke finally looked up to meet Hawkins' eyes.

"Are you ready?" Hawkins asked.

"Yes, sir."

"You're the man of the hour." Hawkins placed the Liopleurodon tooth pulled from the orca nine days ago on the table. "Explain to me this killer-banana's original owner. I don't care about formality."

Luke turned to all of the eyes staring at him. Roosevelt's were curious. Ryan's were resentful. Harris' were proud. Harris didn't know what to expect, because Luke had declined his offer to discuss the presentation in advance. Luke glanced at his notes, looked up, repeated the process, and took a deep breath.

"*Liopleurodon ferox* is best described as a cross between a crocodile and a shark that's the size of a whale. Its head and jaws bare resemblance to a crocodile's while its four flippers give it a seal's agility. It's 25 meters long and 150 tons. Its sense of smell is superior to a vulture's. This means it can smell blood and detect movement from miles away and attack before its victim knows what's coming. It also has an extra-strong rib cage to protect it from attack. Its only weakness is that it has to breathe air."

"How do his jaws work?" Roosevelt asked, turning Luke's presentation into a Q&A session. "You said it was like a crocodile's. Do they work similarly?"

"The Liopleurodon's jaws are its main weapon. Strong muscles connected to its lower jaw cause it to release a tremendous amount of force when it swings up to meet the top. Also, like a crocodile, the teeth lock, so a prey animal can't escape." Luke used his hands to demonstrate.

"How much force?" Hawkins asked. "Do you have any idea?"

"Well, obviously it's never been formally measured, but I made an estimate by comparing the Liopleurodon's size to a saltwater crocodile's. I concluded that a Liopleurodon bite could generate about 70,000 pounds. Or 35 tons."

Roosevelt glanced at the paleontologists in astonishment.

"I take it that's a lot?" Hawkins asked.

"That's enormous," Harris said. "The saltwater crocodile has the strongest bite of any modern animal and its bite is only 3,000 pounds."

"I should point out that the Liopleurodon's teeth can penetrate bone in a way that a crocodile's cannot," Luke said. "That means that not only *can* the Liopleurodon digest bone, but it's designed to do so."

"I see," Hawkins said. "Can it strategize?"

"All predators can. To outsmart their prey."

"Do you have any idea what it wants?"

"My guess is that it's trying to turn the North Atlantic into its territorial sphere," Luke said.

"What does that entail?"

"Attacking anything it perceives as violating its territory until it feels secure as the apex predator. Including ships."

Ross cleared his throat. "If you don't mind, Mr. Jones, can you discuss what sort of prey the Liopleurodon ate? How large were they? What defense mechanisms did they have? You get what I'm asking. It will give a more well-rounded picture of what countermeasures it's used to overcoming."

"The short answer is that the Liopleurodon would eat whatever it wanted," Luke said. "Its preferred prey was Leedsichthys, the largest fish that ever lived. It was a 27-meter long filter feeder, basically a Jurassic whale. Its defenses were its size and traveling in large groups."

"And the Liopleurodon had no trouble killing this fish?" Jenkins asked.

"No more than a normal carnivore targeting its prey of choice. I've personally examined various Leedsichthys fossils that bore injuries clearly delivered by a Liopleurodon or similar pliosaur. Some had healed, some hadn't."

"Jesus Christ," Jenkins muttered.

"Do you know its success rate?" Ryan asked.

Luke was flustered. How could he possibly know that? Just

when Luke started to feel confident—to feel useful—to feel validated—Ryan pierced his bubble. Back to worthlessness—to being a waste of space—to feeling every awkward moment and slight to exaggerated degrees to the point of paralysis and—

"What did animals that didn't have their size as a defense do?" Wood asked, deciding Ryan's question wasn't relevant.

Luke thought for a moment. "Outswim it. There were a variety of animals in the ocean and the Liopleurodon had its pick. Ichthyosaurs were like dolphins. Plesiosaurs were like long-necked seals. There were marine crocodiles, sharks—"

"It ate sharks?" Wood asked, his voice hoarse.

"Like how we eat shrimp," Luke said. "Though there *was* a shark called Hybodus that had horns on its head. They'd stab the Liopleurodon's mouth if the Liopleurodon tried eating it."

"What would happen then?" Hawkins asked.

"The Liopleurodon would probably regurgitate it," Luke said. "But it shows how even sharks had to develop defenses to protect themselves from Liopleurodon and other pliosaurs."

"I assume it preyed on other pliosaurs if given the chance?" Ross asked.

"Yes," Luke said. "*Any*thing in the ocean was on the menu. The same is true now. *Any*one in the Atlantic is in danger. I can't imagine what it's going to do to its environment's food chain."

"What if the environment kills it first?" Ryan asked.

"Reptiles can adapt better than any other type of vertebrate," Luke said.

"That's your analysis of the world since the dinosaurs'

extinction?" Ryan asked. Luke felt a surge of panic, clinging to his credibility. He was happy Kelsey wasn't there.

"What if it reproduces?" Hawkins asked.

"It's a male," Ryan said. "It can't."

Hawkins nodded. That was one less thing to worry about. He had to destroy the Liopleurodon before the Germans made another attempt to capture it. They would need time to regroup. His target was a huge carnivore that wielded dangerous jaws, was fast and agile, and could track its opponents with its sense of smell. Perhaps Hawkins could use that to his advantage. It also had to breathe air. Could he tire and drown it? Or force it to stay at the surface and within his strike range?

"Thank you, Luke, for your presentation. That was helpful," Hawkins said. Luke looked at his notes. He wasn't finished, but was more than happy to cede the attention to someone else. Hawkins turned to Palmer. "You're up next. Are there any legal restrictions we should know about?"

Palmer looked at his own notes. "In what way?"

"Are there any restrictions on killing whales that could be applied to this situation if a legal entity took a broad reading of the law?" Hawkins asked.

Palmer turned the page, scanning desperately for an answer. "I was prepared to speak about what weapons you could use to fight the creature."

"Congress authorized the use of force against the Liopleurodon," Hawkins said. "As far as I'm concerned, I can use any of the conventional weapons at my disposal. What I need is an analysis on possible environmental restrictions."

"Uh…" Palmer flipped through multiple pages. Jenkins shook his head.

"Can we go back to working with Marine JAGs?" he asked Hawkins. "They knew what they were doing."

"I'm doing my best, sir!" Palmer proclaimed. "I only graduated four months ago—"

"Try to get me an answer by the end of the day, Lieutenant," Hawkins said.

"Today, sir?"

"Yes. It doesn't have to be a formal memo. A page is fine. I want us to act as soon as possible. We can't let the Germans make another attempt." He lost focus for a moment. The men exchanged a series of glances. Why was Hawkins so jittery? Hawkins asked the paleontologists, "What do you know about Wilhelm von Branca?"

Ross scoffed. "Branca's the reason why German paleontology has fallen behind the American program. He's good at raising money but not much else. He never looks at the data he's collected or rethinks either the biological or geological basis of paleontology. I'm not concerned about his acting as an advisor to the German government." Ryan nodded.

Hawkins was skeptical of their dismissal. "The pressure's on, but killing it is easier than capturing it." He turned to the blackboard and wrote *options*. "Let's brainstorm. I'll start." He wrote *battleship cannons*. "Say we put blood in the water, the Liopleurodon arrives, and we blow it up with the *Delaware*'s guns. Simple."

"Outrageous!" Roosevelt exclaimed.

"Why?"

"Its body would be blown to smithereens."

"I don't care about you getting a photo," Hawkins said.

"That's not the point. It must be preserved for science," Roosevelt said.

"That isn't part of my assignment."

"It's unnecessary barbarity and would deny the world a major scientific breakthrough."

Ryan signaled that he wanted to speak. "Studying the Liopleurodon *would* do wonders for our understanding of anatomy, biology, and so on."

"Then what do you propose?" Hawkins asked.

"General Wood and I discussed this yesterday," Roosevelt said. "Our opinion is that we should treat this as though we're hunting a sperm whale. There's various sorts of harpoons, harpoon guns, explosive harpoons, lances, and darting guns that we could use to kill the Liopleurodon the way we would a whale."

"But that would require engaging it with smaller ships, yes?" Jenkins asked.

"Yes," Roosevelt said. "The *Delaware* is our base but I think her presence would scare the beast. It's wiser to attack with smaller vessels that won't spook it."

"But those ships would be vulnerable to attack," Jenkins said.

"As they would be for any military engagement," Roosevelt said. "Of course there is risk."

"You're talking about putting my sailors in harm's way for science!" Hawkins said.

"We must be willing to shake off the torpor of over-civilization," Roosevelt countered, "and tap into our innate savagery—"

"You speak of such vile bloodthirstiness?" Hawkins asked. "I'll never approve of such an idea."

"In that case, Captain, I don't know if we can follow your orders." Roosevelt gestured to Wood and himself.

"You will if you want any part of this operation!"

"*One word* to the press and I'll have you replaced!" Roosevelt said.

Hawkins was stunned. He blinked several times. He remembered when Roosevelt leaked a critique of the War Department's decision to keep the Rough Riders in Cuba after the Spanish-American War. Roosevelt's men were dying of yellow fever and his leak brought them home. Of course, part of his motivation was to take maximum political advantage of his war hero status, an action that landed him in the New York governor's mansion. Roosevelt. Always able to see how he could gain by doing the right thing.

Hawkins remained quiet as he worked through his anger while also desperate not to admit defeat. The eyes in the room shifted back and forth between the colonel and captain.

"You know that starting from scratch would delay any move

by at least a week," Hawkins said. "You'd be letting the Germans make a second attempt."

Roosevelt nodded, clutching the delicate olive branch.

"Is there a way to bridge the gap?" Ryan asked. "A way we could attack it with smaller ships but with more dangerous weapons? That way we could kill it without harming any sailors but do it in a way where the body remains intact. That must be possible."

The men nodded, accepting Ryan's framework.

"Why don't we throw a few more ideas on the board?" Jenkins asked. "We could work through them. Is that okay, Captain?" Hawkins nodded. He grabbed the chalk. "The colonel mentioned a few weapons, but let's label them 'harpoons.' Torpedoes, whether from a boat or submarine, would inflict more damage than the paleontologists would like. There's dynamite or mines, but they have the same problem." Hawkins wrote as fast as he could.

"Could we shoot it with a Springfield rifle?" Wood asked. "It would be long range, or at least longer than a harpoon. And more deadly."

Ryan turned to Luke. "Wouldn't a gunshot feel like an ant bite?"

Luke didn't want to upset Wood, though he was pleased that Ryan deferred to him after challenging him a few minutes prior. "More than an ant bite, but, yes, I'm not sure a rifle shot would cause a decisive kill. Unless the bullet struck a perfect spot on its skull, but there's no guarantee that will happen and failure would only agitate it."

Wood put his chin in his hands as he thought.

"Is there anything stronger than a bullet?" Ryan asked. "But that still leaves the Liopleurodon's body intact?"

No one spoke for a few moments.

"What about poison?" Ross asked.

"Naval intelligence reported that the Germans already tried to get the Liopleurodon to ingest a chemical agent by putting it in a meat bag," Hawkins said. "But the Liopleurodon somehow figured it out and refused to eat the bag."

"Perhaps we could put someone in an underwater cage," Roosevelt said. "They could stick the Liopleurodon with a spear laced with poison."

"How would they breathe?" Jenkins asked.

"We could connect an air tube to a ship and—"

"I am not putting anyone in the water with that monster," Hawkins said.

Ross spoke before another argument started. "What about a projectile?"

"Can you elaborate?" Hawkins asked.

"Could we modify a rifle to fire a projectile that injects the Liopleurodon with poison?" Ross asked.

The room's energy increased.

"How soon could this be ready?" Wood asked.

"We don't need to modify a Springfield," Hawkins said. "We could place it within a rifle round's casing. If we pick a poison, I'll send an order to the engineers immediately. We could have it by tomorrow morning. This is why I got you all up so early today."

"Azalea should work," Ross said. "Its nectar is toxic for reptiles."

Hawkins wrote out an order.

"Make sure there's enough for multiple rounds," Roosevelt said. Hawkins nodded. "We should also lace harpoon guns. It would allow us to strike him multiple times at once." He paused. "Lacing harpoons will be simpler than modifying Springfield rounds, anyway. Tell them to ask the Interior Department for—"

"*Thank you*, Colonel." Hawkins rewrote the order and handed it to Jenkins. "Take this to the engineers." Jenkins left. Hawkins smiled and his shoulders relaxed. "Here's the new plan: We'll use patrol boats. Patrol boats don't usually go out that far from the coast but they're small enough that the Liopleurodon won't immediately retreat. We'll put blood in the water. Maybe some fish pieces. The Liopleurodon comes and we attack it with patrol boats from all sides. One of those patrol boats will carry the Spring—"

"Would that not scare the Liopleurodon?" Roosevelt asked.

"How would you propose we control its movements?" Hawkins asked.

"We need a way to drive the Liopleurodon to a couple of patrol boats instead of having them chase *him*. Because he'd just go under the surface and escape," Roosevelt said.

"Okay, but *how*?"

Roosevelt lowered his head to think.

"What if we lit the ocean on fire?" Wood asked.

"*What?*" Hawkins asked, almost snorting from the ridiculousness of the question.

"We'd cover part of the ocean with gasoline and one of the patrol boats would shoot the gas with a flare when the Liopleurodon arrives. That will scare the Liopleurodon so it goes in the other direction. Two more patrol boats will intercept it and shoot it with the azalea. I imagine we'd want to place all of the azalea rounds and harpoons with one or both of these boats, since it's finite and we'll want to maximize the likelihood that we can inject it with a concentrated dose."

"What if it attacks the first patrol boat instead?" Hawkins asked.

"It could be something larger than a patrol boat," Wood said. "But still small enough that it won't scare the Liopleurodon from investigating the area. Perhaps a destroyer."

"Will the gasoline's stench repel it?"

"I imagine there's a low risk of that happening," Luke said, "if there's enough blood in the water." Wood gestured to Luke, as if to say "see? This will work."

Hawkins smiled. "We're getting somewhere." He took a deep breath. So did Ross and Wood. All were tired from getting up early and debating all morning.

"Will all of this be ready by tomorrow?" Wood asked.

"It will have to be," Hawkins said, "unless we want to give the Germans a second chance. I'll send Meyer a telegram. Get what we need. Shouldn't have sent Jenkins off so soon."

Luke leaned back in his seat. He thought he performed well. His future played out in his mind's eye. Harris would get off his back. He'd earned Ross and Ryan's respect, allowing for easy access to the top of the field. That's before mentioning the connections he'd established with powerful men like former President Roosevelt, General Wood, and Captain Hawkins. Most importantly, he had redeemed his father's legacy. The external validation Luke craved—no, obsessed over—would soon be his. His joy faded as Luke looked at the empty seat that Kelsey left behind on the other side of the table. It was still pushed out, a reminder of his love's absence. If only she'd been there to witness his presentation. If only she'd been there to see him shape military policy. Would she believe him if he told her later? If Harris told her? Would Harris cooperate in light of the lecture he had given Luke? But how else was Kelsey to know what Luke had done? How was she supposed to leave Ryan for him if the full weight of Luke's achievement was not made entirely clear? That was the most important thing. The only thing. Nothing mattered if he wasn't with Kelsey. It would be hollow. Meaningless. He had to win her. Would his letter do it? Perhaps. But his presentation was the second step. And she'd missed it. Thanks a lot, Hawkins. He had to find an alternative. A backup plan. Yes. What did women like? Gushiness? The letter covered that. Status? They like that too, and the presentation was meant to secure that plank. What was an alternate way of achieving status? What about him? Roosevelt. The leader of his entire generation. No one alive had higher status than him. How did he get it? Where did it start? Cuba. Roosevelt became famous for his actions in Cuba during the Spanish war. That was it. The idea emerged from his subconscious like the Liopleurodon attacking from the deep.

"Can I go?"

Harris sighed. Why did Luke want to leave already? What did he have to do?

"Go where?" Hawkins asked.

"I want to go on a patrol boat tomorrow," Luke said.

"Out of the question."

"But I've studied Liopleurodon my entire life. I know it. I can anticipate its instincts. I can help."

"If Luke goes, I want to go!" Roosevelt declared.

"Neither of you can go!" Hawkins said.

"I want to go, too," Ryan said. Luke's throat constricted. He looked at Ryan, who smiled back. Ryan saw Luke's play and matched it. Why didn't Luke anticipate that? What was wrong with his brain?

Roosevelt turned to Wood. "You shall join me on this adventure."

"I'm getting a bit old for this, Theodore." Wood smiled.

"Nonsense," Roosevelt said. "It will be like Kettle Hill all over again."

Hawkins said, "I am in charge of this operation, and—"

"Do you believe in the plan or not?" Roosevelt asked.

"Do *you* understand the liability that—"

"Modify our agreements," Roosevelt said. "It's simple,

really."

Hawkins' face dropped. "You can't watch from the destroyer?"

"No. I must be in the action."

Hawkins sighed. "Fine." He turned to Palmer. "Modify the agreements. *Forget* the previous assignment. *Focus* on this for the rest of the day. Get it to me by the morning, *before* the expedition. Can you handle that?"

"Yes, sir. Absolutely, sir." Palmer furiously wrote out his assignment.

"Who wants to go tomorrow?" Hawkins asked. "Raise your hand so Lieutenant Palmer can write your name down."

Everyone but Ross raised their hand.

"Don't be yellow, Benjamin," Roosevelt said.

"I have no intention of dying tomorrow," Ross said.

"The world is divided between warriors and weaklings." Roosevelt's arms folded.

"I admire your original discovery of the Ten Commandments!" Ross said.

Luke turned to Harris. "Why are you going?"

"To look after you," Harris said. Luke smiled. "But if the Liopleurodon eats me, I'm never talking to you again." Luke chuckled. Harris turned to Hawkins. "I jest, but what happens if the Liopleurodon *does* flip a patrol boat?"

"That's *why* I'm warning you all about sitting in on the operation," Hawkins said. His body tightened.

"There can't be a serious risk that would happen," Roosevelt said. "A patrol boat is 70 tons."

"But it isn't impossible," Harris said. "The Liopleurodon is twice that size. Is there anything we can use to defend ourselves if it *does* happen?"

"We could give everyone a harpoon!" Roosevelt said.

"I can see this is going to go swimmingly," Ross said.

Hawkins thought and turned to Luke. "You said it has a good sense of smell?"

"Yes," Luke said. "It's how the Liopleurodon navigates."

"We could attach a bottle of noxious smelling chemicals to everyone's belts as a means to repel it."

"What sort of chemicals?" Roosevelt asked.

"Shark repellent?" Hawkins asked.

"I would suggest 'putrescine,'" Ross said. "It smells like rotting reptile flesh. It will make the Liopleurodon think that a member of its own kind is dying."

"Isn't the Liopleurodon a cannibal?" Roosevelt asked. "Would this not risk making it hungrier?"

Ross' head bobbled to and fro. "Well, I certainly hope not."

…

March 5, 1911

Kelsey stood near the edge of the *USS Paulding*'s deck, watching as the two patrol boats, the *Moosehead* and the *Sea Otter*, moved into their ambush positions about half a kilometer apart. Both ships were a kilometer away from the *Paulding*, which was an 89-meter, 887-ton destroyer that wielded six 18-inch torpedo tubes. The sun highlighted a patch of water the size of a baseball field between the destroyer and patrol boats that the *Moosehead* had covered with chum, blood, and gasoline. The smells of all three blended with the scent of seawater. Kelsey would have gagged had her thoughts not been elsewhere.

Desire, the sensation that gave way to infatuation, resulted in a sleepless night after reading Luke's letter. She'd not felt so much affection since she started dating Dr. Ryan, if not before. That notion—of someone actually wanting her, and not just the status that came with her looks—felt so foreign she had forgotten what it was like. She glanced at the ring on her finger.

Emotions strangled her mind as competing ideas—status versus passion—long-term goals versus theoretical possibilities—clashed like Hannibal and Scipio. She looked to the men on the deck around her. Four sailors carried Springfield M1903 rifles. Another carried a Coston flare gun. A little further down was Captain Hawkins, Commander Jenkins, Lieutenant Palmer, and other members of Hawkins' staff, most of whom held binoculars in their hands. Kelsey turned her head in the other direction and saw Dr. Ross, his weight leaning on his cane, his head under his wool hat, his right hand protecting his nostrils from the stench that rose from the *Moosehead*'s concoction. He was bundled under a thick coat for protection from the ocean's breeze as he hummed the hymn Hawkins had the sailors sing that Sunday morning after reading the Articles of War. Kelsey watched the sad, lonely figure; she did not know Dr. Ross well but sensed his ears may be receptive to her voice.

She noticed the fog on his glasses as she approached.

"The current is going the wrong way," Ross said.

"What's that?" she asked.

"The current's going east. We need it to go west. The patrol boats will face greater resistance given the current's trajectory."

"Hmm." She paused. "Can I ask you a question?"

"Of course, dear. Of what subject?"

"Romantic."

Ross chuckled. "I'm not exactly a 'Romeo.' Frankly, all my attempts at relationships in my early years went terribly."

"I'd like your opinion anyway," Kelsey said.

"I have those in abundance."

Kelsey flipped open her notebook and retrieved the letter. She handed it to Ross. "Luke gave me this yesterday."

Ross' face scrunched as he took it. He raised his glasses and flipped through the letter. It was surprisingly long and had writing on each page. The penmanship implied cycles of careful consideration and sudden surges of thought. He scanned its opening line:

Kelsey,

I know we haven't known each other long, but meeting you has been a light shining through the darkness of my life.

Ross glanced at her. "This seems rather personal."

"I know, but—"

"I'm not sure if it's appropriate for me—"

"Please?" She paused. "I need advice." Ross nodded. He skimmed the letter. It mostly repeated the same handful of points. Some of its most important lines included:

Am I correct in thinking that you're only with Sean because he'll take you to the top of the field? ... I'll fight for you. I'll rise to the top and take you with me ... What do you see in him, otherwise? ... He doesn't treat you like the queen that you are ... I'll give you the perfect life. It will be my mission ... Kids, a house, a dog if you want (my mother's allergic but I don't care) ... whatever support you need to have the career that you want.

The letter climaxed with a poem:

I'd like to turn the deepest of yellows,
Falling, drop by drop, in a golden shower,
Into her lap, my lovely Cassandra's,
As sleep is stealing over her brow.

Then I'd like to be a bull, white as snow,
Transforming myself, for carrying her,
In April, when, through meadows so tender,
A flower, through a thousand flowers, she goes.

I'd like then, the better to ease my pain,
To be Narcissus, and she a fountain,
Where I'd swim all night, at my pleasure:

*And I'd like it, too, if Aurora would never
Light day again, or wake me ever,
So that this night could last forever.*

Ross closed the letter. He saw elements of himself from his youth. "Knows his Ronsard, I see."

"Who?" Kelsey asked.

"Not important. This is—uh—quite something."

"What should I do?"

"What are you asking, exactly?"

"Are you going to make me spell it out?" Kelsey sighed and looked at the concoction in the water. Ross hesitated. "Sean's the pragmatic choice."

"Why's that?"

"He's already established. My family approves of him." She paused. "I barely know Luke. And he's so young."

"There's a point where being too logical is no longer logical," Ross said. "Trust me, I know."

"What does that mean?"

"It's no secret that there's no love lost between Dr. Ryan and myself."

"But that's a scientific dispute, in part," Kelsey said.

"The scientific dispute is secondary. I believe Dr. Ryan lacks character. And that's coming from *me*."

"Does Luke have character?" she asked.

Ross hesitated again. "Mr. Jones still has to grow up. And he's been through a lot. But—deep down—I think he does.

Certainly more than Dr. Ryan." He paused. "Plus, he has passion. He worships you."

"But what if that fades?" Kelsey asked.

"Again, I lack knowledge of the human heart. But if your marriage to Dr. Ryan has an affection deficiency and is *purely* pragmatic, it is doomed from its inception. Mr. Jones is an unknown; that's scary, but at least your relationship wouldn't be destined to fail."

Kelsey chuckled. "Talk about options."

"I think you know what the right one is."

She sighed. "My father won't be happy."

"He likes Dr. Ryan that much?" Ross asked.

"He does. It's one-sided, though. My father doesn't know that."

"What do you mean?"

"Can you keep a secret?" Kelsey asked.

"Of course."

"My father became wealthy through investing in a meat-packing plant in Colorado. I think that's one reason why Sean wants to marry me. But he's also intimidated by it, if that makes sense. So, he wants access to the money but he resents it. It's obvious, frankly. I see the look he makes whenever we visit my parents. I actually think he resents my father as much as he resents you, to be honest."

"Just another reason…" Ross' words trailed off. His eyes squinted.

"What is it?"

He held up a finger, asking for a moment. "Oh my God." Ross breathed rapidly.

"What?"

"Oh my God!" Ross ran toward Hawkins, using his cane at first and then picking it up to run faster. He startled Hawkins' staff. "Captain! Captain Hawkins!"

"What is it, Doctor?" Hawkins lowered his binoculars. Jenkins checked their coordinates. They were southeast of Greenland.

"You have to cancel the attack, sir."

"Are you mad?" Hawkins asked. "Why would I?"

"It's been sabotaged," Ross said. "Dr. Ryan—I think he may be why—"

"Dr. Ross, I understand that you and Dr. Ryan don't get along, but what you're claiming—"

"*Please* listen!" Ross said.

"I have no intention of throwing away this opportunity to kill the monster before the Germans can capture it," Hawkins said. "It mustn't fall into the Kaiser's hands."

"But—"

"Have a little faith, Dr. Ross. Now, if you'll excuse me, I must return to my duties."

Ross turned to Jenkins. "I *cannot* stress how important it is that this be canceled—now."

"We couldn't stop it even if we wanted to," Jenkins said. Ross looked down. He became pale and shivered with anxiety as he returned to Kelsey's side.

...

Luke watched the sunrise on the *Sea Otter*'s deck as the sky became an evolving painting, shifting from black to pink to orange to blue. Nature's beauty was a lifelong source of excitement. He should get up early every morning—with Kelsey beside him. It was free entertainment, as captivating as any work of art ever crafted by man because this was crafted by God. The sky's progression was only the beginning. Beyond it waited the universe, infinite in scale, majesty, and power. Who knew what was out there, what marvels existed to be adored? Stars, planets, other species, all going through their own cycles of life and death. He resented being stuck on Earth. Though the Earth had its own untapped universe to explore, one that was closer and more meaningful. Luke glanced at the ocean's surface. Beneath was another world, virtually none of which man had yet seen. Incredible creatures—predator and prey, monster and magnificent—all part of the same planet, from the same hand as the colors drawn across the sky. That included the ancient monster—evolution's most dangerous creation—that Luke knew was on its way.

Anxiety bubbled below the surface of Luke's mind. He sought to impose calm, but his consciousness struggled to put its pants on as his subconscious darted ahead. Panic surged every few moments, not derived from thoughts, but from his intuition of what was coming and what was at stake if the Navy failed. What if too many poisoned bullets and harpoons missed? What if the Liopleurodon killed everyone on the patrol boats? What if the Germans captured it? What would they do with it? Could it affect the outcome of a future war? Would the Kaiser rule the world? Luke tried taking his mind off his fear. He thought of Kelsey. Her blonde hair. Her embrace. Yes. Think of that. Another surge. Kelsey's image faded. Tainted. Next he thought of his father. A legacy redeemed. If only he'd known. He didn't have to die. Didn't have to leave Luke and his mother. Another surge. Damnit. Think of the sea, where he was more comfortable than he was on land. Of being a great fish. A being of power and grace. No issues of status or love to think of. Just swimming. And eating. And reproduction. And not being killed by sharks. Or the Liopleurodon. Another surge.

Luke shook his head and snorted. He looked at the others. Maybe getting out of his musings would distract him. Professor Harris was nearby. Like Luke, Harris wore a float vest and a belt that clipped to a canister full of putrescine. Harris looked away from the water, staring blankly, focusing on his breathing to stay calm. Luke looked at Colonel Roosevelt and General Wood, sitting together on the other side of the deck, facing opposite the *Paulding* and the concoction zone. Roosevelt's forearms rested on his knees, his hands dangling between his stretched legs. He wore khaki trousers and a blue flannel shirt with yellow suspenders. Atop his head sat a brown felt hat with a blue and white bandanna tied around it. It was the same outfit he'd worn when he rode up Kettle Hill.

Roosevelt noticed Luke staring at him.

"Are you nervous, son?" he asked. Luke didn't answer. He felt lightheaded, partially from skipping breakfast to avoid sea sickness. "It's alright if you are. You can't be brave if you never have fear."

"How about you?" Luke asked.

"I've faced death too many times to register it anymore." Roosevelt tried to smile but failed. "I take it you've never been in the military?"

"No."

"Did you ever think about it?"

"Not really," Luke said. "I have interests in science and maybe art. Not war."

"A pity. War can make strong men."

"And dead men."

"Better to be dead than weak."

"I suppose."

"What are your goals?" Roosevelt asked.

"What do you mean?"

"What are your goals in life?

"I'm not sure," Luke said. "It had been to avenge my father's legacy, but—"

"What happened to him?"

Luke frowned. "He was a paleontologist. He helped discover the Liopleurodon—the fossil, I mean—and argued that it was much larger than any fossils implied at the time. He had *some* evidence but it wasn't enough to convince everyone in the field. Dr. Ross destroyed him in the journals…" Harris turned to Luke and shook his head. "...He fell into depression, and as I said a couple nights ago…"

"I see," Roosevelt said. "I take it the Liopleurodon's discovery completed that goal?"

"Yes."

"And now you wish to become a paleontologist?"

"I guess. It feels different, now that that's finished. Like the purpose is gone."

"Don't you have a passion for prehistory?" Roosevelt asked.

"I do. I just have to rekindle it."

"Perhaps seeing the Liopleurodon will help."

"Perhaps," Luke said.

"What are your other goals?"

"Well…"

"Out with it!"

"There's this girl…"

"Miss Painter?"

"How—"

"You'd make a miserable spy, lad," Roosevelt said. Luke smiled. "You know she's engaged."

"I know."

"Is it just desire? Or do you plan to act?" Roosevelt asked. Harris turned to Luke again, awaiting his answer.

"I'd rather not say," Luke said.

"Be careful," Roosevelt said. "Have you ever thought of writing a novel?"

"Why?"

"Seems like you'd be good at it."

"You've written books, right?" Luke asked.

"Only nonfiction. I should like to write some book that would really rank in the very first class, but I suppose this is a mere dream." Roosevelt paused. "What are your politics, Mr. Jones?" Luke shrugged. "No thoughts on the suffrage movement?"

"Not really."

"Do you think women should have the vote?"

"Sure," Luke said. "I just don't think it will do anything."

"Why's that?"

"Politics is the realm of the Devil," Luke said. Harris shook his head.

Roosevelt laughed. "A charmer, aren't you?"

"I don't mean to offend," Luke said.

"Of course not."

"It just seems that everyone's only out for themselves. They want power, so they can get money and sex. Gratify their shallow desires. The people on top can take what they want and those at the bottom have to restrain themselves or be punished. That's it. That's humanity. Maybe one in a thousand people is actually good at heart."

"You're too young to be this cynical," Roosevelt said.

Luke shrugged. "A man's philosophy is his biography." Roosevelt chuckled.

Harris turned to Luke. "Stick with paleontology. You're on the verge of greatness." Luke nodded.

Roosevelt looked at the sailors standing together near the ship's bow. Two held Springfields. Three held Cunningham & Cogan harpoon shoulder guns, which were designed for whaling but whose blades had been coated in azalea that morning. He thought about how he'd rather be on the *Moosehead* instead of the *Sea Otter*, as it bore the name of the proud beast with which Roosevelt sought to associate. Perhaps he should have asked to trade places with Dr. Ryan. That would have made for an awkward expedition for Ryan, Luke, and possibly Professor Harris, but it would have given Roosevelt a great story for the campaign trail. On the other hand, bearing witness to the Liopleurodon's destruction would more than suffice.

A Marine, wearing a doughboy helmet and carrying a rifle, walked between the group of paleontologists and statesmen. He had dark hair and a sunburned nose.

"Gentlemen." He spoke with a southern accent.

"Do you hold the secret sauce?" Roosevelt asked. The Marine smiled.

"Sure do, Colonel. The boys were up all night workin' on it. Usin' a pump to extract honey and nectar and such. A few shots of these rounds and from the harpoons ought to do it."

Roosevelt smiled like a boy. "Is it loaded?"

"Not yet."

"May I see them?"

"Course." The Marine retrieved a poisoned round and dropped it in Roosevelt's palms. Roosevelt rotated it between his fingers, grinning with delight.

Harris shook his head. "Good *Lord*," he muttered.

"What?" Roosevelt asked. His impression of Harris was set by their debate on the Philippines the night they met.

"Is that safe?" Harris asked.

"I'm no fool, Professor. The azalea is *inside* the casing." He turned to the Marine. "Right?"

The Marine nodded. "Yes, sir."

"How do you know there isn't any residue?" Harris asked. "What if the engineers were sloppy?"

Roosevelt handed the round back to the Marine. "I ought to return this to you before our *friend* has an aneurysm." The Marine took it. "What's your name, son?"

"Curtis. Master Sergeant Curtis."

"Nice to meet you, Sergeant."

"Likewise, Colonel."

"Are you a lifer?"

"Sure am."

"Where have you served?"

"I was part of the pacific'ation efforts in Panama and Cuba."

"Were you?" Roosevelt asked, a cheer in his voice. "Good for you."

"Thank you, sir."

Roosevelt nodded and briefly broke eye contact. "Are you nervous?"

Curtis chuckled. "I was born for this."

...

The Liopleurodon spent the past few hours moving north, tracking the smell of a new feeding frenzy. His momentum kept him at a steady pace, allowing him to exert minimal energy other than using his flippers for course correction. The ocean since emerging from suspended animation was a new world—less oxygen, less reptiles, no mates, a plethora of mammals, bloodbaths that appeared to occur almost daily, and those large metal objects the Liopleurodon associated with trouble and which chipped away at his territory. The Liopleurodon did not know what they were—most didn't have the long necks of plesiosaurs, but they always carried those small mammals on their backs. Worst of all was the metal creature that challenged the Liopleurodon under the water. The Liopleurodon had been spooked and retreated, ceding most of the eastern Atlantic to his rival. That could not be allowed to stand. The Liopleurodon could not tolerate these enemies any longer.

He finally made visual contact with the bloodbath. Three metal surface objects surrounded it. A large object, likely the parent, rested on the surface just west of the blood and meat. Two smaller objects—the offspring—floated close together to the east. Why were they there? Did the blood belong to a dead relative? The Liopleurodon sensed that was unlikely; he had not tasted blood or flesh when biting the object 12 days before. Perhaps the family had killed and feasted upon whatever this prey animal had been. Yes. That made more sense. That explained why there wasn't a body. And now the objects circled their kill, asserting their dominance of the North Atlantic. That was it. These objects were boxing him in, cutting off his food supply, aiming to destroy him.

This *could not* stand. The Liopleurodon *could not* allow any more of these objects to claim segments of what was supposed to be *his* territory. They were challengers. And he had decades of experience with challengers. He *knew* what to do with them.

The Liopleurodon ascended with a flap of his flippers, hoping to signal his arrival and convince the objects to retreat and avoid a fight. A foreign smell was mixed amongst the blood but he did not make much of it. This new world was filled with exotic scents. Sharks and other fish scattered upon his arrival, like usual. The three metal objects did not. They stayed in their place, holding their position for a showdown. That was fine. The Liopleurodon was ready for a fight.

…

Captain Hawkins noticed the shark fins vanish under the surface. His jaw clenched with excitement. This could be it. Hawkins had been unhappy receiving this assignment; hunting an animal was unbecoming of a man of his profession and experience. He was particularly frustrated having to work with an egotist like Roosevelt—why did the President feel the Colonel's presence was necessary?—and status-obsessed intellectuals like the paleontologists. But this was *his* mission, and upon its completion, Hawkins expected recognition, citation, perhaps even a promotion for a job well done. It would certainly make him *unique* among his peers and an interesting chapter in the textbooks future naval cadets would study at Annapolis.

Long, white, intersecting fangs pierced the water. Then came a triangular snout and the rest of the reptile's jaws. Hawkins froze. The Liopleurodon appeared curious—simultaneously larger and smaller than he had pictured in his mind's eye. It was both the sovereign of the sea and just another animal. That was it. His target. A shame. It looked so content. Time for the facade to end.

Hawkins raised his left hand and casually made a fist. The sailor holding the Coston flare gun pointed it at the concoction and fired. A bright red blaze shot from the *Paulding*. At first only one segment of the concoction ignited, but the fire rapidly spread in every direction like the Mongol Horde expanding across Eurasia until most of the ocean's surface in the kilometer between the *Paulding* and the patrol boats was an inferno.

The Liopleurodon could not dive beneath the surface in time. His snout caught fire, causing a triangular flame to rise over the rest. The men behind Hawkins cheered. He smiled. The triangle lowered to surface-level as the Liopleurodon retreated below. Hawkins squinted; the baseball field-sized zone resembled the sun's surface and was hard to look at directly. He felt the heat radiating from it, contributing to Hawkins' anxiety as the plan's next phase began and order gave way to chaos.

...

The Liopleurodon was enraged. Flame-covered gasoline clung to his snout and head, burning his skin, muscle, and membrane. This was excruciating. The water put out most of the fire after several minutes but his jaws continued throbbing.

He had miscalculated. The Liopleurodon hoped that signaling his arrival would convince the metal beasts to withdraw; instead it allowed them to strike first as he forfeited the element of surprise. He would not make that mistake again. The metal beasts—all of them—were his enemies—locked in an existential struggle for dominance and survival. His instincts told him to retreat, to escape the objects' revolutionary attack, but he couldn't back down now.

The Liopleurodon's nostrils opened and sucked in water. The water went to one chamber, scents to another. His nostrils had not been spared; fire had entered and singed them. The Liopleurodon primarily smelled his own burned flesh. But the tracking device was partially active and locked onto the three surface objects. He had to strike back. The parent was several times his weight—too large to attack. That wasn't true of the offspring, which moved toward each other for protection.

The Liopleurodon swam past the hellish surface and ascended.

...

Luke's heartbeat raced as the *Sea Otter* and *Moosehead* moved toward each other. The sailors wanted to increase their firepower in anticipation of the Liopleurodon's likely counter attack. Luke had been thrilled and horrified to see the Liopleurodon come above the ocean's surface. Here was the greatest carnivore of all time, the focus of his life's work, a being so powerful that it would spare him only because killing him wasn't worth the effort.

The *Sea Otter*'s crew was calm as the ship sailed north. They knew their mission well. Luke kept his eyes on the ocean, but he saw two sailors carrying rifles and one carrying a poison-tipped harpoon gun move into position through his peripheral vision. He smiled; a front row seat to a Liopleurodon's demise was the most exciting event of his life. If only his father were here; multiple generations of Joneses would be giddy.

Boom!

The *Moosehead* was thrown off course, even rising in the air, before crashing down a short distance eastward. A wave pounded its port flank as it landed. Cries of "hold fast!" emanated from the *Moosehead* and could be heard on the *Sea Otter*. The *Moosehead* vibrated before stabilizing. Luke jolted to his feet and ran to the starboard side of the *Sea Otter*'s deck, looking to see if anyone had fallen overboard. One sailor had. A few of his comrades worked to rescue him. Luke felt a drop of sadness that Dr. Ryan was not in the water. A harpoon gun on the *Moosehead* fired into the ocean. Was the Liopleurodon there? No. It was clumsiness resulting from the *Moosehead*'s collision, wasting an asset. Luke heard a spike of commotion from the other side of the boat.

He ran to the port side, standing beside Roosevelt. The Liopleurodon's black head, green eyes and the first red stripe at the base of his neck were visible as he looked to determine if he had damaged the *Moosehead*. Several patches of his skin were raw from the fire minutes before. The pliosaur bled from a gash on the right side of his head, where he had struck the vessel.

The Liopleurodon hissed and studied his enemies. He could smell and see the small mammals on these metal objects. Luke couldn't take his eyes off the monster. He watched the black slit in its eye vanish and return as it blinked. Luke and the Liopleurodon had never been so close since the reptile awoke from suspended animation.

Pop! Pop!

Rifles discharged as sailors from both vessels fired multiple shots. Most shells threw water into the air around the Liopleurodon's head. A harpoon sliced the edge of its snout, placing the toxin within its bloodstream for a moment before maintaining its momentum into the deep. Curtis, his Springfield loaded, pointed his rifle but feared missing and froze. Roosevelt turned to him.

"Do it, Sergeant!" Roosevelt ordered. "Do it *now*!"

Curtis fired, but so did a rifle from the *Moosehead*. One of the rounds struck the Liopleurodon's head, blowing away skin and skull and blood, but not coming close to causing a mortal injury. The Liopleurodon hissed and submerged.

"Blast," Roosevelt said. He turned to Curtis. "You can't be timid in battle."

"I'm sorry, Colonel."

"Did your round strike him?"

Curtis sighed. "Couldn't say."

"It's alright," Roosevelt muttered. "I sense this *isn't* over." He turned to the lieutenant standing on the bridge. "How many harpoons hit their mark?" he shouted.

The lieutenant took a moment to respond. "A couple, from what I saw."

"Mine hit it! I think," one sailor said.

"Must do better," Roosevelt whispered to himself. He saw the two sailors carrying Springfields lower their guns. "Get ready!" They raised them.

Several sailors reorganized their positions on the *Sea Otter*'s port side, colliding and bumping into each other as they all moved at once. Luke did his best not to walk into anyone. His emotions were in somersaults, as happened several times a day for most of his life. They went from high to low, from excitement to his default dread and back again. His mind's eye pictured the Liopleurodon lunging at the *Sea Otter* and plucking Luke off the boat, dragging him into the depths below. Luke felt claustrophobic, had trouble breathing, and was tempted to step toward the middle of the deck where there were less people but did not want to appear unmanly to Roosevelt and Harris.

His professor turned to him. "Are you okay? You look pale." Luke nodded. "Maybe you should sit."

"I'm fine," Luke said.

"Riflemen, eyes on me!" the lieutenant shouted. "I want one

of you on each flank. The Liopleurodon could attack from either side if he thinks it's undefended."

"Retract that order, Lieutenant!" Roosevelt said.

"Why?"

"He who defends everywhere defends *nowhere!*"

"But Colonel—"

"He's bound to learn that the ship is a platform and *we're* the real target! Keep your men in place!"

The lieutenant swallowed his anger. "Do as he says."

The riflemen reloaded their guns and pointed them to the water. Sergeant Curtis followed suit. Luke's hands became fists; he anticipated that the next attack would be on the *Sea Otter*.

It wasn't.

It happened faster than Luke could blink. The Liopleurodon pierced the ocean's surface, lunging toward the *Moosehead*'s deck, his jaws extended, his fangs rubbing against each other, his explosive power causing a shockwave of sound as he launched a direct attack on the *Moosehead*'s crew. The sound increased, mushrooming further as multiple rifles and harpoon guns went off at once from both boats. The noise increased a third time as the screams of desperate men merged with the Liopleurodon's roar and metallic *clangs* to form a single cohesive audible wall that not only represented the action but became it in the minds of all present. The Liopleurodon struck the *Moosehead*, shaking it like an elevated punching bag. The noise from the other vessel dissipated as the Liopleurodon submerged once more.

There was a flurry of activity after the Liopleurodon's

second attack. The *Moosehead*'s crew did a body count while Roosevelt, Wood, and others turned to Curtis.

"Well?" Roosevelt asked. Curtis' eyes widened. He looked at Roosevelt, then his Springfield, and then back to Roosevelt. He nodded. "What do you mean? Did you shoot?" Curtis nodded more aggressively. Many of the sailors around them cheered. "How many?"

Curtis checked his magazine. "Got off two more rounds."

"Did you hit it?" Roosevelt asked.

"Can't say," Curtis said. He sighed. "Didn't see where they went."

"You don't have a clue?"

"Not one."

Roosevelt roared as he made his way to the port side, surrounding sailors parting like the Red Sea. They shared the former President's anger with Curtis. Wood noticed an officer on the *Moosehead* give a thumb's up. No casualties.

"Come here, General," Roosevelt ordered. Wood came to him. Roosevelt's cheeks were red; he took off his hat to fan his sweaty face.

"What is it, Theordore?"

"Do we have any idea on the poisoned rifle rounds?" Roosevelt whispered, not wanting to concern the sailors. "Or the harpoons? That was likely our last chance."

Wood took a moment to think. He thought he saw several harpoons from both boats strike the reptile, but it could have been his imagination. He hadn't the faintest sense where the poisoned bullets went.

"I imagine some hit the target," Wood said.

"Enough to bring him down?" Roosevelt asked. "He's a huge animal."

...

The Liopleurodon descended into the ocean's depths. He thrashed his head to and fro. He felt strange. His heart rate increased. His temper shortened. His flippers tingled. His mouth opened and wavered for several moments. He did not know what was going on—or why he felt this way—but he knew the family of metal objects on the surface, and the mammals riding them, were responsible. Just as they were responsible for the fire and bullets and harpoons. They threatened his existence. They wanted his territory—or, rather, they did not want him to take theirs—and would not rest until he was purged from the ecosystem. The Liopleurodon looked up, watching the juvenile objects, as his aggression grew and grew. They had to die. *Everything* had to die. The new world of the ocean rejected him and he would wage war upon it to beat it into submission. This was *his* territory, not the metal objects'. He would conquer the North Atlantic, even if it meant burning it all down in a cycle of unlimited death. *That* was a better fate than submission to the metal objects and mammals.

The Liopleurodon ascended to the surface, more energy coursing through him than he'd felt since his heyday.

...

"Luke, come here!"

Luke joined Roosevelt and Wood. Harris was nearby. "Yes, sir?"

"How quickly would you expect the azalea to kill the Liopleurodon?" Roosevelt asked. He'd restored his hat on his head and instinctively wanted to cross his arms but didn't want to increase his body temperature.

Luke glanced at the ocean and sighed. "Pretty fast. If the dosage was high enough." He paused. "And enough rounds struck it."

"That's what I would think," Roosevelt said. "He's a reptile."

"Why does that matter?" Wood asked. Roosevelt gestured to Luke and Harris.

"Which of you would like to explain?"

"Forget I asked," Wood said. "If that's right, it seems to me that the dosage must not have been high enough and it got away. I could have sworn that multiple harpoons made contact. Probably one of the poisoned rounds, too."

"It's entirely plausible that it will swim a couple of miles from here and die," Harris said, inserting himself into the conversation. "We can't predict these things."

"But wouldn't—"

"What if it was a *medium* amount?" Wood asked, cutting off Roosevelt. "Would it have a stroke and be handicapped? That would disable it, at least. Or would it recover?"

"We'll be here all day if we're going to speculate about every contingency," Harris said. "I'd advise that we wait another 10 minutes and head home."

"The simplest and most likely option is that we failed," Luke said, trying to act on an equal level with the others. "Either the engineers miscalculated or too many shots missed."

"*Really?*" Roosevelt asked. He looked like a disappointed child. He feared he would have to go back to the Oval Office and beg Taft to let him and Hawkins try again.

"I'm afraid—"

Boom!

The *Sea Otter* tilted to starboard as the port side rose. There were no "hold fasts" this time. Everyone on the deck fell—some to their knees, others on their sides. General Wood fell backward, *cracking* the back of his head against the deck before he flipped again.

"Leonard!" Roosevelt shouted before he landed face down, catching himself but having the air knocked out of his lungs. Luke expected the *Sea Otter* to course correct. It didn't. He dug his fingers into the deck as best he could. Skin scraped off of them and his knees. The world was a blur but he saw seawater come over the starboard edge. He tried not to panic, putting as much effort into fighting his emotions as he did in stabilizing his slide.

Rows of sailors rolled over each other and formed an avalanche of men. Several fell into the ocean. Many tried to grab one another or the deck or the railing. Luke slid, hurting his fingers and knees further. He steadied himself, taking a moment to catch his breath and wince in pain. He needed a plan. A way to climb to the port side, which was now the highest point of the *Sea Otter*. Maybe there he could wait for rescue. Of course, there was a sports field of fire and the most powerful reptile in history between him and the *Paulding*, so that didn't—

A chair struck Luke's back, knocking the wind out of him and causing him to lose his grip on the deck. Luke blacked out, regaining his senses just before hitting the water, which caused him to black out again. He plunged into the ocean, sinking until his float vest halted his descent. The cold shocked Luke's senses. He regained consciousness and saw the *Sea Otter* above him. He had to move before it trapped him below its mass. He noticed many dark objects in the surrounding indigo hue. Some were men. Others were flotsam. Luke looked up, desperate to find Professor Harris or Colonel Roosevelt. He didn't see them. Then he looked for the Liopleurodon. Where was it?

The green eye caught Luke's attention as it surveyed the destruction. The eye—and the intersecting fangs—reflected light from the fire and rising sun over the surface. Luke didn't know the Liopleurodon's intention. Did he plan to attack? The *Sea Otter*'s men were at his mercy. Luke's lungs burned but he ignored them. He couldn't take his eyes off the pliosaur. It was his favorite species to ever exist—far more than humanity—but he feared it—its greatness—its power. Luke felt as though the Liopleurodon's eye, that black slit surrounded by green, was locked onto him, because it knew that Luke had a greater connection to him than anything else in the ocean.

Luke acted on instinct and pulled the lever on his belt. Orange dye engulfed him, signaling the putracene that would keep the Liopleurodon at bay. He lost sight of the monster. Luke looked down. He didn't see it there. The *Sea Otter* was mostly submerged now and was uncomfortably close. That and his lungs' tantrum convinced Luke to swim to the surface. His vest helped.

He took the biggest breath of his life. He coughed several times and breathed again. The coughing scratched his throat. His eyes stung, but he wasn't sure if that was from seawater or tears. He sneezed from the salt in his nose, so now seawater, tears, and mucus covered his face. He wiped his face and then put it in the water to wipe it again. He saw the sinking *Sea Otter* and wondered how many sailors were trapped beneath it. His eyes were red from the salt and from being deprived of oxygen for so long. He tread water and looked around. Many sailors did the same.

Harris floated on the surface a short distance away. His face was sideways, half of it submerged underwater.

"Professor!" Luke shouted. He swam in Harris' direction. "Professor, I'm coming!" It took a moment to reach him. Luke rolled Harris's face away from the water. Harris had a broken nose and possibly other injuries. Blood ran down his right cheek. He was unconscious.

"Oh God! Oh God! Hang on!"

Luke saw a large piece of wood flotsam. He dragged Harris to it. Luke grabbed the flotsam and angled it with one hand while pushing Harris onto it with his other. He struggled. Then he angled Harris' head so he would not drown in his own blood. Luke put his own weight on the flotsam and it sank. It wasn't large enough for both of them.

"You stay here!" Luke rolled off and the flotsam bounced up, keeping Harris over the surface. Luke found his own piece and climbed aboard. He swam with his legs, directing it to Harris' side. Luke caught his breath. He saw that most of the sailors from the *Sea Otter* were treading water but knew the original group had been larger.

He couldn't find Roosevelt, Wood, or Curtis. He turned to the *Moosehead*, which was incoming to pick up castaways while also being cautious of another Liopleurodon attack. Luke put his head under the surface but couldn't see the Liopleurodon. He suppressed the desire to panic, determined to rise to the occasion. Harris needed him. He saw the fire and the *Paulding* in the distance.

...

"Nobody panic!" Hawkins ordered. His staff looked to him. "We have to remain calm." He turned to Jenkins. "Go to the bridge. Tell them to prepare the torpedo tubes and circumnavigate the fire zone. I've had enough of Roosevelt's games."

"Shouldn't we prioritize finding survivors?" Jenkins asked.

"The *Moosehead* will help them. I want the Liopleurodon's guts for dinner. Now go!"

"Yes, sir!" Jenkins left. Hawkins opened his lips to instruct his staff.

Boom!

The *Paulding* shook. Hawkins swung his arms, trying to catch his balance and avoid falling over the ship's railing. Two members of his staff grabbed him, putting him back on his feet. Three of his subordinates were less lucky, as evidenced by the splash below. Hawkins caught his breath. He had to rescue them, but it wasn't safe to put anything in the water.

"Captain! Captain! Look!"

Hawkins pivoted to where his staff member pointed.

"Oh my God."

...

Luke was stunned, both that the Liopleurodon would ram an object six times its size and that it made such an impact. The dying flames allowed Luke to see the commotion around the *Paulding*. He saw three sailors in the water. He didn't pay much attention to them. But something *did* catch his eye—Kelsey's blonde hair and Ross' shiny scalp were unmistakable.

Luke's heart was in his throat. Kelsey was in danger. He had to help, but distance and fire made that impossible. He saw Ross swim toward her. All that Ross had done to him—destroying his father, the tsunamis of arrogance—all would be forgiven if Ross kept her safe. Calm lowered Luke's shoulders for the first time all day. Ross—more than anyone, even Roosevelt—epitomized the intellectual prowess that always appeared beyond Luke's grasp. He'd know what to do. Thank God for him.

Water burst on each of Kelsey's flanks. Then came the teeth, each one a spike. Then the scales—some burned, some bleeding—attached to the jaws that surrounded Kelsey. Luke couldn't see the details of her face as it left the world forever. The Liopleurodon's jaws snapped shut. His head and neck rested above the Atlantic's surface. Blood poured down the side of the Liopleurodon's snout, a result of slamming his head into multiple ships, especially the *Paulding.* The Liopleurodon's eyes—usually green, now featured red spider webs from inflamed arteries. The red was highlighted by the fire that sat between Luke and the Liopleurodon, which, from Luke's perspective, framed the Liopleurodon's head like a bust mantle. An evil image. Worst of all was the Liopleurodon's jaws curving upward at the back, a demonic smile that mocked Luke.

Luke could not process what he witnessed and stared at his enemy as though they were the only two beings in existence. Luke and the Liopleurodon—weak and strong—pathetic and dominant—a worm and the master of evil.

Pop! Pop!

Sailors on the *Paulding* fired their Springfields at the Liopleurodon. Some rounds struck his snout, causing minor injuries. The Liopleurodon roared at the *Paulding* and submerged, finally retreating, desperate to recuperate.

Luke vibrated, not from the cold, but from the magnitude of what he had witnessed. The ocean's current carried Luke and his flotsam away from the *Moosehead* and the capsized *Sea Otter*.

Chapter Six
Alliances

March 7, 1911

Roosevelt rested in the *Delaware*'s medical bay. The dreadnought was docked in New York Harbor. White curtains separated the beds, most of which were filled with survivors from the disaster two days prior. Roosevelt was sweaty and pale; he'd lacked an appetite since recovering consciousness. He sensed—and tuned out—the other patients' fear and distress.

Edith's letter wrinkled in his hands.

Last night, I slept better because I held your letters to my heart instead of having them under my pillow. I felt I was touching you when I pressed against me what your hand had touched.

This separation is reminiscent more of when you fought in the Spanish War than your African safari last summer. Strange, as this is another hunt. But I find it absolutely essential not to break down for the sake of the children, as I did in 1898 and as other wives surely must have done during the four years of the Civil War. Always I have a longing and missing in my heart but I shall not write about it, for it makes me cry.

The children ask for you to write us again. They want an update on your campaign.

Try not to miss me or the children too much. I don't want to unman you.

Your Lover

Roosevelt felt his eyes water and resisted crying. He knew that Edith would take charge of his care if she were on the *Delaware*. His subconscious screamed at him for leaving her to go on another adventure. Edith—the woman who'd saved him in his darkest hour—there was no one he was more desperate to see, to hold.

He opened his diary and placed her letter in a page where he had written:

March 2, 1911
Thoughts on Principals:
Good

- Gen. Wood—Would never shoot a retreating man. The Nineteenth Century ideal. Among the finest men I've ever met.
- Ben Ross—The smartest man I know. Big head. Bigger heart.
- Kelsey Painter—Competent and pure.

Mixed

- *Comm. Jenkins—must learn to think for himself. Pigheaded at times.*
- *LT Palmer—needs more experience.*
- *Will Harris—Idealistic and foolish. Not malicious.*
- *Sean Ryan—?*

Bad

- *Capt. Hawkins—a jellyfish.*
- *Luke Jones—Reminds me of brother Elliot.*

Roosevelt heard metal strike metal. It repeated every few moments and became louder each time. Dr. Ross' walking stick. The curtain retracted and Ross entered.

"The nurse said you were awake."

"I see you held onto your cane during your dip in the ocean," Roosevelt said. Ross had forgotten how weak Roosevelt could look.

"This is my spare," Ross said. "Do you mind if I sit?" He gestured to a small wooden chair meant for medical professionals.

"Please," Roosevelt said. Ross leaned his cane against the bed and sat so his elbows rested on his knees.

"How are you doing?"

"My black care is back." Roosevelt referred to his depression. "I wish I'd been left to die in the Atlantic."

"You don't mean that."

"Yes, I do. It would have been a valiant death."

"There's still good for you to do amongst the living."

"Not if I live without honor." Roosevelt broke eye contact. "At least I got one thing out of all this."

"What's that?" Ross asked.

Roosevelt formed a thin smile. "I have always been unhappy, most unhappy, that I was not severely wounded in Cuba in some striking and disfiguring way. That isn't true this time." Ross was silent as Roosevelt pulled off his blanket, revealing that his right leg had been amputated and replaced with a wooden peg. Roosevelt's smile widened as he looked at it.

"I wish you weren't so morbid, Colonel."

"It's a lasting reminder of my efforts," Roosevelt said. "My failed efforts."

"I suppose my nightmares shall be the lasting reminder of mine."

"I'm so *sorry*, Benjamin."

"She was such a pretty girl. So much potential." Ross stared blankly. "A better person than I'll ever be and she wasn't even 30. And that monster—right next to me." He teared up. "I saw her face transition from dread, to relief from seeing me near her, to the *absolute* terror of her last moments…" His voice dissipated and he wiped away the stream on his cheeks.

"It wasn't your fault, Benjamin," Roosevelt said. Ross nodded. "No, it wasn't."

"Yes, it was," Ross said, getting ahold of himself. "I knew it was dangerous. I shouldn't have let her stay on the deck."

"How could you have known that the Liopleurodon would attack the *Paulding*?"

Ross hesitated. "You should know they found General Wood yesterday."

"Really?" Roosevelt sat up, surging with energy. He appeared like his usual self.

"Yes. They tried to return him to Washington but he refused. He's back in his room."

"He's on the *Delaware*?"

"Yes," Ross said. "He was injured but he's resting. He'll probably need to rest for the remainder of the day."

Roosevelt smiled. "Any other updates?"

"Mr. Jones is still lost at sea," Ross said. "Captain Hawkins plans to declare him dead if he isn't found by the end of today."

"A pity," Roosevelt said, "though it's better for a young man to die in battle than to grow into a weakling."

"That's disgusting," Ross snapped. "I had my issues with him. But I think he could have *been* something. Especially if he and Miss Painter were a couple. They would have been *great* together. Each was exactly what the other needed. She would have guided him into maturity. Given him purpose. He would have given her the family she wanted and an entry point into the field as a married woman. And the professional collaboration." He shook his head. "Really—they would have led their generation for decades."

Roosevelt studied Ross' face. He hadn't realized that Ross felt so strongly about them. "What about Will Harris?"

Ross sighed. "Still unconscious. They're not sure he'll ever wake up. Apparently he broke several ribs. And I think an arm and a leg. I don't remember which ones but they were on opposite sides of his body. Oh, he fractured a wrist, too." Roosevelt was tempted to say "good for him" but didn't. He knew that would just upset Ross further. "I never told him this—I wish I had, when he was awake—but I respect him more than any other colleague I've ever had. It's not that he's smarter—he's not—at least, not in terms of intellect. It's that he was the master of his emotions, instead of the other way around. I've tried so hard to be like that. To be logical. *Truly* logical." He remembered his conversation with Kelsey. "The number of years I've spent suppressing my emotions. Only to have them rebel against me. Starve them of what they demand. He never had that problem. And I envy him."

Roosevelt wasn't sure how to respond. Ross appeared to sink into himself and then shifted in his seat. "Have we ever discussed how your father helped sponsor the Natural History Museum?" Ross asked. "I owe him for establishing the institution where I've spent most of my career."

"He was a great man," Roosevelt said softly. "How have you liked having Osborn as President?"

"It's hard to match President Jesup. History will see his reign as the museum's golden age. Expeditions in the North Pole, Siberia, the Congo, and elsewhere. But it's refreshing that President Osborn is a professional scientist."

Roosevelt frowned. He made a fist. "I'd *so* hoped to make

the Liopleurodon's carcass the centerpiece in the museum's entrance. Add to my father's legacy."

"I remember when you invited me to have dinner with your father. Such a fascinating man. The Senate missed an opportunity when it rejected him for New York Customs Collector."

Roosevelt's frown deepened. "That's what killed him. Bowel cancer struck immediately thereafter. Took him in two months. Only 46. That's absurd. I'm already older than my father was when he died." His eyes watered. "That man was *everything* to me. He was the only one I told *everything* to. Why are you bringing this up? Do you want to make me sadder than I already am?"

"Of course not," Ross said. "I'm just thinking about how you and I are frequently together during crises. I did my best to be there for you when he died. Get your mind off of things."

Roosevelt brushed away his tears and squinted. "You kept asking for my opinion on scientific matters." He laughed. "Was that what that was? Why you sought my advice on homework while I grieved?"

"I was *more* than capable of doing my own homework," Ross said. "I thought it would distract you."

Roosevelt laughed harder. "You *truly* are one of the most peculiar men I've ever met. Though that's true of all you paleontologists."

Ross froze. "That's actually a good segue to something I'd like to discuss."

"Yes?"

Ross took a deep breath. He expected to face resistance. "I've concluded that Dr. Ryan is a saboteur." Roosevelt betrayed no reaction. "He likely freed the Liopleurodon from Naval Station Newport and switched out the azalea for some sort of stimulant."

Roosevelt took a moment to process Ross' words. He shook his head. "That's absurd. All of this has been the work of a German spy."

"Oh, please."

"I'm serious."

"Okay, fine. Who?" Ross asked. "Who's working for the Kaiser?"

"I don't know," Roosevelt said, breaking eye contact. "It could be anyone. But this is part of his masterplan to bring down our country and rule the world. Honestly, Benjamin, the Germans have already attempted its capture."

"I'm not denying that," Ross said. "But I don't think they freed it and I don't think they—"

"How else do you explain the German Army button found in Naval Station Newport?"

"Dr. Ryan planted it there as false evidence to throw the government off his trail."

"You realize how that sounds, don't you?" Roosevelt asked.

"Can I make my case?"

"Of course."

"And you'll have an open mind?" Ross asked.

"Yes."

"Okay. First, there's the fact that he was opposed to the Navy killing the Liopleurodon when we first saw it at Naval Station Newport becau—"

"Hardly unreasonable," Roosevelt said. "It's a magnificent creature and it's a miracle of nature that it survived."

"But you wouldn't prioritize its survival over human life."

"That's right. But how do you know that Dr. Ryan would?"

"I'll jump to my main point: I think that Dr. Ryan is trying to frame me," Ross said. "I recommended that poison be used and he switched it to a stimulant so it would look like I was responsible. He's trying to destroy me professionally so he can take my position as the leader of our division at the museum and in the field as a whole."

"That analysis is a bit self-centered, is it not?"

"I'm *convinced* this is true. But he might have other motives, as well. I'm still piecing it together."

"How do I know that *you're* not the saboteur and you're framing *him* to eliminate a rival?" Roosevelt asked.

"Colonel, please. After all of our shared history—"

"I will not allow myself to be manipulated with sentimentality, Benjamin."

Ross sighed. "What if you didn't have to believe me?"

"What does that mean?"

"I have to inform Captain Hawkins about this. That will likely trigger investigations into Dr. Ryan and myself. I'm *confident* that I'll be proven right."

"What if it plays out differently? What if you end up in jail?"

Roosevelt asked.

"That's a risk I'm willing to take. Dozens or hundreds may die if I don't." He paused. "He can't be allowed to sabotage our efforts again."

Roosevelt was torn. Ross *seemed* genuine, and he was making a big gamble. But what if it was a move? What if he was opening himself to legal vulnerability as an ultimate bluff, a last role of the dice to convince Roosevelt that he was sincere? Would Ross do that? Really? Roosevelt watched his old friend, weighing whether to make his own gamble.

"Is it possible that Kelsey was helping him?" Roosevelt asked.

"No."

"What about Luke Jones?"

"No," Ross said. "I think he's acting alone."

"How would you explain why he went on the *Moosehead* and put himself in harm's way?"

"Another effort to cover his tracks. And an attempt to appear manly to Miss Painter in his feud with Mr. Jones."

"That's another problem," Roosevelt said. "Do you realize that you're accusing him of causing his fiancé's death? That he sacrificed her *willingly* as part of this plot?"

"Colonel, I think Dr. Ryan is a *monster*. I don't think there's anything he *wouldn't* do to get his way."

Roosevelt broke eye contact. He still suspected the Germans were pulling the strings. But what was the harm of triggering investigations into Ross and Ryan, to be certain? Especially if

Ross *was* right? He restored eye contact.

"What should we do?"

Ross smiled. "So, we're allies?" Roosevelt extended his hand. Ross shook it.

"I assume you want me to try and convince Hawkins?" Roosevelt said.

"No."

"No?"

"I need you to distract Dr. Ryan for a few hours," Ross said. "Make sure he doesn't leave the ship. *I'll* go and talk to Captain Hawkins. I'm closer to him, and *you're* closer to Dr. Ryan."

"I barely know Dr. Ryan."

Ross chuckled. "Colonel, you can't possibly have a *worse* relationship with him than I do."

…

Dr. Ryan spent the morning packing his bags. His eyes strained from the low lighting; his room, like most rooms on the *Delaware*, lacked a window. He thrice checked that he had not forgotten anything only to learn that he had. Of course he had. No matter how hard he tried, nothing succeeded, nothing reached his standards. How could he not find space to pack everything he'd brought aboard? That didn't make sense. Whatever. He glanced at Kelsey's bags, which he'd brought to his room as a contingency. He paused, pushing aside emotions he didn't have the time to feel. The excitement of their relationship had faded over the years. Their engagement had not restored it and it had not transitioned into a steady partnership as expected. But now he knew what he had taken for granted. His eyes wetted against his will. No. Not now. Too late. He gave himself a moment to sit on his bed and reflect.

Clank. Clank. Clank.

Roosevelt arrived in his doorway and watched as Ryan dried his eyes. Ryan glanced at the former President's pegleg.

"I'm still getting used to it," Roosevelt said. "I hope to replace it with a leg made of Liopleurodon bone by year's end. I've always venerated the empty sleeves of Civil War veterans. This shall be my equivalent." Ryan remained quiet. Roosevelt gestured to the bags. "You're abandoning the cause?"

"Colonel," Ryan said in a voice barely louder than a whisper, "I just watched my fiancé get eaten by a sea monster. With her *died* any interest I have in this operation." He paused. "Also, I was unaware the Navy would try again after how badly the last attempt—"

"And let the Germans win?"

Ryan's face fell, breaking eye contact and looking at his feet. "Did they kill her? By switching the poison with a stimulant?"

"To the best of my knowledge." Roosevelt studied Ryan. Was this pathetic creature responsible for all that Ross accused him of doing? Had he not been through enough? Ryan fought to remain stoic in Roosevelt's presence. Roosevelt came closer and gestured to the bed. Ryan nodded. Roosevelt sat next to him, angling his body so his pegleg was fully extended.

"You must treat the past as the past," Roosevelt said, "the event as finished and out of your life. You should never speak one word of the matter again."

"I'm not sure I'm *strong* enough for that."

"You mustn't be *weak*, Doctor. You'll rebuild."

"For what purpose?"

Roosevelt hesitated. From within his subconscious came a memory he had fought to suppress—the night the light went out of his life. He had not spoken of it—had tried not to *think* of it—for decades. Yet here was a man in pain. A man who needed not just sympathy, but empathy.

"Are you aware that I was a widower?"

Ryan nodded after a few moments. "Yes. I remember reading that."

"In fact, I lost my dear mother to typhoid the same day." Roosevelt paused. "Same house." He retracted into himself but pushed himself to keep going. "But my darling Alice—it *really was* love at first sight. My *first* love. And I was *determined* to win her. Especially after my father passed." He chuckled. "What a torturous experience that was. And when we wed, I was so happy that I didn't dare trust my own happiness. No man ever loved a woman as much as I loved her. There was nothing on Earth left to wish for." He reached out and took Ryan's hand, squeezing it. Ryan hesitated, awkward at first, but accepted the gesture. Roosevelt cried. "When she died in childbirth—and my mother—I almost went crazy. I—*I*—"

Roosevelt fell silent. He fought the emotional explosion from the Pandora's box that he'd opened. He felt wave after wave of chills. He shivered and let go of Ryan's hand to wrap himself in a fetal position.

"Hey. *Hey*," Ryan said. "You're okay."

Roosevelt nodded, reconquering his emotions.

"Let us no longer speak of such sorrows," Roosevelt said. "Tell me. What is your favorite work of literature?"

Ryan glanced at his bags and then at the open door and then at Roosevelt's face, which, besides a pair of puffy eyes, had regained its composure.

"I don't really read fiction—"

"Oh, my boy, you mustn't *starve* your soul," Roosevelt said. "A good poet does as much for our country as a good manufacturer. For American writers I'd recommend starting with Poe and Hawthorne. But globally, the two best writers of our time are Kipling and Tolstoy."

Ryan nodded, not wanting to be sucked into the conversation but uncomfortable with being rude.

"Tolstoy is the best but I find his books are filled with a sexual decadence. It bothers me, and if you're a man of character, it will bother you too. He also never comments on the actions of his personages. He relates what they thought or did without any remark whatsoever as to whether it was good or bad. It reminds me of how Thucydides wrote history. This tends to give his work an unmoral rather than an immoral tone, along with the sadness so characteristic of Russian writers. But *Anna Karenina* is perhaps my favorite novel of all time. I read it to stay awake when I hunted and captured a group of hooligans who stole my boat during my time in the Dakotas. But I hardly know whether to call it a very bad book or not. There are two entirely distinct stories in it driven by two wonderful characters. The first is Levin, and his courtship of Kitty. That storyline is not only very powerfully and naturally told, but it is also perfectly healthy. Anna's story most certainly is not, though of great and sad interest; she is portrayed as being prey to the most violent passion, and subject to melancholi—"

Ryan sprung to his feet. "This is all very interesting, Colonel, but I really must—"

Roosevelt stood to block him. "Nonsense, my boy! I *insist* on this little chat." Both glanced at the door. Ryan saw his escape route but Roosevelt played for time. "I think reading that book would be of great service to you, given what it says about relationships. Both healthy and unhealthy."

"I'll keep that in my mind." Ryan gestured to his bags.

"I know you're familiar with the bounty of specimens I gave the Smithsonian last year, but have you heard of my hunt for the white rhino?" Roosevelt asked.

Ryan's face flashed red. "I don't believe so, but—"

"I began planning the journey as my presidency wound down. We bought weapons and equipment, selected ammunition, drew up maps, and so on. I was so excited that I had difficulty focusing on my presidential duties." Roosevelt laughed. Ryan's eyes bulged in his face. Roosevelt guided them back onto the bed. "My talks with other hunters informed me that I had to go to the Northern Guaso Nyiro River, which is north of Mount Elgon. There, I hoped to find a bull elephant. But the rare white rhino was in northern Uganda. At Lake Victoria I acquired a crazy little steam launch—a couple of sailboats, rowboats, things like that—and we embarked for hundreds of miles down the Nile to a place called the Lado Enclave. That's where I hoped to find the white rhino. Now, luckily for me, the Enclave had passed from Belgian to British control upon King Leopold's death, meaning it was no longer restricted to his use."

Ryan's eyes widened as he realized what Roosevelt was doing. He had to find a socially acceptable way to end the story.

"If you'll excuse me, Colonel, I'm hoping to catch the train at—"

"No, no, Dr. Ryan. I don't know when I shall see you again and it is important to me that you know what that *other* hunting adventure was like. Now, where was I? Ah, yes. To get to the Lado Enclave, my team and I had to pass through the islands near Lake Victoria's northern shore where an epidemic had killed hundreds of thousands of Ugandans. But nothing was going to keep me from my target. Now, millions of black rhinos lived in the area, but the white rhinos neared extinction, and I was desperate to acquire a specimen for our museums."

Ryan's veins flared in his forehead from anger.

"The conservationist in me wanted to protect its kind but it was overruled by my inner naturalist who *knew* they were destined for extinction anyway and it was for humanity's betterment to have a specimen for study. Oh! I forgot to mention our encounter with the British police on the Nile! That's a separate story in itself."

Ryan's face turned pale. His head dropped.

"You'll love this," Roosevelt said. "So, there we were…"

…

Dr. Branca paced in circles in the corridor outside of Michaelis' cabin aboard the *Thüringen*. Bags protruded from under his eyes. Michaelis' words, "I'm not done with you," repeated in Branca's ears for the past four days. What were Michaelis' plans for him? Did Michaelis know that Branca instructed the engineers to coat the ketamine canister in citrus to make it unappetizing for the Liopleurodon? All the evidence said that he did. Branca had underestimated him. Branca had hoped to give the Americans the opportunity to destroy the Liopleurodon but the American effort more than failed. It was a *catastrophe*. What was wrong with them? Michaelis kept Branca on the *Thüringen* to leave him within his grip. The question was why. What was Michaelis planning? Would he grind him into powder? He couldn't kill Branca, could he? Branca was a semi-public figure. He was the dinosaur guy—the man who discovered the Brachiosaurus that all the children loved. There would be an outcry—well, at least an out-moan—if the government killed him. But Michaelis could destroy his career. Everything Branca dedicated his life to was at Michaelis' mercy. A word from Michaelis could bring the entire government down upon him. Branca, and the museum, could be destroyed. Science's advancement, Branca's life's work, crushed because he didn't want to give the military a weapon. *Another* weapon. God forbid the government lacked another tool to spill the blood of young men like Hans, Branca's son-in-law. But how could Branca fight back? He lacked the status of a military leader such as Michaelis, especially in an authoritarian country like Germany. The court of public opinion wasn't a viable option. Could Branca kill him? That didn't sit well with his pacifism. And how would he? How would he even get close? Maybe Branca had to run. Get Edith and Hans and their kids and *leave* Germany. Leave the museum and rebuild in America or Austria or wherever. Dr. Benjamin Ross would give him a job, right? Ross liked him. Right? It wasn't ideal, but running might be the best option. If Michaelis let him. If Michaelis didn't destroy him before Branca could flee. If—

The door to Michaelis' cabin opened. Branca heard Mozart's Requiem playing at a high volume. "Mors slopebit et natora/Cum resurget creatura/Judicanti responsura." A lieutenant poked his head through the opening.

"The Vice Admiral is ready to see you."

Branca nodded, barely containing his panic. Why had Michaelis asked for him? Had the Liopleurodon been spotted since the American failure two days prior? Branca followed the lieutenant.

Branca didn't pay much attention to the cabin. It was less fancy than one might expect for a Prussian officer. A thin layer of light shone through the skinny windows on the opposite wall.

Photos of the Kaiser and of Michaelis' family sat on his desk, which was unsurprisingly well-organized. Michaelis, behind the desk, tracked Branca's nervous shivers as he entered. Gunther stood behind Michaelis, holding his cap in his hands.

Michaelis gestured with two fingers on his right hand to the record player, signaling for the lieutenant to kill the music. The lieutenant did so.

"Nice to see you, Doctor." Michaelis' tone bore a watered-down version of the charm he had shown when he and Branca first met. Thankfully, it lacked the venom from their encounter after failing to capture the Liopleurodon.

"Likewise, Vice Admiral," Branca said, trying to sound confident. He looked at Gunther and nodded. "Rear Admiral."

"Am I correct in my understanding that you know English?" Michaelis asked.

Branca nodded. "Yes, sir. Can I help with a translation?"

"In a moment. The American's awake."

"American?"

"You haven't heard? We picked him up when we visited the site of their disaster." Michaelis turned to the lieutenant and delicately said, "Retrieve our guest, if you don't mind."

"Yes, sir." The lieutenant left.

Branca turned to Gunther, who didn't make eye contact. Michaelis' hands were clasped on his desk, a professional ready to pounce. Branca's emotions bubbled under the surface, which he fought to hide. His mind raced to find ways to counter Michaelis, but it was empty. He scanned the desk. Was there a weapon he could kill him with? The thought made Branca squeamish, and he would undoubtedly be executed if that happened, but at least he would take Michaelis with him and exact revenge on the Vice Admiral for abusing his power by torturing Branca the way a cat would a mouse. He cursed the Americans for failing, from President Taft down to the average sailor. *What was wrong with them?*

Fifteen minutes passed before the lieutenant returned. He dragged the American by the arm. The American was a young man, perhaps 20 years old. He sported a goatee and surprisingly long hair—decadent Americans—which was wet and looked terrible. Other distinguishing features included a cut on his bottom lip, bandages circling his left wrist, and the dead stare in his eyes. The lieutenant guided him to a chair opposite Michaelis' desk. Branca watched from the room's right flank.

Michaelis looked at the lieutenant. "You couldn't have washed him?"

"I'm sorry, sir. He was uncooperative."

"That's all right." Michaelis turned to the American. "Young man, I am Vice Admiral William Michaelis, commander of the *SMS Thüringen* for the Imperial German Navy. I am deeply honored to meet you. What is your name?"

Branca recognized the charm offensive that Michaelis had given him when they met. This time it was turned up to 11. Branca waited for the American's response. Michaelis turned to him.

"Translate that, if you don't mind."

"Oh! Of course." Branca repeated Michaelis' words in English. The American was unresponsive.

"Did you translate correctly?" Michaelis asked.

"Yes, sir."

Michaelis smiled and watched the American. He had ways of making this young man *talk*. The youngster must have been scared out of his mind. Michaelis dialed the charm up to 13.

"I understand that you were advising the American government in its operation to kill the Liopleurodon. That's *very impressive* for a man your age."

Branca translated. The American was unresponsive.

"I'd like to reach an arrangement between us," Michaelis said. "Man to man. I'll have you delivered safely home to your parents, but I'd like something first. I need some information about your government's decision-making." He paused. "Can we make a deal?"

Branca translated. The American finally showed signs of life. He raised his head, looking Michaelis in the eye.

"Or *what*?"

Branca was stunned by the American's courage. He translated for Michaelis, whose smile imploded.

"I'm not sure you understand the sit—"

"I watched the woman I love *die*!" the American shouted. His eyes held an animalistic intensity. He raised his bandaged left wrist. "I already *tried* to kill myself! So tell me—what exactly are *you* going to do to *me*? What could you *possibly* threaten me with that I haven't already been through?"

Branca translated as quickly as he could. Michaelis slammed his fist on the desk. Branca was amazed that Michaelis lost his temper.

"*Arrogant* child!" Michaelis regained his composure but only with partial success. "Why did your government inject the Liopleurodon with methamphetamine? Do you realize the exponential growth of danger this has added to the situation?"

Branca translated. The American squinted.

"What the Hell are you talking about? We tried to use azalea. And *your* government switched it. You probably gave the order yourself so your *precious* Kaiser can rule the world like a modern Genghis Khan. Barbarians." He paused. "*You* killed Kelsey."

Branca translated. Michaelis' face became red.

"I have had the Kaiser and Admiral Tirpitz *breathing* down my neck for an answer to what is going on!" He seethed and again regained his composure. He turned to Gunther and whispered. "There's clearly been a penetration of the American operation."

"Was it us?" Gunther asked.

"Do you really think our 'friends' in the Army could pull this off?"

"What about the Tsar?"

"Possibly," Michaelis said. "But I suspect it was an American. Probably a capitalist who hopes to profit from a war. Whoever it was also likely released the Liopleurodon from the Americans' grasp at the beginning. Let's assemble a list of—"

Branca learned toward them. "If it helps, sir, I have a professional relationship with most top American paleontologists, and—"

"Silence!" Michaelis turned to the lieutenant. "Take this *child* back to his room. You should do the same, Dr. Branca."

The lieutenant grabbed the American's arm and guided him out of the cabin. Branca followed, seeing the direction that the lieutenant took the American, in awe of the young man's bravery.

Michaelis and Gunther spoke in the cabin.

"Figure out which officer is in charge of the American operation," Michaelis ordered. "I want to send him a telegram."

...

"Bring him in."

Lieutenant Palmer left the cabin, giving a moment for Hawkins' depression to secure his psyche within its dark grip. He'd lost six sailors when the *Sea Otter* capsized. Then the monster killed Kelsey Painter. Luke Jones, that slithering creature who Hawkins had been told would be the mission's maestro, was missing and likely dead. The former President, the celebrity thrust upon Hawkins, was injured for the rest of his life. Worst of all, the Liopleurodon was more dangerous than ever and could be anywhere in the North Atlantic.

Hawkins waited for word from Washington. Was he to continue the mission? Was his career over? He knew that shouldn't be his biggest concern, but it was hard not to resent how his life's focus was in pieces. Hawkins long believed that men needed order to exist, that it was a prerequisite for man to lower his guard and be civil. Nothing unleashed man's dark side like chaos, because in chaos man had no guarantees of protection and so had to defend himself at all costs. Such extremism did not allow for multiple, conflicting interests to coexist—domination and suffering were the only outcomes until order was restored.

Palmer returned with Ross.

"Please remove your headgear, Doctor," Hawkins said. Ross nodded and complied. He held his wool hat in one hand and his cane in the other. Hawkins smiled, too tired to restrain himself. Ross was the adult among the paleontologists, the one he could do business with. "What can I do for you, Dr. Ross?"

"Captain, I believe that Dr. Ryan is a saboteur." Ross went straight to his core point, desperate to trigger the investigation and knowing that Roosevelt couldn't distract Ryan forever.

Hawkins and Palmer exchanged a glance.

"Are you saying he's a German spy?" Hawkins asked.

"It's possible," Ross said, knowing it was easier to work within the narrative than arguing that the Germans weren't involved.

"Are you aware that he received a background check before the Navy Department granted him permission to partake in this operation?"

"How thorough was that background check?" Ross asked.

"The government didn't have a lot of time given the urgency of—frankly, Dr. Ross, Dr. Ryan is an established professional,"

Hawkins said. "Why would he cooperate with a hostile government?"

Ross leaned forward, his weight on his cane. "You have to understand, Captain. Metaphorically speaking, Dr. Ryan wants to rule the world just as much as the Kaiser." Hawkins laughed. Ross didn't blink. "He has *no limit* to what he thinks he deserves. I'm talking about a man—a man who once told me his parents were 'well meaning but couldn't keep up with him intellectually.' A man who went into paleontology because he thought it would be an easy field to dominate only to be blocked by my—"

"That is quite enough, Dr. Ross. You're wasting my—"

"Or maybe he's an environmental extremist!" Ross said. "Or —or maybe he wants to start a war! Or—"

"This is *nonsense*. I thought you were a reasonable man, but —"

"You *must* listen to me!"

"No, you must—"

"You are doing a *bad* job leading this operation, Captain!"

"How *dare* you!" Hawkins leapt to his feet, slamming his fist onto his desk. His face became red. "It was *your* plan to use azalea that killed *six* of my men!"

"Because Dr. Ryan replaced it with a stimulant! He's trying to fra—"

"When would he have done that?" Hawkins asked.

Ross sighed. "I don't know. But clearly someone—"

"Exactly." Hawkins sat down. "You see the worst in him, and so you've found a conclusion that you like and you're forcing the evidence to support it. But your evidence isn't stable."

Ross looked at his feet, the weight of defeat coming down upon him. Hawkins' rejection was crystallizing. Ross didn't know what other argument he could give. He saw Kelsey's expression in his mind's eye—the last one she ever made—when the Liopleurodon's jaws surrounded her. Ryan *couldn't* get away with it. He *couldn't*—

The door flew open and Jenkins burst into the cabin. "Captain!"

"What is it, Commander Jenkins?" Hawkins asked. "I'm wrapping up—"

"Captain, we just received this from Secretary Meyer," Jenkins said. "It's a telegram from Vice Admiral Michaelis."

"*Michaelis?*" Hawkins asked, snatching the envelope from Jenkins' hand. He had suspected that Michaelis was directing the German effort to capture the Liopleurodon. Ross studied every twitch of emotion on Hawkins' face as he read the telegram. It shifted from a fading redness to pale to burgundy.

"What does it say?" Ross asked.

Hawkins took a moment to process and respond. "I—I can't believe…" He turned to Jenkins. "He says he picked up an American student from our failed attempt to neutralize the Liopleurodon."

Jenkins and Ross exchanged a look.

"That must be Mr. J!" Jenkins said.

"Of course it is!" Ross said. "Mr. Jones is *alive!*" He turned to Hawkins. "Captain, we have to—"

"I'm not finished!" Hawkins barked. Everyone froze. "Next, the Vice Admiral says that he'll return the student to us if the United States and Germany agree to cooperate to capture the Liopleurodon—for the world's benefit."

Jenkins said, "That's the cockiest thing I've ever heard. He's —"

"He's blackmailing me." Hawkins placed his chin on his right fist. He looked at the telegram. "There's more. He says he's convinced that someone on my team sabotaged our efforts to neutralize the Liopleurodon and that if I hand over the names of the paleontologists advising me that *his* paleontologist will help determine if any of them is the traitor."

Ross snorted. "Branca."

"Is there anything else?" Jenkins asked.

"He ends by promising that the German Navy had nothing to do with freeing the Liopleurodon or sabotaging our mission and that it must be one of our own people." Hawkins slammed the crumpled telegram onto his desk.

"Do we think he's telling the truth?" Jenkins asked.

Ross said, "I am *telling* you that Dr. Ryan is—"

"Quiet!" Hawkins shouted. "Let me think." He stared blankly for several moments. Everyone awaited his words. "I don't intend to respond to Michaelis."

"But what about Mr. Jones?" Ross asked.

"I'm not negotiating for a hostage."

"We have to rescue him."

"Out of the question," Hawkins said.

Palmer lifted the Navy's legal manual. "Sir, Article 341 of Navy Regulations says that when an American citizen is injured or threatened through a violation of international law—wait, this says you're supposed to report the facts to the Secretary of the Navy. Here! It says the commanding officer has responsibilities for the actions taken—"

"Enough, Lieutenant!" Hawkins said.

"I'm sorry, sir."

"That's all right."

"Do you think Michaelis is sincere that the German Navy isn't responsible for the sabotage?" Jenkins asked.

"I don't know," Hawkins replied.

"I think he's telling the *truth*, Captain," Ross said.

"Of course *you* do." Hawkins looked at Ross. He wondered if Ross was playing him. But what if he wasn't? He turned to Jenkins. "Is Dr. Ryan still on board?"

Ross spoke first. "Colonel Roosevelt should be preventing his departure."

Hawkins winced. "You brought Roosevelt into this?"

"I did, sir," Ross said. "I'm telling you the truth. As well as I understand it."

Hawkins turned back to Jenkins. "Escort Dr. Ryan to the brig." Ross restrained himself from jumping with joy. Hawkins turned to Palmer. "What authority do I have to restrain a civilian contractor?"

Palmer flipped through the manual. "What about this? Article 809(1) of Navy Regulations says the commanding officer can restrain or surveil any person *not* in the armed forces of the United States who is found under irregular circumstances within the command—"

"I'm not sure this is the proper context for that statute, but—whatever. It'll do." Hawkins turned to Jenkins. "Do as I've commanded."

"Yes, sir." Jenkins left. Ross smiled. Pressure dissolved from his body.

"Don't be so jubilant, Dr. Ross," Hawkins said. "I want you under lockdown in your room until I can sort out what's going on."

"That's fine, sir," Ross said. "I have nothing to hide."

Hawkins smiled. "We'll see."

...

"...I slept under a mosquito net every night with nothing on, on account of the heat. We also burned mosquito repellent all night long, which mixed together with our collective sweat. We finally reached our destination on the banks of the White Nile two degrees north of the Equator. We were in the heart of the African wilderness. I was lucky not to die from dysentery. All the other members of the party were down with it or with fever. One gun bearer had died of fever and four porters of dysentery. Two were mauled by beasts. In a village on our line of march, near which we camped and hunted, eight natives died of sleeping sickness during our stay."

Ryan hadn't moved as Roosevelt recounted his tale. His eyes were so bulged and wide he had barely blinked.

"I was determined not to quit, for this was the *only* chance the Smithsonian would get for receiving the white rhino specimen. I eventually shot five white rhinos and Kermit, my son, shot four more. The white rhinos were a rather pathetic prey as we shot most of them while they slept or were emerging from sleep. A bigger problem was the fires that burned the jungle grass and the papyrus. The fires turned the night sky red, not dissimilar to the patch of sea water we covered in gasoline the other day. But all in all, the mission was a success. A white rhino shall be on display at the Smithsonian in Washington. I don't know. It might already be there."

Roosevelt paused. Ryan blinked, first only once and then several times. His eyes were dry and stinging. Was he done? Ryan moved his head for the first time in an hour. His back was stiff.

"There is a delight in the hardy life of the open, and no words can describe the hidden spirit of the wilderness, or can reveal its mystery, its melancholy, and its charm." Ryan slumped back down. "That is why I have always viewed office life with a critical eye. It softens a man's masculinity. Hunting is man's birthright, and I for one—"

Ryan had focused so little for so long that he did not hear the approaching footsteps and was startled as Commander Jenkins and half a dozen sailors entered the doorway.

"Please come with us, Dr. Ryan," Jenkins said.

"What?" Ryan asked.

"Captain Hawkins has ordered for you to be held in the brig," Jenkins said. "He's launching an investigation into potential sabotage."

Ryan leapt to his feet. "This is outrageous! By what right—" He turned to Roosevelt, who averted his gaze. It *was* all a ploy, including the bonding over tragedy. He turned back to Jenkins. "By what law can you arrest *me*?"

"Article 809(1) of Navy Regulations," Jenkins said.

"Show me the statute," Ryan demanded. "I want to read it."

"You can review it later," Jenkins said. "You'll be speaking with Lieutenant Palmer tonight."

Ryan scanned his room for an advantage, a way to resist. He found none. "Very well." Ryan lowered his guard. "May I bring my things?"

"I'll arrange for your bags to be brought to you," Jenkins said.

"Thank you." The sailors escorted Ryan out of the room, leaving Jenkins and Roosevelt. Roosevelt watched Ryan go, torn. Ryan's sadness had seemed genuine.

"So, Dr. Ross roped you into this, too?" Jenkins asked. Roosevelt nodded. "Do you trust him?"

Roosevelt was about to declare "with my life!" but he hesitated. He glanced at his pegleg. "I *think* so."

Jenkins pivoted to leave but paused. He turned back. "Luke Jones is alive."

"Really?" Roosevelt said. "Good for him."

"The Germans have him."

"Oh my. Has Hawkins planned his next step?"

"He's not going to negotiate," Jenkins said. "The State Department will deal with it once the crisis is over." Roosevelt nodded and Jenkins pivoted again but once more turned back to the colonel. "How sore is your throat? Do you need any water?"

Roosevelt's eyebrows ruffled. "I'm fine. Why do you ask?"

...

March 8, 1911

The sperm whale used his echolocation to monitor the Liopleurodon as it floated passively under the pitch-black water. A missing pectoral fin and pliosaur teeth embedded in his blubbery neck were evidence of his attacker. The Liopleurodon, rampaging from methamphetamine and head trauma, had struck head-on and underestimated the mammal. The whale's sonar blasts left the reptile stunned and, it appeared, his brain scrambled. The whale was satisfied with his successful defense and rose to the surface to rest, still tired from diving to the ocean's depths during the day.

The Liopleurodon's eyes opened. His consciousness came back online and his olfactory senses identified his opponent. The Liopleurodon's jaws spasmed as his heartbeat resumed. His flippers, bleeding from the whale's bite, moved briefly at first and then with more energy as the Liopleurodon and the methamphetamine gripping his psyche kicked into action.

The Liopleurodon felt a surge of energy. He targeted the whale from below, ignoring the pain he felt from their initial skirmish. He grabbed the whale's fluke in his jaws and threw his weight downward. The whale thrashed about and tried countering the pliosaur's attack. The contest of strength was resolved with a *crack* after several minutes.

The crocodilian jaws released the whale. The whale, his tailbone shattered, sank into the darkness. The Liopleurodon tracked the whale through smell, monitoring his fidgeting jaws and flippers, indicating that he still lived for the moment. The Liopleurodon decided not to deliver the fatal blow, allowing his enemy to drown. Sharks closed in, wary of the sperm whale's lethal bite.

The Liopleurodon rose above the water to breathe. He looked at the moon and roared, asserting his dominance over the *entire* ocean. He was the king of all the carnivores that ever lived. He thrashed his head to and fro, his psyche on fire from methamphetamine. He wanted to kill everything he could find. The North Atlantic was *his* territory and no one else's. Everything within his territory had to be at his mercy—to be a potential meal through minimal effort. Nothing should fight back. Anything that could had to be eliminated. Then he would sit atop the pile of corpses and soon-to-be-corpses, an empire of death where he was the emperor to do as he liked, when he liked. He wanted the easiest and most enjoyable existence for his golden years but it required effort upfront while he had energy, especially with this extra boost. All life in the ocean was on a platter for his choosing.

He put his head underwater and smelled a huge metal object violating his territory dozens of kilometers away. He moved in that direction to eliminate the threat.

…

Dr. Ryan was a sweaty mess in the brig. His clothes were dirty, his hair forming blonde clumps, his right wrist handcuffed to his chair's armrest. Ryan was surrounded by iron bars, between some of which were windows. A short silver table sat outside the bars near the locked door. Ryan stared at his lap as the two sailors guarding him droned on and on.

"Did you hear they opened a new stadium at Clemson?"

"When?"

"Today. Or yesterday, I guess."

"Where's Clemson?"

"I think it's in one of the Carolinas. I think."

"I've always wanted to visit the Carolinas."

"Really?"

"Yeah."

"Why?"

"I had a friend who traveled through them on their way to Florida. Said the food was good."

"Why would anyone go to Florida?"

"I don't know."

"You don't know?"

"I don't know. He probably told me but I don't remember."

"That's interesting."

"What's interesting?"

"That is."

"I think so too. So, what are they calling the field?"

"What field?"

"The one in Clemson."

"Oh. I don't know. R-something. I think."

The door opened, sparing Ryan from this commentary. He looked up to see Lieutenant Palmer placing his pad and pen on the silver table.

"Evening, gentlemen," Palmer said.

"Evening," a guard replied.

"Sorry I'm getting here after midnight."

"Makes no difference to us. We got the nightshift."

Palmer reached into the bars and placed a mug on the desk in front of Ryan. "I brought you some coffee. I thought it would warm you up." He sat down.

Ryan glanced at it. "Thanks," he muttered. "I noticed Commander Jenkins never brought me my bags."

"Sorry about that."

"Will I get them in the morning?"

"That's not up to me."

"I see."

"Are we good to get started?"

"Why not?"

Palmer looked at his pad. "Dr. Ryan, you're being accused of sabotaging the United States Navy's operation to destroy the Liopleurodon and possibly of being a German spy." He looked up. "How do you respond to this claim?"

"It's *so* classy that you're accusing me of effectively *killing* my fiancé."

"Doctor—"

"By the way, I've yet to be told exactly what authority my detainment falls under."

"Article 809(1)."

"Which says what?"

"Uh…" Palmer flipped through the manual.

"Because I'm going to *sue* you personally—and Hawkins—for false imprisonment and emotional distress unless I'm satisfied that my detainment is lawful."

"Let's—let's calm down. Is that okay, Dr. Ryan?"

"Sure. Let's calm down."

"I'm sure you have nothing to worry about. Let's just—let's have a conversation. Is that okay?"

"Yes. That's okay."

"How did you feel when you first saw the Liopleurodon in Naval Station Newport?"

"I was in awe. Who wouldn't be? It was the most amazing thing I'd ever seen."

Palmer wrote down Ryan's answer. "Why did you volunteer to be an advisor for the operation?"

"It was Kelsey who wanted to go. But I had to go so she could go."

"Why did Miss Painter want to go?"

"I'm not sure. Adventure, I guess."

"Why did you decide to propose to—"

"Actually, let's wait a second."

"Yes?"

"I'd like a lawyer. Before we continue any further."

"We don't have one available."

"Then we're done."

"Wait—but—"

"The Fifth Amendment gives me protection from self-incrimination and the Sixth Amendment gives me the right to a lawyer in federal criminal proceedings. This is federal law. You're a federal employee."

"I—uh—wait." Palmer flipped through the manual.

"Didn't they teach you *anything* in law school?"

"Yeah, but—"

"I'm not a lawyer and even I know this."

"Okay."

Ryan snorted, mocking Palmer's inexperience. "You're not prepared, *are* you, Lieutenant? *Very* unprofessional."

Palmer was frustrated from being mocked by those older than him. He closed the manual and placed it, his pen, and his pad together. "Have it your way. Enjoy your night." He stood up.

"Wait!"

"Yes?"

"You're being manipulated."

Palmer sat down. "What do you mean?" He pulled out his

pen and pad.

"I assume you've already spoken to Dr. Ross?"

"I'm not going to say—"

"I assume you have. And I assume he told you that *I* sabotaged the azalea—that I might have even released the Liopleurodon from the Navy's control—out of some vendetta against him. Does that sound familiar?"

"Uh…"

"Typical. You realize that this is likely all *his* doing, right? That I'm a professional rival and so he's trying to frame me?"

"Why—why would he—"

"Are you aware that Luke Jones effectively ended Dr. Ross' career by identifying the Liopleurodon at Naval Station Newport? That Dr. Ross launched his career by debunking Andrew Jones'—Luke's father—his theory about pliosaur-size and Luke validated his father and proved that Dr. Ross was wrong? There's your case, Lieutenant. Dr. Ross is trying to destroy me and restore his image in the profession. I'm surprised the government even appointed him as an advisor to this operation, if you want to know the truth."

Palmer wrote down Ryan's words. He considered mentioning that Luke was a German hostage but decided against it. "You're both accusing each other of the same thing."

"But because he did it first his accusation is more valid?"

"I'm just saying that you're both accusing the other person of *serious* crimes out of your professional rivalry when this event is playing out on the world stage."

"I never said that wasn't part of his thinking."

"What does that mean?"

"Dr. Ross was born into money. That's why he sucks up to the Captains of Industry and thinks there should be no limits on the accumulation of wealth. It's why he thinks women shouldn't get the vote. I wouldn't be surprised if he's trying to help Roosevelt get elected so, if there's a war, Roosevelt will intervene and end it quickly before Europe's colonies can rise up or communism starts toppling governments."

Palmer scribbled his notes faster. "Um—are you saying the former Pres—"

"I have no idea if Roosevelt is helping him. Probably not. Though this whole thing is clearly in his interest if he wants to challenge Taft in next year's election."

"How was it in Colonel Roosevelt's interest to inject the Liopleurodon with a stimulant?"

"More publicity? Or maybe you're right. Roosevelt probably isn't involved in the plot."

Palmer finished writing his notes and scanned them to make sure he didn't miss anything. "Okay. This is all very interesting." He glanced at Ryan. "I'll talk to Captain Hawkins about all of this in the morning."

"Sure, sure. Hey, Lieutenant, before you go—just one more thing."

"What?"

"Sorry for being rude to you earlier. It's just—I watched the love of my life die a few days ago and now I'm locked to a chair.

It's upsetting, you know?"

"Sure. I understand."

"Great. Sorry again."

Palmer gathered his things and stood up. "Well, goodnight."

"Goodnight."

Chapter Seven
Here Lies Wolfe Victorious

March 8, 1911

Neville Chamberlain completed tying a Victoria Knot around his collar in his dressing room as the *SY Jupiter* shifted to port. He looked at his reflection in the mirror that sat atop an oak dresser. He sought to evaluate his appearance but couldn't focus; waves of panic, the source of which he couldn't consciously grasp, eroded his efforts to calm his mind. Chamberlain took a deep breath, fighting to convince himself that his decision was correct, that his gamble would work.

It's a big ocean. It's a big ocean. It's a big ocean.

His thoughts briefly turned to Hoskins & Company, wondering if there was a chance his company built the *Jupiter*'s berth. Why did he make the transition to politics? He was *good* at business. It was a natural fit for his temperament. What if he lost the city council election? Would it be mentioned in his obituary? Or what if he *was* elected and his political career went badly? Was that how he wanted to be remembered?

Poor Anne. His ambitions had even warped their wedding. The guest list was formed of businessmen, Birmingham political connections, and representatives of the United Hospitals Committee. Not exactly the embrace of friends and family, but even their wedding had to advance his electoral chances and the *Jupiter* only had so much capacity.

The true source of his anxiety lay elsewhere. It took all of Chamberlain's connections to convince the Defense Ministry to authorize the *Jupiter*'s voyage, and even then they advised him with all the emphasis they could muster to cancel the journey. The look that bureaucrat gave, that condescending, demeaning look—but Chamberlain was behind in the last straw poll and he was *certain* that this display of courage would reverse his fortunes. Sweat built up on his palms. He wiped it on his pants and finally evaluated his tie.

Was that the best he could do?

Knock knock.

"Come in!"

The cabin door opened. Winston Churchill entered. "The groom wished to s-see me?" He stuttered.

"Yes," Chamberlain said. "To help calm my nerves."

"I'll make my best effort," Churchill said. "Thank you for inviting Clemmie and myself. *Most* generous and thoughtful." He spoke as though they were words he was supposed to say but didn't believe.

"You're quite welcome, Winston," Chamberlain said. Churchill was an important connection in the Liberal Party and the guest with the highest political office. Chamberlain looked in his direction and saw that Churchill held a briefcase. "Is that what I think it is?"

Churchill sighed and combated his own anxiety. He had more experience at this. "I don't expect we'll see it. But I wanted a contingency plan. In case…"

"It's a big ocean," Chamberlain muttered. He glanced at his outfit in the mirror. "Anne's passion is archaeology, funnily enough. Though I'm not sure this is what she means." Churchill smiled half-heartedly. "What do you suspect are the chances that Asquith will name you as First Lord of the Admiralty?"

"Is-s this really what you want to discuss on your wedding day?"

Chamberlain shrugged. "I'm dressed. The ceremony's not for a few hours. And, you know, this will distract me."

Churchill sighed and leaned against the bed. "I'm optimistic. Or at least I *ought* to be. There's no use in being anything else. I've done what I can as Home Secretary and—" He paused as the ship lurched. Both men became anxious but realized it was just the current.

"You were saying?" Chamberlain asked.

"Herr Lloyd George and I are still locking horns with McKenna over his proposal for *more* naval expansion," Churchill said. "I'm sure you recall from our previous discussions that I don't buy into fears of imminent war with Germany—"

"Right. Right."

"—and the working class will turn on the rich if we don't establish a minimum wage. But the Tories control the House of

Lords and will veto any Liberal proposal along those lines."

"I see."

"If only we could *abolish* that chamber." Churchill stared at his feet. They were silent for a moment. "I think my work on prison reform is nearing completion."

"What is that again?" Chamberlain undid his tie.

"You'll need to read the Liberal platform if you want to become an MP one day." Churchill laughed. "It will codify the distinction between criminal and political prisoners." He spoke with his hands, signifying the division. "That way we can relax conditions on the latter."

"Sounds dry, honestly. I see why you want to switch to the Admiralty."

"Have you already forgotten what happened last month?" Churchill asked. "Or, I suppose two months ago now."

"Well, sure—"

"But that doesn't happen everyday."

"You're talking about getting whipped by suffragettes for suggesting a male referendum on—"

"I'm talking about investigating the murder of East End policemen—"

"Right. Right. My mind's playing tricks on me."

"The groom needn't apologize." Churchill opened his jacket, revealing a Webley Model 1909 pistol in a holster clipped to his belt. "That's when I got this."

Chamberlain smiled. "Do you come armed to *every* wedding?" Churchill didn't answer. Anxiety set in, leading to awkwardness. Chamberlain sought to break it. "Tell me a story."

"What?"

"Tell me about how you escaped the Boers."

Churchill thought back to the event that made him a national figure. "It's not that complicated. They surrounded our forces at Estcourt and the brass decided to evacuate to Ladysmith 60 kilometers north. Herr Haldane invited me along. He was my friend and was a veteran of earlier battles with the Boers. But it was a folly plan because train tracks are fixed in place and the Boers could ambush us. They attacked with artillery and put rocks on the tracks. The man beside me lost an arm. A number of officers surrendered with their little handkerchiefs just so. I was determined not to get caught and made a run for it but I left my revolver on the train. They got me, along with everyone else. They put us in a school that had been converted into a prison. My plan was to take over the prison and with this force capture the Boer President. The others thought this was too complicated and came up with the less *interesting* plan of jumping over the fence while a separate group distracted the guards. They told me not to come. Said I *talk* too much. But I insisted. The guards wouldn't move and my comrades gave up and decided to get dinner. I went without them. But then I realized I hadn't brought supplies and couldn't speak the local language. And the Boers were upset because I'd left a cheeky letter saying goodbye."

Chamberlain laughed. His shoulders relaxed. "What happened next?"

"They searched the neighboring town for me. You can

imagine—"

Boom!

Churchill fell from the bed. He slipped from consciousness for a moment. He coughed. His lungs wouldn't inhale, causing him to gag and to feel too weak to move. He panicked. His body tensed and his skin tingled. Try again. Air. Okay. That was good. Next his forehead throbbed. Did he land on it? He'd tried to land on his forearms. His eyes opened and he saw Chamberlain had fallen so his left elbow took the brunt of the impact. Churchill coughed again. "Must stand," he whispered as he grabbed the bed and pulled himself up onto one knee. He paused.

A big ocean indeed.

Boom!

Churchill fell again. The fall was shorter but the impact was worse because it built on the pain from the previous one. The hope that his head was not concussed flashed through his thoughts. His forehead hurt more now. He touched it. It was wet. That was all right. It wasn't the first time. He rallied his energy. This was no time for dillydallying. Keep buggering on. He again grabbed the bed. Perhaps a 37 year old shouldn't fight this sort of battle.

Chamberlain was still on the ground.

"Come!" Churchill barked. "Come! Let us *see* the action!"

Chamberlain's face rose, looking at Churchill as though he were an alien. "Are you mad? We'd be best to wait here!"

"*That* would be mad! The creature will tear this ship apart unless we *fight* back!"

"I'm staying!"

"Oh, suit yourself!" Churchill took a deep breath, pulled his pistol from its holster, and ran out of the room. He was halfway down the hall when he realized he'd left the briefcase. He went back and grabbed it. "I'm going to need this."

Churchill made his way to the deck where dozens of Birmingham and London elites had been socializing minutes before and were now on their knees or bellies. Some clung to the mast. Several tables had toppled. Cocktails were everywhere.

Boom!

The starboard flank was struck a third time. It briefly lifted out of the water and landed with a *thud*. Churchill tripped but clung to the deck's railing. Several wedding guests fell into the water. He coughed, still recovering from his fall. He watched the water and moved further down the deck to where he expected the monster to appear, returned his pistol to its holster, and placed the briefcase down. He was unsure if he should open it or use the pistol. Churchill replayed the attacks through his mind, calculating the space between them. He lacked time. He retrieved his pistol, already loaded, and pointed it to the water. His finger sat on the trigger.

Churchill saw a current along the surface a few meters from the *Jupiter*'s flank, detected a hint of green, and fired. The bullet struck the water but he knew the animal was too deep for the bullet to reach before losing momentum. The green disappeared. He looked at the wedding guests treading water. A 30-something woman in a red dress was the most attention-grabbing. Churchill feared for her life.

His jaw clenched. Typical that Lord Britannia had to clean up after the Germans and Americans. Especially the Americans. They lost the monster from between their fingers and then injected it with a stimulant. Only God knew why. God and maybe Taft. The Americans always did the right thing after trying everything else and were still in the process of trying everything else. Churchill heard footsteps behind him. He turned. It was Chamberlain.

"Make s-sure an SOS is sent!" Churchill ordered. Chamberlain hesitated. "*Now!*" Chamberlain withdrew inside, both to do as Churchill instructed and to check on Anne.

Churchill heard gasps and turned to see a large current incoming. Churchill screamed and fired multiple shots from the semi automatic pistol. Several hit the current but it didn't slow down and struck the *Jupiter* the hardest time yet. The *Jupiter* dipped to port. Churchill felt his feet leave the bottoms of his shoes. He grabbed the railing before the starboard flank came down. It *crashed* into the water, which splashed into Churchill's face and blocked out the screams from other passengers. He was on his knees and couldn't see but felt both the pistol and briefcase leave his grasp. The pistol went into the Atlantic. That was fine. It was on the brink of jamming from residue buildup.

He restored his vision and saw the briefcase wasn't far away. He grabbed and opened it, revealing pieces of a Lee-Enfield rifle that he started assembling.

"Come on. Come on," he muttered. His focus carried him

forward, determined to be ready before the creature struck again. He focused so intensely that he didn't hear the wood *cracking* behind him. A shadow encircled him. Gasps caught his attention. He looked and saw that the sail mast had come loose. It plummeted into the deck as multiple passengers dodged it as best they could. Churchill wasn't close but clutched his face and eyes. The mast's impact sounded like a cannon firing. He prayed he hadn't been struck by wood splinters.

Churchill dropped the rifle and fell on his side. Dust had invaded every opening on his face—his eyes, his ears, his nostrils, his mouth, his cuts. Tears emerged and mixed with the dust to form muddy substance under his eyes. He willed himself into sitting upright so he could load the rifle. Drops of blood fell from his face onto the deck. His eyes stung. He loaded a 10 round magazine and heard more gasps.

What now?

Churchill saw what now. The mast had broken through the railing and much of the *Jupiter*'s starboard side. Waves striking the *Jupiter* exacerbated the problem. The yacht's two halves formed a V as the mast sank deeper, its base barely touching the deck. Both halves tilted to starboard, throwing more passengers on the overcrowded deck into the water. Loved ones and colleagues clung to each other.

The woman in the red dress swam toward the *Jupiter*. The yacht capsizing made the deck accessible. Her father followed her, ready to lift her as best he could. Churchill watched a black object emerge behind the man. He aimed his rifle.

Passengers screamed as the Liopleurodon's jaws grabbed the man. Churchill fired but the round missed, causing the water to burst near the Liopleurodon's head. The woman turned to see her father's horrified face one last time as it was pulled under the surface. The Liopleurodon vanished.

"Blast it," Churchill said. The woman made it to the *Jupiter* and grabbed its shattered railing. None of the passengers moved to help her. All were determined to maintain their grip and not fall into the water given the steep angle of descent.

They heard the wailing of a man treading the Atlantic's surface. It blocked out every other sound. He was too tired and too cold to swim to the *Jupiter*. The current pushed him in the yacht's direction, but it was too gentle to get him there before he would drown or be eaten. He saw a piece of plaster that had broken off from the ship floating nearby. One of its edges was jagged. Sharp. An escape. The man used what energy he could muster to grab the plaster. He pulled it closer and felt relief, turning away from the passengers so they didn't have to watch. He closed his eyes, smiled, and raised the plaster with his right hand while exposing his left wrist.

The Liopleurodon lifted the man in the air. His screams and the passengers' gasps competed to be heard. His screams won. The man stabbed the Liopleurodon's gums with the plaster, attacking it the only way he could. It dug into the Liopleurodon's flesh but the reptile barely registered the pain. His teeth punctured the man's chest.

Churchill aimed for the Liopleurodon's lower jaw and fired.

Blood burst in every direction. This the Liopleurodon felt and he dropped the man back into the water. The Liopleurodon lowered his head so he could see the *Jupiter*. Churchill got his first good look at him. Red veins pulsated in his green eyes. Burn marks, collision marks, and bullet holes distorted his facial features—not that he was nice to look at before.

The Liopleurodon's roar sounded like a reptilian *hiss* mixed with a deep baritone. He was furious that the *Jupiter* violated his territory and was determined to destroy it and as many of these small mammals as possible, particularly because, like the family of metal objects from three days ago, it had struck him with a stinging long range attack.

A wave of fear moved through the guests.

Pop!

Another of Churchill's rounds struck the Liopleurodon's upper mouth, blowing away two teeth. The Liopleurodon's roar spiked. Then he dove beneath the surface to circle the *Jupiter* from below.

Many of the guests looked at Churchill, who kept his rifle raised for several moments before lowering it. He turned to the guests in the water. How many had drowned? A dozen? More? Churchill pointed to the living.

"Don't just sit there. Help them!" he ordered the guests on the deck. He raised his rifle. "I'll keep the beast at bay."

Some of the passengers, especially those closest to where the *Jupiter* was split near the water, did as the Home Secretary instructed. The woman in the red dress was the first helped.

Further out, the man whom the Liopleurodon had briefly grabbed could no longer feel his legs. His torso was riddled with tooth-punctured holes and he bled from the mouth. He sank beneath the surface, still alive, but too weak to resist the elements.

...

"Thank you, Lieutenant," Hawkins said to the officer who escorted Ross to his cabin.

"Sir," the lieutenant said as he exited. Ross had not brought his hat this time and placed his weight on his cane. Neither Hawkins nor Palmer, who stood to the captain's left, had a friendly expression.

"Good morning, gentlemen," Ross said. Hawkins stared at Ross, trying to peer into his soul.

"Please begin, Lieutenant," Hawkins said, his eyes still on Ross. Ross turned to Palmer as Palmer looked at his notes.

"I spoke with Dr. Ryan last night." Palmer waited for Ross to respond. He didn't. "As you can imagine, he denied all of the claims you made against him. And he made counterclaims."

"I see," Ross said. "Are you entertaining them?"

Palmer turned to Hawkins, who was silent. Ross, exhausted from the previous days, was taken aback. How gullible were they? Why did Hawkins have that look in his eyes?

Palmer continued. "He said that it's *you* who are trying to frame *him* to remove a professional rival and that you're trying to save your career after Luke Jones proved that his father was cor—"

Ross chuckled and shook his head. "That lying son of a bitch."

"Watch your language, Doctor," Hawkins said. Ross restrained himself from telling Hawkins to go to Hell. "Please continue, Lieutenant."

"No," Ross said. "No, I need to respond to that." Palmer looked at him. "I am *not* proud of what happened with the Joneses. It is an embarrassment and black mark on my record as a professional scientist. But it's an exaggeration to say that my career is over and it's *outrageous* to claim that I—"

"That's enough, Doctor," Hawkins said. He turned to Palmer. "Proceed."

Palmer glanced at his notes. "Dr. Ryan also argued that advancing Colonel Roosevelt's electoral chances aligns with your political vi—"

"Are you *serious*?" Ross said.

"Let Palmer finish," Hawkins ordered.

"I will not," Ross said. "These claims are absurd." His hand waved in exasperation. "They are made out of whole cloth meant to waste our—I don't even agree with Colonel Roosevelt politically. He's much more progressive than I am."

"The argument was that Roosevelt would enter a European war before colonial or communist uprisings would occur," Palmer said.

Ross' mouth dropped for a moment. "And so he's claiming

that I freed the Liopleurodon, sabot—honestly, gentlemen, you can't expect me to respect your intelligence if you don't dismiss this argument at this moment."

"That is quite enough, Doctor," Hawkins said.

"No, it isn't. These are attacks upon my reputation. And that piece of filth is protecting his own misdeeds by—"

"An emotional reaction isn't helping, Doctor," Palmer said. "These are just claims. I never said I believe them."

Ross nodded and calmed down. "You're right. I apologize."

"I think what makes the most sense is if you and Dr. Ryan are both removed from the *Delaware*. Investigations would commence," Palmer said. "You'll likely be detained until charges are brought or released if not."

"*Ridiculous*," Ross muttered. He knew this was a risk, but deep down he'd thought the Navy would see Ryan for what he was without needing to investigate Ross too. He turned to Hawkins. "Know that I will defend against these charges in court if I must. The nondisclosure agreement can be broken under legal necessity."

Hawkins' anger had grown exponentially since Palmer told him of Ryan's claim against Ross. Now, he was almost seething from the web of lies he had to navigate from these people who were meant to *help* him. Especially Ross. He was supposed to be the good one. Now, he might be the saboteur who killed his men. He might be the Kaiser's pawn.

"If you did this," Hawkins said, "I will slit your throat and build a jail on top of your corpse."

"Captain!" Palmer exclaimed.

Ross stepped toward Hawkins' desk, leaning forward. "I will make sure the *world* knows the degree of incompetence—"

"Accusing a man of murdering his fiancé," Hawkins said. "You *disgust* me. You're the one with a clear motivation. Who's actually been to Europe. To *Germany*."

"Go ask Roosevelt who—"

"I don't care what that *clown* thinks."

The cabin's door flew open and Jenkins burst in carrying a form, doing his best not to crush it. "Captain!"

"Commander Jenkins," Hawkins sighed, "you're making a habit of interru—"

"Captain, w—"

"Please come back la—"

"This is an emergency." Jenkins stood next to Ross. Hawkins made a fist to lower his temper. Too many things. All at once. Couldn't process them all.

"What is it?" Hawkins asked.

"We received an SOS," Jenkins said.

"Explain."

"It's from a British yacht. Se—"

"Wait." Hawkins turned to Palmer. "Lieutenant, escort Dr. Ross back to his room." He looked at Ross. "You're under lockdown."

Ross glared at Hawkins with resentment but then followed Palmer out of the cabin. Hawkins and Jenkins were alone.

"Is it the Liopleurodon?" Hawkins asked.

"Yes." Jenkins handed him the paper. "These are the coordinates."

Latitude: N 50° 44' 11.2385"
Longitude: W 32° 42' 59.5612"

Hawkins' eyes scrunched. "This is the middle of the Atlantic."

"That's right."

"What was a civilian—the British government must have approved of this."

"I agree."

"Why in the—"

"Sir," Jenkins said, catching Hawkins' attention. "Secretary Meyer wants us to intervene."

Hawkins' eyes widened. Blood drained from his face. He'd been traumatized by the disaster three days ago that cost the lives of six sailors under his command. Now a large civilian vessel was under attack. His worst fear, the worst contingency, made reality. Except this was even worse because the saboteur was still on his ship and neither Ross nor Ryan could be removed before the *Delaware* set sail. Plus, Luke was still in German hands. The Germans. They likely also received the SOS. How would they respond?

"Sir?" Jenkins asked.

Hawkins nodded. "Set the course. I'll come to the bridge shortly." He paused. "Have the *Delaware*'s guns and rescue boats ready. This ends today."

...

Branca did his best to sit still in his room aboard the *Thüringen*. He was on the brink of a nervous breakdown. His hands jittered. He needed to think straight and resisted his emotions' coup attempts. Focus. Use reason. He had a terrible hand to play. Michaelis had all the power. Maybe Branca's best option was to jump off of the *Thüringen*'s deck and escape. He could survive that, right?

What a ridiculous thought. What was the point of saving his career if he was dead? Of never seeing Edith or his grandkids again? Besides, Branca's career was a secondary concern. His main goal was keeping the Liopleurodon out of Michaelis' hands. That left Branca with one option. It was a million-in-one shot. When should he make his move? His timing had to be perfect.

The *Thüringen*'s movement startled him. What was happening? Did Michaelis get word of the Liopleurodon's location? Was the second attempt to capture it underway? Maybe Branca was too late. Maybe Michaelis had a plan in place and had already won. It was over. No. Branca had to take his shot. He *had* to try. He rallied the strength to leave his cabin and saw several officers and sailors moving into action to do their duty. Branca approached one who looked like an officer.

"What's going on?" Branca asked.

"The sea monster is attacking a British yacht."

Branca froze. What idiot chose to go sailing? "So—so we're going to rescue the passengers?"

"I guess so." The officer did not hide his annoyance with Branca's questions. This was a nightmare. Innocent people were going to die—no, were already dying. And there was *no doubt* that Michaelis would take advantage of the crisis to try and capture the Liopleurodon again. This was it. Now or never.

"Do you object to me leaving my room?" Branca asked.

"I don't care what you do," the officer said.

Branca nodded graciously, leaving the officer to go about his business. He moved in the direction that he saw the lieutenant take the American the previous day. He spent over half an hour peering into rooms before he found his man, who was sitting on his bed in a semi-fetal position. His arms wrapped around his right thigh as his left leg extended to the ground. His left wrist was still bandaged from when he stabbed it with a wooden spike broken off from the flotsam platform.

Branca took several breaths. He whispered the phrase, "I have a proposition for you" three times in English. He opened the door.

"I have a proposition for you." Branca spoke with a German accent.

The American turned his head and looked up at Branca, a glazed expression in his eyes. "What kind of small talk would Mona Lisa make with the ghost's wallpaper? What sort of jelly would she want?"

Branca wondered if his English was worse than he realized. He closed the door behind him.

"I need you to get outside of your head for a minute," Branca said, remembering that this young man was coherent yesterday. The American nodded. His face scrunched as though he were in pain. "What's your name?"

"Luke Jones."

"Nice to meet you, Luke." Luke nodded. "I am Dr. Branca."

Luke made eye contact, wearing desperation like a mask. "Can I get your permission to commit suicide?"

Branca froze. He was fairly certain he knew what Luke meant. He glanced at Luke's bandaged wrist.

"Why do you care what I think?" Branca asked.

"I would feel more comfortable with someone's permission," Luke said. "I'm ready to do it, but I'm concerned it might upset my mother."

"Of course it would upset her. She loves you."

"I guess."

"You have no reason to commit suicide, Luke."

Luke's arms gripped himself tighter. "You don't even know me."

"That's fair," Branca said. "What happened?"

Luke shuddered. "The woman I love is dead. What's worse is it's my fault. I wanted to go on the mission to destroy the Liopleurodon because I wanted to impress her. She only watched the attack because I was there. I—" He choked up. "I should have protected her and I—I failed."

Branca had to get Luke to think clearly. He had time to spare. For now.

"Have you ever heard of—should be the same name in English—have you ever heard of Marcus Aurelius?" Branca asked. Luke shook his head. "He was a Roman emperor. But he's most famous for a book of philosophy that he wrote to himself. Marcus mostly repeats the same couple of ideas over and over again. He says that the key to happiness is to separate what we can control and what we can't and to base our identities on what we *can* control. What happened to your woman was outside of your—"

"What you're talking about would never work for me," Luke said.

"Why's that?"

"Because my mind has a mind of its own. And it tortures me. It doesn't let me focus or think straight. It goes all over the place. It makes me react to things in ways that I regret. I know I'm going to regret it later but my other mind doesn't care. And I'm powerless to stop it. I'm just its puppet."

Branca shifted strategies. "Luke, the Liopleurodon is attacking a yacht full of people as we speak. That's why the ship started moving. Dozens of people will die if we don't do something."

"Good," Luke said curtly. "They'll be put out of their misery. Life's not worth it."

"You don't actually believe that."

"Yes, I do. Life is suffering. The bad outweighs the good for almost everyone that's ever lived."

"Then why do people cling to life?"

Luke hesitated. "They're cowards."

"Or maybe you're wrong," Branca said. Luke looked at his lap. "There's more. The German government plans to transform the Liopleurodon into a weapon. They think it will help them in a future war. It might even *convince* them to start a war. Imagine a conflict the size of the Napoleonic Wars in the Industrial age. I *really* can't stress—" He could tell that Luke wasn't listening. Luke had withdrawn back into his own mind. His eyes watered. "What is it?"

"I'll never be happy without her."

"You can't have preconditions on happiness," Branca said. "All problems in life are temporary."

"Kelsey's death is permanent."

"But her time on Earth was temporary no matter what. It was just a question of whether it would end sooner or later. And your emotions are temporary too."

"A person's existence *is* reality," Luke said. "*Their* reality. We can't tap into objective truth. We're within our perceptions. So the death of a loved one—or of ourselves—" Luke couldn't complete his thought. "If life is temporary anyway, why *shouldn't* I speed up my own demise? If nothing matters?"

"Because in the time you *do* have there's good you can—"

"If life doesn't matter that much, why do you care if some aristocrats are killed or if there's a global war? If our existence is just temporary?"

"I was talking about putting things into perspective," Branca said. "We should still strive to make the best of this world while we're in it."

"That's impossible," Luke whispered.

"I'm sorry about what happened to your woman, but you *really* must focus on the big picture here."

Luke's eyes narrowed. "What if this isn't about her?"

"What's it about?"

"I'm not capable of living a happy and productive life. There's something wrong with my brain. It sabotages me. I can feel it. Failure and misery are inevitable. I'll never rise in society —never get what *I want* from others—because I can never meet their expectations. I have to accept that. And it's *okay*. I'm not going to fight reality. But I shouldn't have to spend the rest of my life being miserable either. So suicide—it's an escape. There's no conditions that have to be met or *can* be met that will change that."

Branca turned from Luke and looked to his right. His efforts weren't working. They were counterproductive, if anything. Luke didn't care about appeals to morality. But Branca had one final card to play.

"You're telling yourself a story where a happy ending is impossible," Branca said. "You have to change the story. Maybe the story isn't that you and Kelsey live your lives together in bliss. Maybe the story is that you *avenge* her death. Maybe that's your purpose now."

Branca watched Luke's reaction. Luke processed Branca's

words.

"I know what you're doing," Luke said.

"What am I doing?"

"You're manipulating me."

"Perhaps. But does that mean what I'm saying is wrong?"

"No," Luke whispered. "Revenge against a wild animal is a strange concept."

"Why?"

"Because animals lack a capacity for reason or planning."

"I know plenty of humans who are like that."

Luke smiled. "I'm serious. The Liopleurodon doesn't know that it hurt me. It just acted. It saw a snack and it acted."

"Objectively, sure. But we live in our perceptions. Not in reality. So to you, the Liopleurodon murdered your true love, did it not?"

Luke pictured the moment after the Liopleurodon killed Kelsey, when its head vertically sat over the ocean's surface. The Liopleurodon's closed jaws looked like a smile surrounded by flames—a demon laughing at Luke. He closed his eyes, desperate to escape the image.

"We can't fight it," Luke said. "It's an unstoppable force of pure evil."

"No. It's mortal. Like you and me."

Luke blinked several times, his mind working through multiple questions at once. "What would be the purpose of my existence afterward? Assuming we win?"

Branca hesitated. "I'll help you decide."

"Do you promise?"

"I promise."

Luke's jaw clenched. He absorbed his new purpose. Branca studied his face, which telegraphed that he was thinking about how to fight the Liopleurodon.

"I have a proposition," Branca said.

...

"Captain's on the bridge!"

Jenkins and other officers turned to salute Hawkins.

"Not now!" Hawkins barked. His eyes were swollen. He opened and closed his fists multiple times to maintain his focus and to keep his nerves at bay. It didn't help that the bridge was overcrowded and fed a subtle claustrophobia. He turned to Jenkins. "Have we made visual contact with the *Jupiter*?"

"We have." Jenkins pointed to a series of windows with curved tops. Hawkins saw the *Jupiter* in the distance and identified two separate pieces on the ocean's surface. Smoke rose from an orange hue.

"My God," Hawkins muttered. "Are our guns ready?"

"They are," Jenkins said.

"Good. I want to blow that monster to pieces." Hawkins heard a faint melody. Where was it coming from? He took a series of short steps toward the wheel, squeezing his way through the crowd of officers until he could see the deck. The *Delaware*'s band played "Yankee Doodle Dandy" in their starch white uniforms. Hawkins took a step back.

"Isn't there a risk of hitting civilians?" Jenkins asked.

"Our presence will scare the Liopleurodon away," Hawkins said. "Then we'll hit it from a distance." Jenkins was uncomfortable relying on a plan that depended on the Liopleurodon's cooperation. Hawkins closed his eyes to feel a moment's peace. He was desperate to kill the Liopleurodon quickly. He could still salvage the operation but couldn't afford another mistake. No more mistakes.

"Captain!" an officer on the port side of the bridge cried. "Look!"

Hawkins, Jenkins, and some of the senior staff crowded near the officer's window. A large object emerged from the distance. It was east of the *Jupiter* and difficult to see through the yacht's smoke.

"It's the *Thüringen*," Hawkins declared. Pressure swelled in his chest. Palmer looked at Hawkins and Jenkins, anticipating their reactions.

"What should we do?" Jenkins asked.

"We keep going," Hawkins said. "We *don't* back down. I'm not going to let Michaelis chase us away."

"What about the Liopleurodon?"

"What about it?"

Jenkins leaned closer to Hawkins so no one could hear him. "Sir, we can't fire our guns at it. It risks causing a brawl with Michaelis."

"How else do you recommend attacking it?" Hawkins said,

louder.

"That's what *I'm* asking."

Hawkins closed his eyes again. He felt dizzy. He thought the Germans might respond to the *Jupiter* attack but didn't think they'd arrive so quickly. Michaelis must have had the *Thüringen* ready to sail. Hawkins hadn't prepared for this contingency. It felt as though his mind wasn't working. Process. Faster. *Think*. Jenkins was right. Firing the *Delaware*'s guns in the *Thüringen*'s direction would trigger a diplomatic incident at best, a skirmish at worst. Hawkins couldn't take the risk.

"How about the rescue boats?" Hawkins asked.

"Sir?"

"Are they ready?"

"You want to deploy them?" Jenkins asked. "They'll be vulnerable if the Liopleurodon is still active."

The pressure in Hawkins' chest increased. Sweaty. Eh, why —too many people. Can't. Think. Of course Jenkins was right. Hawkins should have thought of that first.

"We could arm the rescue boats with harpoons. Or with Gatling guns. In case the Liopleurodon attacks them," Hawkins said.

Jenkins' face scrunched. "Perhaps we should—"

"Captain!" a lieutenant commander shouted as he entered the bridge. "Captain!"

"*What?*" Hawkins said. "What is it, Lieutenant?"

"It's Sean Ryan!"

"What about him?"

"He escaped."

Hawkins and Jenkins froze and exchanged a glance. "What do you mean?" Hawkins asked.

"He escaped the brig," the lieutenant answered.

"Wasn't he being watched?"

"Y-yes, sir."

"And?"

"Sir." The lieutenant paused. "The sailors watching him are dead." Hawkins was silent. "Sir?" Hawkins remained silent. The lieutenant looked at Jenkins.

"He killed them?" Jenkins asked.

"Yes. He stabbed them to death."

"He had a knife?"

"No. He broke a window in the brig and killed them with a glass blade."

Jenkins turned to Hawkins, who didn't respond. He looked back at the subordinate. "Wasn't he chained down?"

"Yes, but—I wasn't there to see it, but he must have manipulated the guards."

"And then murdered them," Jenkins whispered. The other officers all stared at him. "And now he's loose on the ship."

Palmer fought to avoid panicking, terrified that Ryan might target him.

An argument broke out among the officers. "How did he get to the poisoned rounds and harpoons?" one asked. "Why was he even *allowed* in the room with the engineers?"

"We were looking for Germans," another said. "Who ever

heard of an evil paleontologist?"

"What is it about that profession that attracts such eccentric personalities?"

"Is he working for the Germans?"

"Pro—"

Jenkins heard a scream behind him. He turned to see Hawkins. Hawkins leaned forward and held himself in place with his hands on his knees. His jaw vibrated.

"Cap—"

Hawkins broke into manic laughter. It started out soft but became louder within seconds. His body shook and his face became red. The other officers were horrified.

"We-we'll figure it out," Jenkins said.

Hawkins took a deep breath and Jenkins wondered if he had stabilized. He didn't. Hawkins laughed even louder and his knees buckled. Other officers caught him before he hit the ground. Another burst of laughter.

The officers turned to Jenkins for leadership. Jenkins took a moment to think. He inhaled.

"The *Delaware* is under lockdown until Ryan is found. Deploy the rescue boats." Maybe Hawkins was right. This was their only option. "Give each one a rifle. In case the Liopleurodon attacks. We're going after the civilians."

The officers went into action executing Jenkins' orders. The Navy Band played "The Star-Spangled Banner" on the *Delaware*'s deck. The music blended with Hawkins' laughter.

...

"Careful with that!" Lieutenant Commander Joachim ordered his crew as they moved the *Nautilus* into its launch tube in the *Thüringen*'s stern. Eight men gripped four separate cables attached to the *Nautilus*' snout. They heaved and grunted as they aligned it with the slanted track that led to an opening through which they could see the *Thüringen*'s wake. The front of the *Nautilus* finally laid its weight against the gate levers that held it in place; the levers' release would remove the only obstacle to the prototype one-man submarine from entering the Atlantic. "You'll be paying for its repairs for the rest of your life if you so much as scratch my baby. No matter how many checks the Kaiser signs for you."

The other sailors laughed and rested. Joachim saw one subordinate slap another on the back for a job well done. Joachim's chest filled with dread as he looked at the *Nautilus*. He had not sat in the pilot chair since his encounter with the Liopleurodon five days before. It had taken two nights for him to sleep again after that episode. The Liopleurodon's features, especially its evil smile, were seared into his consciousness. Joachim was desperate not to be in the water with the Liopleurodon again but anticipated that Michaelis would demand it. That left Joachim with choosing which he feared more—the Liopleurodon's jaws or Michaelis' wrath. The choice wasn't easy.

The sound of a door opening behind Joachim interrupted his

concentration, as did the gasps of his crew. Was Michaelis there? He turned around and his body clenched at the image before him. A disheveled young man—sweaty, strangely long hair, a cut on his lip and a bandage on his wrist—held Dr. Branca within his grip. The young man's left arm wrapped around Branca's torso; his right hand held a knife to Branca's throat. Small droplets of blood already dripped onto Branca's shirt collar.

Joachim looked into the man's eyes. They revealed an unthinking barbarism, an anger and hatred that Joachim had never seen in a civilized person. Joachim glanced at Branca, whose jaw was tight and who looked desperate to avoid further harm. Sweat fell from his mustache. His head faced far to the right to protect his throat from the man's blade.

"What do you want?" Joachim asked.

"Is that a submarine?" the young man shouted in English. Joachim didn't know English. He turned to his subordinates for a translation.

"H-he's asking if that's a submarine," Branca translated.

Joachim was confused. He'd heard that the *Thüringen* had picked up an American when it investigated where the Liopleurodon defeated the *Delaware*'s forces. This was him, presumably. But how did he get a knife? And how did he know about the *Nautilus*?

"The Liopleurodon killed the woman I love," the American said. "I won't rest until it's dead." Branca continued translating.

"I can't allow you to take the *Nautilus*," Joachim said. He raised his hands, hoping the American would calm down.

"Why?" the American asked.

"You're an American civilian and this is a valuable piece of German military equipment," Joachim said. "Surrendering it to you would be treasonous."

The American, looking deranged, said, "You're going to give it to me or this man's blood is going to be all over the ground."

Joachim looked first at Branca's desperation and then at the American's barbarism. Was it an act? That was the only explanation for how the American knew about the *Nautilus*. Unless he was a spy, but that was even more far-fetched. It *had* to be an act, though the scrapes on Branca's throat were real. Whether or not it was an act was besides the point—the American wanted to take the *Nautilus* to kill the Liopleurodon. He had almost no chance of succeeding. Not even Joachim, who could pilot the *Nautilus* better than anyone, could expect to survive a fight to the death with a Liopleurodon on methamphetamine. But that wasn't the point either. Whether the American or submarine came back in one piece, or however many more ships the Liopleurodon preyed upon, were not Joachim's concerns, especially since Joachim could blame the American for the *Nautilus'* disappearance. The American and Branca gave him a way out, and he seized it.

"Okay, okay," Joachim said. "You win."

The American's face calmed. "Really?"

"Yes," Joachim said. "I can't allow such an esteemed scientist to be killed."

A subordinate leaned toward Joachim. "Should we ask the

vice admiral first?"

"No," Joachim said. "There's no time." He gestured to the *Nautilus*, giving it to the American on a platter. The American released his grip on Branca, who dropped to his knees and coughed. Two German sailors lunged to his sides to help him.

Joachim and the American approached the *Nautilus*' cockpit, which was open. Joachim turned around, his hands behind his back. "Get Branca over here." The sailors helped Branca to his feet and walked him to the *Nautilus*. "Ask the American whether he's ever piloted a submarine before. I want to know whether I should cover the basics."

Branca translated. The American looked at Joachim.

"No," the American said. "And I should warn you, I'm bad with details."

...

Ross laid on the bed in his room aboard the *Delaware*. His face was red as he thought about Hawkins. All of that effort—recruiting Roosevelt, building the argument, gambling his future. Ross had really believed that Hawkins would see the light, that Ryan would be thrown in jail, and that the Americans could target the Liopleurodon again without sabotage. Saying he was willing to be investigated was a rhetorical device and a gamble. Now it was real and it likely meant the end of Ross' career, even though he was confident that he would be released without charge. Hawkins was a fool. How could he consider Ryan's story to be true for even a second? How did such a man achieve his rank? And now the *Delaware* was at sea after Ross heard Jenkins say a British yacht had sent an SOS. Another job for Hawkins to bungle.

Knock knock.

"Come in," Ross muttered. He took a deep breath to increase his energy. "Come in!"

"It's locked," a voice said. Ross grumbled as he stood up and opened the door. Roosevelt was at the entrance, wearing his combat uniform. "Care to stage a mutiny?"

"What do you mean?" Ross asked. "What's happening?"

"We're in a standoff with a German dreadnought," Roosevelt said. Ross took a moment to process that information. Events were spinning out of control. "My understanding is that Hawkins won't fire on the Liopleurodon now. He's sending rescue boats to save the civilians."

"They'll be massacred."

"Exactly. General Wood and I have recruited a group of sailors and officers," Roosevelt said. "We've commandeered a rescue boat of our own. We're going after it."

Ross chuckled. "I take it Hawkins doesn't know?"

"Of course not," Roosevelt said. "Not since the campaign of Crassus against the Parthians has there been so criminally incompetent a commander as Hawkins."

Ross nodded. He assumed Roosevelt was there to recruit him. This *would* trigger legal ramifications. "Do you want me to go with you? I'm under lockdown and this isn't my cup of tea."

"How do you feel about being bait?" Roosevelt asked.

"For the Liopleurodon?"

"Not exactly. Dr. Ryan escaped the brig."

Ross panicked for a moment. Then he smiled and offered Roosevelt his hand. Roosevelt took it.

"I want to see you when this is over," Ross said. "Be careful."

Roosevelt had the toothy grin made famous in campaign posters. "Good luck, Benjamin."

"Thank you, Colonel. You as well."

…

Vice Admiral Michaelis stood on the *Thüringen*'s deck. He held his hands behind his back. Just to his rear and slightly to the right was Gunther, who was at the front of his staff, all awaiting his imminent victory. Michaelis' face bore a small smile, the only evidence of the jubilation that he restrained beneath the surface. He'd won. This was the best day of his career. The day that he would be associated with in German history books. 8 March 1911. The day Germany captured the Liopleurodon and humiliated its two greatest enemies. How many British aristocrats were dead because the British Defense Office had approved of the *Jupiter*'s voyage? And the Americans—look at the *Delaware*, powerless to act because of the *Thüringen*'s presence. Michaelis was going to take the Liopleurodon out from under them. Would Prime Minister Asquith face a vote of no confidence? Would President Taft be impeached? That might be Michaelis' thoughts getting carried away, something he usually stopped himself from doing, but who could blame him? He was on the brink of acquiring the perfect weapon to unleash upon an enemy port in a future war, a factor that could be decisive to German victory. Most importantly, Michaelis would be guaranteed to be Tirpitz's successor once the old man finally retired.

God, what a day. Was it true that the Liopleurodon was red, white, and black—the same colors as the German flag? Michaelis was eager to confirm whether this was the case.

Enough celebration. He needed to strike. Michaelis turned to Gunther. "Rear Admiral."

"Yes, sir?"

"It's time to deploy the *Nautilus*," Michaelis said. Gunther looked concerned. Michaelis was surprised he had to spell it out. "We're going to force the Liopleurodon to the surface. Have the ketamine and harpoons ready. I do not want the Kaiser's newest weapon to be damaged. Then deploy rescue boats to save some civilians. We can rub extra salt into Washington and London's wounds."

Gunther still didn't respond. He'd been praying that the *Nautilus* wasn't part of Michaelis' plan. He glanced at the other officers.

"What is it?" Michaelis asked.

Gunther remained quiet but then shouted at the officers behind him. "Send Joachim up!"

Michaelis' eyebrow arched. Why was Joachim on the deck? The *Nautilus'* deployment would be delayed. Why did Michaelis have to do his subordinates' thinking for them? Joachim emerged from the group, joining Michaelis and Gunther.

"What is the problem, Lieutenant?" Michaelis asked with as friendly a tone as he could muster.

"Sir…"

"What is the matter?" Michaelis smiled. "You can tell me anything."

Joachim took a deep breath. "Sir, the American stole the *Nautilus*." Joachim and Gunther watched Michaelis' face. His expression held for several moments and then collapsed all at once.

"Is this a joke?"

"No, sir."

"*How* did this happen?" Michaelis screamed.

"Sir, please don't yell."

"I'll *more* than yell! I'll have whoever's responsible hanged!"

"No one is responsible, sir," Joachim said. "The American took Br—" he forgot Branca's name due to stress, "He took the dinosaur scientist hostage."

Michaelis froze. "*What?*"

"He barged in with a knife to the man's throat and said he'd kill him if we didn't let him take it," Joachim said.

"And so you *gave* it to him?"

"We couldn't let him—"

"Couldn't *let* him?" Michaelis asked. "Do you think I *care* if he guts that traitor?" Joachim was shocked hearing his commander say something so heartless. "Why would the American want the *Nautilus*?"

"Because the Liopleurodon killed his—I guess she's his wife, sir," Joachim said. "He wants revenge."

Michaelis' eyes darted in every direction. Right. Left. Right diagonal. He thought the words, "Where's Branca?" but lacked the strength to say them as he realized the truth. Branca had made a master chess move. The *Nautilus* was a priceless piece of machinery, an innovative weapon that, like the Liopleurodon, would have given Germany an advantage in a future war. *And* it was a prototype. *And* it was gone. Michaelis looked at the seawater between the *Thüringen* and the *Jupiter*. Somewhere under the surface was the *Nautilus*. Piloted by that deranged American child. It didn't matter whether he or the Liopleurodon emerged the winner.

Michaelis would exact his revenge on Branca. No. He wouldn't. That was the point. Michaelis' revenge required the authority to deliver it. And Michaelis would soon have *none*. His career was over. His face became pale as he felt his world crashing around him. He considered jumping off of the *Thüringen*'s deck.

No. That wasn't how a *man* faced defeat. He would return to Germany and endure whatever punishment the Kaiser had in store.

...

Roosevelt put his weight on his left knee. His wooden right leg extended as far as the rescue boat stolen from the *Delaware* allowed. He glanced at his reflection in the sapphire sea and saw the outline of his blue, polka dot handkerchief that remained tied around his felt hat. The rippling wind chilled his skin and vibrated the German-made sword that was clipped to his belt. He'd used it in the Battle of Las Guasimas in Cuba. The sword's handle was wrapped in a traditional Navy shark-skin hilt. A harpoon shoulder gun was within reach under his wooden leg. The gun had a steel barrel and an iron breech block. It was loaded and cocked; two spare lances were nearby. A .38 Colt Model 1895 pistol, salvaged from the *USS Maine*, sat in a holster on his belt.

He was determined that that day, March 8, 1911, would replace July 1, 1898, the day he charged Kettle Hill, as the great day of his life. He would return to America either carrying his shield or laying on top of it. Any man who felt the power of joy in battle knew what it was like when the wolf rose in the heart, for no triumph of peace was quite so great as the supreme triumphs of war, for peace was not the end, righteousness was the end, and when the Savior saw the money-changers in the Temple he broke the peace by driving them out. At that moment peace could have been obtained by keeping quiet in the presence of wrong. But instead of preserving the peace at the expense of righteousness, the Savior armed himself with a scourge of chores and drove the money-changers from the Temple.

Roosevelt's enemy was the Liopleurodon, the largest and most powerful carnivore of all time. Conquering it was his ultimate challenge. He did not know if he was up to the task but knew their survival was mutually exclusive. Which was the hunter and which was the hunted would soon be revealed.

Roosevelt took his eyes off the water to briefly look behind him, seeing General Wood and the three sailors they had recruited who rowed the boat oars. Roosevelt was grateful to these men. They placed themselves in greater danger than any since Cold Harbor in '64 to save innocent lives and slay the monster. He saw that Wood was red in the face; Roosevelt's junior by less than two years and still following him into action. Perhaps Roosevelt was ready to forgive the times Wood cut his forehead and wrist while they fought with swords in the White House.

The rescue boat was now half a kilometer from the southern half of the *Jupiter*. Most of the wreckage was underwater. The fire was past its peak. The wedding guests forming a single mass became more distinct as Roosevelt got closer. Several guests huddled together, surrounded by blankets, desperate to warm themselves after falling in the ocean. What fool wanted a wedding on the Atlantic in March anyway? Many corpses floated around the debris.

At the southernmost endpoint of the wreckage was a stocky man in a Gieves and Hawkes Classic Pinstripe Jacket holding a Lee–Enfield rifle. The man watched the ocean, clearly in charge of defending the wedding guests from the Liopleurodon. Roosevelt had an epiphany. He recognized the man. It was Winston Churchill, whom Roosevelt had never considered an attractive man; a vulgar fellow who was no gentleman for he did not stand when a lady entered the room. Still, Churchill's memoir of journeying in Africa formed a blueprint for Roosevelt's hunting adventure the prior summer.

Churchill's jaw nearly dropped when he saw the former President's rescue boat approach from the south. He lowered his rifle.

"Get out of here!" Churchill shouted. "The mons-ster is circling below!"

Roosevelt ignored Churchill. "You people will drown if we flee!"

Churchill was amazed at the arrogance of this man and of the Americans. This was the best they could do? One rescue boat with a former President? No, clearly Roosevelt was acting alone and putting himself, his crew, and the wedding guests in danger. The Americans were likely paralyzed due to the *Thüringen*'s presence. They'd lost the guts to do what was necessary, typical of a rising great power. The New World indeed.

Churchill tried again. "Go back! You're not doing us any good if—"

Sound spiked on both sides of Churchill, but he heard the crowd gasping to his right first. The *splashing* sound of the Liopleurodon's jaws piercing the ocean's surface came a moment later, though the whole event occurred within milliseconds.

Churchill was right to say that the Liopleurodon was circling the *Jupiter*, but it had kept a special eye on him since it was he and he alone who struck it with the long range weapon that the Liopleurodon despised. Churchill's distraction and lowering of his rifle gave the Liopleurodon the perfect opportunity. The pliosaur seized it. Killing Churchill was a prerequisite to destroying what was left of the *Jupiter* and its passengers. Otherwise he would wait for the metal objects to sink and for the mammals to drown. Churchill saw the largest carnivorous jaws in history lunging toward him as the Liopleurodon's fangs formed a cage of railroad spikes around him.

Churchill fired point-blank into the Liopleurodon's jaws but failed to halt the reptile. His mind couldn't process what happened but registered pressure on both of his sides and felt knives stab his body. His perception of reality rose through the air.

The wedding guests gasped as the marine reptile clutched their savior in the narrow part of his jaws, expecting it to drop the Home Secretary into the back of its throat.

Roosevelt smiled. The Liopleurodon gave him an opening as his crocodilian head lifted into the air and exposed his throat. Roosevelt raised his harpoon gun and fired, eyeballing the trajectory. The harpoon struck the Liopleurodon's throat but missed the windpipe. The Liopleurodon *roared* in pain, opening his jaws and dropping Churchill before he could bite down.

"Winston!" Clementine cried as her husband landed in the water. The Liopleurodon submerged. Chamberlain leapt into the

Atlantic. Another man followed. They grabbed Churchill and pulled him onto the *Jupiter*'s wreckage. A crowd surrounded the Home Secretary, though a space was made for Clementine. "How is he?"

Chamberlain searched for a pulse but couldn't find it. He turned to the crowd. "Is anyone here a doctor?" he asked, revealing his lack of knowledge of his own wedding guests. A doctor was found and he made his way through the group. The doctor confirmed that Churchill was breathing, though he was unconscious and had suffered multiple puncture wounds.

Roosevelt watched as the five-meter triangular head moved along the ocean's surface. It first swam toward the *Thüringen* and then turned to attack Roosevelt's boat.

"Keep a distance from the yacht!" Roosevelt shouted to the men behind him. He made a split-second calculation of weaponry and decided the harpoon gun was his best chance since it combined distance and power. The drawback was that it had to be reloaded. Roosevelt moved as fast as possible, loading another lance and cocking the weapon.

The Liopleurodon flapped his flippers, closing the distance to Roosevelt's boat. Roosevelt aimed and fired. The harpoon overshot the Liopleurodon, which struck the boat. However, dodging the harpoon sacrificed the Liopleurodon's speed and decreased his attack's power. Roosevelt and his crew wouldn't have known this as they spun along the ocean's surface, feeling queasy as they slowed.

Roosevelt grit his teeth and changed tactics. He drew his

sword.

"Come on! Let's settle this! You and me!"

The pliosaur approached once more, again attacking on the Atlantic's surface. Roosevelt marveled at the Liopleurodon, envious of his power as his three-meter jaws opened. Roosevelt was cocked, screaming and lunging with his sword, stabbing the top of the Liopleurodon's mouth. Blood burst from where the sword struck.

The Liopleurodon shrieked and Roosevelt surged with joy. The adversaries moved in opposite directions as if on cue, the Liopleurodon raising his head to escape and Roosevelt pulling back to strike again.

"What fun!" Roosevelt shouted as he swung for the Liopleurodon's throat, already bleeding from the harpoon wound. Roosevelt missed and the Liopleurodon turned to submerge.

Roosevelt took a second to catch his breath, careful not to lose his balance with his pegleg. He knew the Liopleurodon was done playing with him. That was fine. Roosevelt's brain raced as he calculated ways to score a mortal blow. He needed to access a weak point so he could stab the reptile to death. Roosevelt couldn't let the Liopleurodon dictate the terms. No amount of stabbing the Liopleurodon's mouth would kill it. He had to access someplace more vulnerable. If the Liopleurodon did as he predicted, such an opportunity was imminent.

He turned to his men. "Brace yourselves!"

Roosevelt faced forward, not wanting to see the terrified look on the faces of the sailors who risked their lives so he might obtain glory. He bent his left knee, hoping he had the power to leap.

The boat remained remarkably still as it rose in the air. The sky became several meters closer. Roosevelt jumped but his pegleg was caught on the boat's edge, breaking his momentum. He tripped downward, plunging into the ocean along with his men and the now two pieces of his boat.

Roosevelt was stunned, furious at himself for his miscalculation, taking several seconds to open his eyes. He couldn't see the Liopleurodon, partly because it had left his view and partly because his pince-nez glasses were nowhere to be found. Roosevelt saw the rough outline of his sword below him. He returned to the surface, took two deep breaths of air, and dove.

He prayed both that the Liopleurodon would spare him for a moment and that he would experience the heroic death he craved as he swam several meters to retrieve his sword. Roosevelt grabbed it with his left hand, flipped over, and broke for the surface.

Roosevelt opened his mouth prematurely, swallowing a mouthful of seawater. He coughed and shook his face from side to side. Once he was no longer disoriented, he used his right eye to look around, first at the *Jupiter*'s wreckage, and then at Wood and the sailors who all treaded water and clung to the back half of the rescue boat. Roosevelt swam to the front half. He was alone. He prayed that the Liopleurodon would come for him and not for his men. He gripped his sword and was tempted to retrieve his pistol but knew that water had destroyed it. Besides, guns had proven ineffective in combating the sea monster.

He briefly looked at the *Thüringen*, which kept its distance. As did any German rescue efforts. What were *they* waiting for? Surely, they wouldn't want Roosevelt to kill the Liopleurodon. Perhaps they hoped the Liopleurodon would kill him first, though saving a former American President and taking him prisoner would be the propaganda scoop of the century.

Roosevelt had to get such concerns out of his mind. His life, the lives of his men, and the lives of the *Jupiter*'s guests all depended on his ability to make a decisive blow. He had *one* chance to succeed. He looked at the half of a boat he held. It was upside down and he lacked the strength or leverage to flip it over. He climbed onto it while clutching his sword. The boat sank slightly but supported his weight. Roosevelt looked in every direction with his good eye, desperate to identify the Liopleurodon's attack before it came.

Roosevelt coughed. Water irritated his eyes and throat and dripped from his mustache. His skin was pale from the cold. He shivered, but that was from both the cold and from fear.

He saw a dark mass move below him. As before, the Liopleurodon knew which target was the greatest threat and wanted to eliminate that threat first. Roosevelt tracked him as best he could, but he eventually lost sight of the marine reptile. He coiled his left leg against the boat and held his sword in his right hand. The mass reappeared. It moved toward him. This was it. He leapt as high as possible.

The Liopleurodon pulverized the flotsam but Roosevelt was in the air, coming down on top of the monster. Roosevelt screamed a scream that could be heard for kilometers as he landed on the center of the Liopleurodon's head, stabbing his sword perpendicularly into the Liopleurodon's left nostril. Blood sprung in every direction, landing on Roosevelt's face and hands.

The Liopleurodon roared and raised his head. Roosevelt held onto his sword and the top of the Liopleurodon's head for dear life, knowing it sought to shake him off and that this was a contest of strength he was *doomed* to lose. He acted on instinct, retracting his weapon by pulling the blade from the pliosaur's nostril. Ideally, he could strike at the Liopleurodon's throat but that was not an option so he settled for the next best thing. He leapt forward with his three good limbs as the Liopleurodon turned to the left.

Roosevelt stabbed the Liopleurodon's right eye.

The Liopleurodon spasmed, throwing his head upward and shrieking in pain. Roosevelt lost his grip on his sword, which remained in the reptile's eye, and fell. The Liopleurodon's triangular jaws became smaller and smaller until they vanished once Roosevelt landed in the water.

He sank for several moments, absorbing the chaos of the past minutes. Roosevelt's need to breathe startled him into action. He swam to the surface and away from the Liopleurodon. The Liopleurodon's cry—a shrill, reptilian wail—was deafening. Roosevelt looked at the beast as he put distance between them.

The Lipleurodon's left eye, the good one, tracked him along the sea's surface, but the pain of his right eye distracted him. Finally, his instincts took over and the Liopleurodon submerged.

Roosevelt treaded water. He looked at his men, who still held onto the back half of the rescue boat. He looked at the *Jupiter*'s wreckage, which was close to being entirely under the surface. Roosevelt was out of options. He searched for the harpoon gun but couldn't find it. He retrieved his pistol from his holster, but as he predicted, it was waterlogged and useless.

He was out of weapons and lacked any ability to strike his enemy again. He had failed. He would die, as would the men he dragged into harm's way, the *Jupiter*'s castaways, and anyone involved in additional American or German efforts to kill or capture the Liopleurodon. A series of images flashed in his mind: His father saying, "You must make your body." Edith saving him from the deepest valley. His bunnies scurrying around the White House for the first time.

Roosevelt closed his eyes, accepting his fate. His would be a heroic death, the valiant sacrifice he always wanted, a martyr to be celebrated by future generations. He was at the Liopleurodon's mercy, awaiting a final attack that would end his time on Earth.

The attack did not come.

...

A few minutes earlier, noise burst through the radio speaker on the *Nautilus'* dashboard. Luke assumed it was German but it sounded like gobbledygook. He saw a switch under the speaker and flipped it down with his right index finger. He suspected the Germans were demanding that he return their submarine.

"Boo hoo, Huns," he whispered to himself. "Don't take me hostage next time."

Luke's body temperature climbed and dropped in cycles. He felt the sweat build up on his forehead and where his hair touched his cheeks. He fought to slow his breathing so he didn't hyperventilate, and then to breathe deeper so he wouldn't pass out.

Clear your head. Clear your head.

His subconscious ignored him; every emotion somersaulted within it, wilder than ever and beyond his control.

He wished it was easier to see out of the *Nautilus*; he could see only a few meters forward and above through a periscope and was blind to anything below or to the sides. He thought he was a few hundred meters above the ocean floor and wasn't at risk of crashing. Or so he hoped.

Joachim's lessons ran through his mind as he glanced at the joystick. Pull back to go up, push forward to go down, and starboard or port to move in either direction. Joachim had said that the *Nautilus* was slow to turn, which Luke's experiment after leaving the *Thüringen* had confirmed. Just right of the joystick was a red button. It fired the torpedoes. The *Nautilus* had three on each flank in two torpedo tubes. Joachim said that a torpedo blast had a five-meter radius. Luke hoped he was a good enough shot.

Luke glanced at the ocean's surface every few moments. It was a couple hundred meters above him and was an open space every time he looked, besides the occasional dot of flotsam or oil picked up by the current. That finally changed.

The multitude of black marks appeared in the upper right corner of the *Nautilus*' periscope. Luke closed his left eye as his right was glued to the lens that sat at forehead level. He elevated himself in his seat, causing the seatbelt that covered his shoulders and torso in an X to squeeze his sides. He pulled the joystick back and to starboard to correct his trajectory. Of course he'd been sailing at the wrong angle.

The *Nautilus* ascended until Luke got a clearer image. He counted four ship halves on the surface, each sinking at a different rate. The two larger pieces likely belonged to the yacht that Branca mentioned. Luke was unsure of the smaller pieces. Maybe they were a failed American rescue mission, though Hawkins only sending one boat was strange. Luke also saw that most of the surface was coated in the yacht's oil. The Liopleurodon came into view; he thrashed his head back and forth near the smaller boat pieces, all of which became larger within the periscope's image as Luke approached from the southeast.

Luke paused the *Nautilus*' ascent. He wanted to be close enough to strike the Liopleurodon but not so close that the Liopleurodon sensed he was coming, though the pliosaur appeared distracted. Probably chewing on some poor soul. Luke pulled back on the joystick ever so gently until the Liopleurodon sat within the periscope's crosshairs.

This was it. An ambush.

Luke pressed the red button. A torpedo fired from the *Nautilus*' starboard torpedo tube. Luke had his widest smile since Harris arranged the dinner at Delmonico's as he watched the weapon rise from the depths. He aligned it perfectly. He did his task correctly. For once.

The torpedo disappeared from sight before detonating. The blast consumed the entirety of Luke's view within the periscope. He felt content and expected to see the Liopleurodon's carcass sink to the seabed. Just wait until Hawkins and Roosevelt and Dr. Ross and all the others saw the German submarine that Luke had stolen. They'd give him the Medal of Honor. He was eligible for that, right?

The blast dissipated and the surface became visible. Luke's jubilation transformed into terror as he saw the Liopleurodon turning to face him, descending by flapping his flippers. He'd fired the torpedo from too great a distance.

Luke whispered an expletive.

The reptile dove and his image became clearer within the periscope. Luke noticed Roosevelt's sword sticking out of the pliosaur's right eye. What was going on at the surface? Had pirates joined the fight? Luke saw the Liopleurodon's left nostril was bleeding. That was good. The Liopleurodon depended on his directional sense of smell to navigate and his radar unit was compromised, though his right nostril worked and could track the *Nautilus* with greater ease than Luke could track him. It was clear the Liopleurodon had recently suffered various injuries. His face and torso were riddled with wounds from blades, gunshots, collisions, and scorch marks. The Liopleurodon bull-rushing the *Nautilus* juxtaposed his demonic smile.

The pliosaur remembered the submarine from their first encounter five days earlier. The *Nautilus* had challenged the Liopleurodon for the stinky chum bag, violating the Liopleurodon's territorial claim. The Liopleurodon had ceded the eastern Atlantic to avoid a showdown with this strange metal creature, but the challenger had tracked him down in the mid-Atlantic and burned the Liopleurodon's tail. It wanted a fight and the Liopleurodon, stimulated on methamphetamine, sought to destroy the *Nautilus*, his greatest rival for control of the North Atlantic.

Luke shouted the same expletive over and over as he turned the joystick to port, making a 180 degree turn and fleeing. He prayed this product of German engineering could outpace the ancient marine reptile. He had hoped to kill the Liopleurodon with its back turned, knowing he had virtually no chance of winning a battle. Now, he needed to put distance between himself and his enemy to form Plan B.

Luke's prayers went unanswered. The Liopleurodon easily caught up to the *Nautilus* and struck its stern, biting above the *Nautilus*' battery-powered engines. Luke gasped as the *Nautilus* shook, vibrating in his seat, though his seatbelt protected his head from colliding with the cockpit wall. He visualized the

Liopleurodon ripping his submarine apart. Instead the Liopleurodon released his adversary. The *Nautilus*' armor was far too strong for the Liopleurodon to penetrate or grip from that angle, and he shattered several teeth by trying. The Liopleurodon ascended. Luke lost contact with it.

His inclination was to put space between himself and the predator and to then turn back and fire again. A second option popped into his mind. The small boat pieces on the surface implied the Americans were present. Or the British—an ally—right? It couldn't be the Germans; they'd never place themselves in harm's way to save civilians. The French? Nah. When were they ever useful? It was *probably* the Americans and *possibly* the British. Luke considered retreating aboard the *Delaware* and letting someone else avenge Kelsey's death. Maybe Ryan would do it? Luke could show him how to pilot the *Nautilus*. Or a sailor? No. Luke *had* to fulfill the cause of which Branca spoke.

A third option occurred to Luke. The battle began with the Liopleurodon positioned above the *Nautilus*, leading it to bite the submarine from an awkward angle. But the Liopleurodon had been the main focus of Luke's studies his entire life. He knew more about it than anyone on Earth and he knew that it shared its signature hunting strategy with the great white shark.

Luke's eyes widened and he slammed the joystick to port, gambling it wouldn't break. It didn't, and the *Nautilus* banked left, narrowly dodging the Liopleurodon's attack from below. Luke saw the 150-ton monster ascend past his submarine in a black and red blur.

The Liopleurodon burst through the ocean's surface, his three-meter jaws biting a mouthful of air before slamming into the water like a breaching whale. The combatants were now between the *Delaware* and the *Jupiter*. Luke took a deep breath, thankful his instincts had worked for once. The Liopleurodon would have broken the *Nautilus* in half if Luke had not evaded the attack. Luke tracked the Liopleurodon's white underbelly as the reptile submerged. It was Luke's turn.

He pushed the joystick so the *Nautilus* descended at a 45 degree angle, increasing the distance between the belligerents. He knew the Liopleurodon was following him and waited until he thought it was safe to turn the submarine around. He moved the joystick to starboard. It took several long moments until the Liopleurodon came into his periscope's view. The predator was attacking but Luke had a brief window of opportunity and he used it, pressing the red button twice.

A torpedo fired from each torpedo tube, first from the port side, then the starboard.

The Liopleurodon's right nostril detected the torpedoes fire. He did not recognize these objects but his reptilian mind was wary of any metallic long range attack and remembered how the *Nautilus* scorched his tail. He used the seal-like agility afforded by his flippers to dodge the port-side torpedo. It detonated behind the reptile, leaving the predator unscathed. This placed him directly into the path of the starboard-side torpedo, but he spun in the other direction, masterfully evading the second detonation without pausing his descent.

Luke had no time to be awestruck by his adversary's agility. The Liopleurodon slammed into the *Nautilus* and dragged the submarine deeper.

...

Dr. Ross stood at the edge of the *Delaware*'s deck on the port side, a few meters in front of a staircase and a series of doors that led to the ship's interior. He was alone; he held his cane in his right hand and witnessed the scene unfold as well as he could despite his nearsightedness. He saw the *Jupiter*'s ruins and the *Thüringen* beyond them. He also watched as half a dozen rescue boats left the *Delaware* to help the *Jupiter*'s survivors.

Ross was unsure what had transpired between Roosevelt, the Liopleurodon, and the Germans. Had the colonel slayed the beast? Or the reverse? He had expected an update by now—some way to know who had won. The lack of news led Ross to think that the Liopleurodon must have killed Roosevelt, because its presence made communication to the *Delaware* impossible.

He saw a white triangle as the Liopleurodon's jaws rose above the water between the *Delaware* and the *Jupiter*, the pliosaur's underside facing Ross. He shuddered at his insignificance as the reptile breached and snapped its jaws before landing on the ocean's surface, taking a breath, and submerging.

What was going on? Why was the Liopleurodon so close to the *Delaware* when its victims were several kilometers to the east? Ross didn't know but was certain its presence meant that

Roosevelt was dead. He had battled the Liopleurodon and lost. Wood, and the sailors they'd recruited, were also dead. The plan had failed. Roosevelt was the last hope. Now the Liopleurodon would kill the *Jupiter*'s remaining survivors. Then either Germany would capture it or the Liopleurodon would escape. What a disaster. Roosevelt's death was a national tragedy and the *Jupiter*'s destruction would be mourned by civilized men the world over.

Ross looked at the *Thüringen*. He suspected that Luke was on that ship, a hostage to an authoritarian government that wanted to transform the Liopleurodon into a weapon. Why did the bad guys keep winning?

"Hello, Ben."

Ross' jaw tightened as he heard the voice behind him. He held his breath and turned around. Dr. Ryan was a horrible sight. Patches of dried blood covered his hands, arms, and shirt. His blonde hair was disgusting. He held a blood-stained glass blade that he'd used to murder the guards in his right hand. His fingers bled from gripping it. He smiled, satisfied that he had Ross pinned near the railing.

"Hello, Sean."

"I'm curious," Ryan said. "How did you figure it out?"

"It wasn't hard. You're not that clever."

"Is that it? You love to talk."

"It was something Miss Painter said," Ross muttered. Ryan's eyes narrowed, feeling anxiety at her mention. "Do you feel any remorse for what you did to her?"

Ryan fought off his emotions. He didn't want to react. "I didn't intend that to happen."

"But it did!" Ross snapped. "It happened because of *your* actions." He paused. "You should know that Mr. Jones is alive. The Germans have him." Ryan's face was blank as he processed that information. "I'm going to dedicate the rest of my life to bringing him home and mentoring him so he fulfills his potential, as Professor Harris intended. You remember Professor Harris, don't you, Sean? Another good person whose life you destroyed." Ryan still didn't react. "You should also know that Miss Painter was going to leave you for Mr. Jones. She saw through you. Saw the person you are."

Ryan had had enough of Ross' verbal barrage. He was supposed to be the one with the power. He raised the blade. "I'm going to enjoy throwing what's left of your carcass into the ocean."

Ross scoffed. "Oh, I'm *so* scared."

"I did the right thing," Ryan said. "I didn't mean for so many people to die, but the Liopleurodon's survival was part of God's plan. It was His intent. I couldn't let this masterpiece of nature perish."

"This reflects your 'big picture architect' view of God?" Ross asked. "That He's a guiding force?"

"Precisely. That's why it's important that the Liopleurodon lives for as long as possible."

"Oh, please. Don't act like you're a moral crusader. You didn't do this for nature or for God."

"What?" Ryan asked. "You think I'm working for Germany?"

"No," Ross said. "You did this because you were *bored*. I saw the look in your eyes at Delmonico's. Life was crushing your soul. You weren't the revered scientific genius that you'd dreamed of being, and Miss Painter may have looked good on your arm but she was a bad match because she wanted love and you're not *capable* of it. So the Liopleurodon's discovery brought excitement to your life. I bet it was fun to engage in a battle of wits with me and the government. You might even believe that you did it to preserve nature, but I know you better than you know yourself. And let me tell you, Sean, you're not pretty."

"The government? Ha! Yes, I've been *very* impressed with them," Ryan said. "Do you realize that I freed the Liopleurodon from Naval Station Newport by paying some young people? It wasn't even that expensive."

"Is that so?" Ross asked as he looked up behind Ryan. Ryan turned to see two sailors holding Springfield rifles, given to them by General Wood. They pointed the rifles at Ryan. His eyes widened.

"Even *you* should have seen that coming," Ross said. "Did you really think you could outsmart me, Sean? You're an *inferior* mind. More than that, you're a worthless pile of scum who murdered dozens of innocent people because you were *bored* with a life that most people would dream of having."

Ryan knew he was out of options. He'd lost. But he could

still fulfill his final objective.

He lunged at Ross, swinging his glass blade down on his enemy. Ross raised his cane to block him. The men collided and the sailors hesitated to fire, afraid they might hit Ross. Ross' cane blunted Ryan's attack, but Ryan's blade still struck Ross between his chest and left shoulder.

Ross yelped and Ryan smiled as he pushed Ross toward the railing. Ryan growled like a leopard. Ross' glasses fell from his face. He wanted to look behind him to evaluate how much space he had but knew it was a mistake. Ryan pushed the blade deeper and jumped to gain more leverage and momentum.

Ross realized that played to his advantage. He took a step back with his left leg to appear unbalanced. Ryan thought his opponent was weakening and jumped again to push the blade deeper, hoping it would prove fatal. Ross' knees buckled, dropping his weight and falling backward. Ryan landed on top of him and lost his grip on the blade.

The men hit the deck. Ross punched Ryan's ribs and pushed him off. Ross rolled to his right, trying to get away from Ryan. Ryan lunged at Ross, desperate to grab his blade. It was still lodged in Ross' torso.

The sailors saw that the paleontologists were separated. They fired at Ryan simultaneously. One bullet struck his chest and the other hit his stomach.

Ross froze until he was certain that Ryan was dead. He sat on the deck, coughing and touching the blade but not attempting to remove it. He breathed slowly, his chest swelling with pain. It was disorienting.

"Mr. Ross!" one of the sailors shouted as they ran down the stairs. "Mr. Ross! Are you okay?"

"That's *Dr.* Ross!" he exclaimed as they reached him. "And I am. Thanks to you boys."

...

The Liopleurodon pulled the *Nautilus* close to the seabed, his jaws grabbing the submarine near the cockpit on the port side. He wanted to hold the *Nautilus* still and drown it, as he would a shark. But the *Nautilus*' engines kept buzzing, and the Liopleurodon grew frustrated with how to strangle his adversary. The day's incessant combat, along with the methamphetamine and the transition to the twentieth century, had deteriorated his mind until he felt nothing but the urge to destroy.

Tears streamed down Luke's face and onto his lap and hands. He was in the Liopleurodon's grip and knew it was only a matter of time before the reptile ruptured the submarine's armor. He felt the *Nautilus* shake, a feat the Liopleurodon accomplished with its thick, sturdy neck. Luke's mind was an anxiety swamp and contained no other substance.

"Think! Come on!"

He pushed the joystick to starboard, but the Liopleurodon's 35-ton bite force held the *Nautilus* in place. Luke tried the other direction and shifted the joystick to port. The Liopleurodon was surprised by this shift of momentum. His grip weakened. Luke turned to starboard again. The rapid thrusts wiggled the *Nautilus* from the Liopleurodon's bite. It broke free, spinning in an out-of-control descent.

Luke screamed as he saw the seabed get closer and closer through the periscope. He pulled the joystick back as far as he could. The *Nautilus* stabilized less than 30 meters above the reef-covered ocean floor. Luke calmed down. Most of his body was covered in tears and sweat.

He looked into the periscope as he rose to 50 meters over the seabed. He couldn't see the surface. His anxiety grew from being this deep. He wondered if he could retreat to the surface and have the Liopleurodon chase him within range of the *Delaware*'s guns. Why hadn't Roosevelt accepted that idea? Luke would already be back in New York if he had.

He adjusted the *Nautilus*' position until he could see the Liopleurodon in his periscope. It appeared to be resting and its mouth bled from biting the submarine.

"What are you up to?" Luke asked. He again wondered if he could take advantage of the Liopleurodon's exhaustion to escape to the surface. Then the image of the monster grabbing Kelsey, its jaws surrounded by fire, appeared in his mind's eye.

No. Retreat wasn't an option. One of them wasn't leaving this fight alive. The Liopleurodon, his energy recovering, tracked the *Nautilus* with his good eye and nostril. He felt similarly about this territorial challenger. Each combatant was wounded but each was determined to destroy the other in a battle of annihilation.

The Liopleurodon's front flippers rose, beginning the next phase. Luke knew he was too close to his enemy and didn't want the pliosaur to strike or bite his submarine again. He looked in the periscope and took only a moment to aim before firing the fourth torpedo.

The reptile surged with energy as he dodged the torpedo and swung to the *Nautilus'* starboard flank, spinning 360 degrees like a crocodile's death roll. He flapped all four flippers simultaneously, slamming into the submarine's side at a 90-degree angle. Luke didn't have time to react. His face struck the dashboard. His seatbelt pulled him back. His head and neck slammed into the cockpit seat behind him. He was dizzy, as though punched in both his face and the back of his head in rapid succession. His head felt like a ping pong ball.

An explosive sound caught Luke's attention. Had something ruptured? He looked into the periscope and saw water dissipating in the distance. He turned to the dashboard and put two and two together.

He'd hit his head on the red button. Great. He'd wasted the fifth torpedo. One shot left.

Thud!

The Liopleurodon struck the *Nautilus* again, hitting its nose and yanking Luke deeper. Luke questioned how many more strikes the *Nautilus* could take and looked into the periscope to see how close they were to the seabed. Darkness. Were they beyond sunlight's reach? No. Luke saw fangs.

The Liopleurodon bit the cockpit. The *Nautilus'* armor was

all that stood between Luke and the Liopleurodon's mouth. A dagger-like tooth pierced the periscope. Luke noticed the walls around him start to cave and heard metal creek.

The most powerful weapon in the Animal Kingdom's history pressed down on the cockpit. The metal objects and the mammals that clung to them were a continuous thorn in the Liopleurodon's side since awakening from hibernation. The *Nautilus* was the worst of them all. It had to be obliterated. Then he would eviscerate what was left of the *Jupiter* and hunt other metal objects wherever he could.

Luke tried to free the *Nautilus* the way he had earlier. He moved the joystick in every direction. Forward, back, starboard, port. Anything to break free from the Liopleurodon. But the Liopleurodon had a better grip this time and the *Nautilus* couldn't escape. Luke's tear ducts were empty as he kept rotating the joystick, desperate for a miracle.

Boom!

"What was that?" Luke asked, panicking. The *Nautilus* shook, vibrations emanating from the stern. Luke's fear halted his mind from thinking through what that meant. Then it popped into his conscience: one of the *Nautilus'* two engines had ruptured.

Luke screamed an expletive with what little energy he had left. His head fell. So weak. He was hopeless. Beaten. Dessert. He felt ashamed, the sort he'd felt his entire life but greater than ever. Not because his death was imminent. He didn't care about that. It was because he'd failed to destroy the Liopleurodon and avenge the woman he loved. It was going to get away with it. It was going to get away with it. It was going to get away with it. The thought repeated multiple times in Luke's mind. The Liopleurodon murdered Kelsey and was going to swim away, forgetting all of this, and build its empire across the North Atlantic, the unconquerable master of the deep. Luke was destined to be forgotten, one mere obstacle among many in that empire's construction. A victim among the pile.

Why couldn't he get his way? On anything? Ever? His father's implosion, alcoholism, and suicide. Dr. Ross embarrassing him at the restaurant. Kelsey's commitment to another man and death. All of these events, plus every other humiliation and slight that Luke had experienced over the course of his life—culminating in defeat in his nemesis' jaws—could all be blamed on one thing. His mind. The defect in his brain that gave him ambitions but wouldn't let him fulfill them and then mocked him for trying. It was the real enemy. God! There were times Luke wanted to wrap his fingers around his brain and strangle it.

The cockpit walls creaked again.

No. No. No. It couldn't end like this, with the monster getting away with it. That was the *most* important factor. The Liopleurodon *did not* survive to see tomorrow. Nothing else mattered. *Nothing*. Luke wiped mucus from his nose and tears from his eyes and cheeks. His jaw clenched. He had to think more creatively and take more risks.

The cockpit walls came closer. Luke expected to see the tips of the Liopleurodon's teeth penetrate at any moment. Clearly, he couldn't use the *Nautilus* size or momentum to break free. He looked at the red button.

"One more," he whispered, exhausted. He was not sure where exactly the Liopleurodon's jaws were clamped upon the *Nautilus'* bow. He didn't think that either torpedo tube was inside the crocodilian incisors, reducing the risk that the torpedo's detonation would strike the cockpit. There was still a risk, however, that the torpedo might hit the Liopleurodon's head or neck and then detonate. In that case, the resulting explosion could still kill Luke.

Whatever. The only question that mattered was whether or not the Liopleurodon survived. Luke took a deep breath and paused. He pressed the red button.

The final torpedo fired. It passed the Liopleurodon and descended under the combatants before detonating. The blast shattered part of the coral reef and singed the Liopleurodon's tail and rear flippers. The *Nautilus* shook but was far enough from the blast that it was unharmed. The Liopleurodon released the *Nautilus*, thrashing his massive head in agony.

"Yes!" Luke cried as he looked into the periscope and saw blue. The periscope was damaged—it had been punctured and resembled a spider web—but was still usable.

Luke pulled back on his joystick. The *Nautilus* rose with its one working engine. He sailed away from his enemy. He paused after a few moments and adjusted his angle so he could see the Liopleurodon below. The Liopleurodon kept himself steady with synchronized flipper strokes. It turned to the left and saw the coral reefs stretched along the ocean floor with its good eye. That was its best bet. Its jaws weren't strong enough to break the submarine's armor, but slamming the *Nautilus* onto the seabed with all 150 tons of its strength might crack the vessel like a walnut.

"Come on," Luke muttered, anticipating his enemy's plan. The Liopleurodon's flippers swung wider, rising to implement his idea. Luke pushed down on the joystick, descending. The combatants looked doomed for a head-on collision but the Liopleurodon banked to the right, hoping to dodge the *Nautilus* and attack its flank. Luke shifted the joystick to port, striking the Liopleurodon's underside and front left flipper. The Liopleurodon's reinforced rib cage absorbed the blow but his flipper bones shattered.

Luke was below the Liopleurodon. He looked into the periscope and turned the *Nautilus* until he saw the reptile above him on the port side. He saw its jaws and, though the periscope was cracked, believed it was smiling at him with its demonic grin. Luke roared with adrenaline as he pulled back on the joystick, rising so the Liopleurodon could barely dodge his ascent. The Liopleurodon was too tired and too battered to outmaneuver the *Nautilus* again. Luke spun the *Nautilus* around, looked into his periscope, saw he was facing the Liopleurodon at a perpendicular angle, and pressed the joystick forward with all his strength.

Luke screamed as the *Nautilus'* nose struck the

Liopleurodon's rib cage and slammed the pliosaur into the ocean floor. He felt the *Nautilus* shake as it absorbed the impact. Sand and shattered coral consumed the combatants in a cloud of chaos and darkness.

The Liopleurodon spasmed under the *Nautilus'* weight. He threw his head to and fro, using his momentum to attempt escape. When that failed he turned toward the submarine and snapped his jaws three times. His enemy was beyond his reach. The Liopleurodon played his last option, spinning like a crocodile's death roll. It worked. The *Nautilus* lost its positioning and fell. The nose and cockpit struck the seabed and it plummeted to its starboard side. Water friction split its hull. It landed on the ocean floor as an enormous metal L. More sand and coral rose and fell.

The dissipating debris revealed the Liopleurodon lying on the seafloor, surrounded by shattered coral. He tried lifting himself but his reinforced rib cage and two left flippers were crushed. He had to breathe, exhausted and having had the air knocked from his lungs by the impact. But he was immobile. The Liopleurodon tried moving again but could not. Bubbles emerged from his jaws as his lungs filled with water. The last thing the Liopleurodon saw was sharks circling above, attracted by the commotion.

Luke hung at an angle within the X-shaped seatbelt that covered his torso. His forehead bled. So did his bottom lip, which was torn, the blood dripping into his mouth, nostrils, and face. The cockpit's hull was pierced. Water seeped inside. Luke took several moments to regain focus, disoriented from the collisions. He coughed as the blood from his bottom lip dripped into his mouth and nose, taking a moment to wipe it and slow it down. He closed one eye and peered into the periscope. The periscope was damaged beyond functional use but Luke caught a glimpse, a small glimpse, of the red and black entity sitting on the ocean floor, motionless.

Luke smiled. He laughed, though he didn't have any oxygen to spare. He did not know if the Liopleurodon was dead or dying but it made no difference. Luke filled with jubilation, more than he'd felt all his life. He felt, perhaps for the first time, genuinely happy and unburdened.

"I'm coming, Kelsey," Luke said with what air remained in his lungs. He passed out.

Epilogue

March 8, 1915

"Welcome to the Oval Office," Roosevelt said after Major Butt opened the door.

Dr. Ross was silent as he entered. A small rope connected his cane to his left arm. He pushed Harris' wheelchair. The paleontologists looked glum, as though devoid of energy. Harris had let the hair on his head and face grow out. Ross glanced around, noticing a glass cube on the President's desk that contained the Liopleurodon tooth pulled from the orca. The wall opposite the desk wielded portraits of Washington, Hamilton, Lincoln, and Grant. An open circle of furniture was in the Office's center. Senator Lodge sat on the left end of a couch. Roosevelt approached its right flank; he had grown more skillful at maneuvering with his pegleg. Ross placed Harris on the right side of the opposite couch and took his seat facing the President. Glasses of cocoa were placed on the table between the four men.

"I was delighted when you agreed to see me," Roosevelt said, angling his peg leg so it didn't touch the table. "I've been looking forward to this small commemoration for the anniversary of *that* day."

Harris looked at his immobile feet. He had not even been conscious when the events that Roosevelt referred to occurred.

"I assume a photographer is coming," Ross said. He spoke softly, trying not to antagonize his throat. It became difficult for Ross to breathe or speak after Ryan stabbed him.

"There isn't," Roosevelt said.

"So you've wrung enough adulat—" Ross had a coughing fit, having spoken too loudly. His face became beet-red.

Roosevelt claimed credit for the Liopleurodon's destruction. The press was more than happy to cooperate and he became the most popular American since Washington resigned as the head of the Army. Anyone trying to correct the narrative would fail. No one did. Taft, whose treaties were rejected by the Senate and who unintentionally helped a conservative government win power in Canada, knew that resisting Roosevelt was a fool's errand and stepped aside in 1912. Woodrow Wilson, the Democratic Party nominee, won only a handful of Deep South states.

Roosevelt gestured to the cocoa near Ross if he needed a drink to open his throat. He grabbed his own glass and took a sip.

"Can we enjoy this reunion without bickering?" he asked. "You can imagine the stress I've been under since the Ferdinand assassination last summer."

"Is our entry into the war inevitable?" Ross asked.

"It is our duty to act," Roosevelt said.

"But will Congress cooperate?"

"I have the votes whipped in the Senate," Lodge said. "Soon

we'll have the support we need in the House for a joint session."

"What about the pacifist movement?" Ross asked.

Roosevelt snorted. "I don't take them seriously. If Lincoln acted after the firing of Sumter the way the pacifists desire to respond to European events, in one month the North would have been saying they were so glad that he kept them out of the war and the Union would have died."

"I thought the entire point of our operation was to avoid a war," Harris said.

"The mission's goal was to deny the Kaiser a chance to use the Liopleurodon as a weapon," Roosevelt said. "We succeeded."

"I also suspect that Asquith wouldn't have adhered to Britain's 1819 treaty with Belgium if Germany could unleash that monster on their ports," Lodge said, "meaning that Germany would have already conquered Western Europe."

"Besides," Roosevelt said, "the war will be over quickly if our boys in blue display an ounce of the courage that Luke Jones demonstrated."

"Please don't glorify his death," Harris said. "He was a good kid. None of it should have happened."

"He was the *best* of us," Roosevelt said. "His sacrifice saved dozens of lives. Do you not see poetry in that he and the beast were lost to the world together at the bottom of the Atlantic?"

"You haven't learned a thing," Ross said. "Not a thing from that entire operation."

Lodge turned to Roosevelt, wondering if the President was going to dismiss his guests from the Oval Office. He didn't. He sat quietly. Whatever they had been through together did not permit it.

Harris leaned forward. "Sean Ryan bears the bulk of responsibility for what happened, but you took advantage of the circumstances for your own ambitions. Your hands aren't clean either."

"I saw an intersection between a genuine threat and my political fortunes," Roosevelt said. "It was clear to me from the outset that the Germans would try to capture the Liopleurodon. It didn't matter whether or not the German Army button was a ruse. I know the Kaiser. I know how he thinks. How his high command thinks. Now, you might not like it but that's how men in the real world operate. Okay? That's politics. And I think a lot of good is coming from it."

"A war?" Harris asked.

"Peace!" Roosevelt declared. "Our entry will end the war quickly so it doesn't lead to lasting resentment. We'll restore Germany as a respectable member of the world order, as Metternich did with France after Napoleon's defeat." He paused. "I also plan to build a World League of Peace and Righteousness."

"What does that entail?" Ross asked.

"The League will arbitrate disputes between states and will urge them to contribute military forces for use against any country that refuses to carry out the League's decrees or that violates other nations' rights," Roosevelt said.

"That sounds like it would require the Senate to ratify a

treaty," Harris said. "How is it any different than what Taft failed to do?"

"Senator Hitchcock on the Foreign Relations Committee has already guaranteed me his support for this project," Lodge said.

"Peace shall be the cause of the rest of my life," Roosevelt said. "And I don't just mean peace between countries. My administration passed the most progressive agenda in history in my first two years in office and will enact a permanent arbitration mechanism between capital and labor by the time I retire." He sipped his cocoa. "I also intend to appoint General Wood to lead the American Expeditionary Force in Europe and if he does his job well I plan for him to succeed me in '21. What I am doing will shape the rest of this century."

"The President will be remembered as an equal of Washington and Lincoln," Lodge said. "He may even become their superior."

"The legacy you always wanted," Harris said. Roosevelt made no reply and took another sip.

"Will it be possible to extradite Dr. Branca after the war?" Ross asked. "I refuse to believe that Mr. Jones managed the theft of the German submarine on his own. Dr. Branca sent him to his death and he did it knowingly."

Roosevelt sighed, briefly breaking eye contact. "You must *move on*, Benjamin."

"I'm not sure I can," Ross said. His eyes watered, hurting his throat again. He turned from the others to pull himself together. Melancholy hung over the gathering. No one spoke for several minutes. The reunion appeared a failure when Roosevelt attempted to salvage it.

"Perhaps we can take a cruise around the world when I leave office. It would be a more appropriate commemoration of our shared experience. I'll retire in March of '21, assuming I win in '16. That will be the operation's tenth anniversary."

"Sounds nice," Ross said. He looked at the Liopleurodon tooth on the President's desk. "It's been four years since I've been on the water."

Acknowledgments

I discovered Liopleurodon, like millions of others, when watching the BBC's *Walking with Dinosaurs* as a child. The animal dominated my thoughts for the next seven years. At 14 I read Steve Alten's *MEG* series, and I wanted Liopleurodon to get its own book. None existed, so I wrote what became *Liopleurodon: King of the Carnivores*. The book was set in the present day and featured much of the same cast as *The Master of the Deep*, including Luke Jones and the other paleontologists.

King of the Carnivores reached number 72 on Amazon's bestseller list for Sea Adventures and was well received by the intended teenage audience. But older readers questioned why modern weaponry couldn't kill the Liopleurodon quickly. That led to my contemplating how the story would work if set in an earlier time period. I initially considered World War II, but that felt too similar to *Raiders of the Lost Ark*. I settled on the early twentieth century, where Theodore Roosevelt could be a major character and he and Luke would race against the Kaiser's Germany.

I want to thank my wife, Amanda Makhoul Zucker, who supported my decision to rewrite *King of the Carnivores* into a historical/science fiction adventure and who never stopped encouraging me. She also proofread the novel more than once.

Thank you to Dustin Prisley and Kian Williams for discussing my plan for *The Master of the Deep* early in the planning stage.

I also want to credit the sources that helped inform me about the different elements in *The Master of the Deep*. The BBC's portrayal of Liopleurodon in programs such as *Walking with Dinosaurs* and *Chased by Sea Monsters* was the main influence of my version of the animal in this book.

Daniel Ruddy's *Theodore Roosevelt's History of the United States*, Evan Thomas' *The War Lovers*, and Doris Kerns Goodwin's *The Bully Pulpit* all informed my portrayal of Theodore Roosevelt. Goodwin's book also influenced my portrayal of Taft.

Candice Millard's *Hero of the Empire* was the main source I used for Churchill's monologue about the Boer War.

David Foster Wallace's "This is Water" speech influenced Will Harris' monologue.

Darrin Lunde's article "Teddy Roosevelt's Epic (But Strangely Altruistic) Hunt for a White Rhino" was the source for Roosevelt's monologue on his African safari.

Finally, I want to thank you, the readers. I hope you enjoyed *The Master of the Deep*.

About the Author

M. B. Zucker has been interested in storytelling for as long as he can remember. He is the author of *The Eisenhower Chronicles*, a biographical novel about General and President Dwight Eisenhower, and *A Great Soldier in the Last Great War*, a novel set in the Battle of the Bulge. Mr. Zucker earned his B.A. at Occidental College and his J.D. at Case Western Reserve University School of Law. He lives in Virginia with his wife and dog.

Follow Mr. Zucker on Twitter at @MBZuckerBooks and @MichaelZucker1 and on Instagram at @m.b.zucker.author

Contact him at mbzucker1890@gmail.com

HISTORIUM PRESS

www.historiumpress.com

2022

CPSIA information can be obtained
at www.ICGtesting.com
Printed in the USA
BVHW052038240523
664819BV00006B/66